T0346848

By Mandy Morton
The No. 2 Feline Detective Agency
Cat Among the Pumpkins
The Death of Downton Tabby
The Ghost of Christmas Paws
The Michaelmas Murders
Magical Mystery Paws
Beyond the Gravy
The Ice Maid's Tail

A Pocket Full of Pie

The No. 2 **FELINE** Detective Agency

MANDY MORTON

This edition published in 2021 by Farrago,
an imprint of Duckworth Books Ltd
1 Golden Court, Richmond TW9 1EU, United Kingdom

www.farragobooks.com

ISBN: 978-1-78842-305-2

*A cautionary tale for all my fellow broadcasters,
and for Nicola with love.*

Chapter One

The success of The No. 2 Feline Detective Agency had brought a number of personal opportunities to Hettie Bagshot and her sidekick, Tilly Jenkins. The town had embraced them as heroes, and barely a week went by without the local paper singing their praises. Hettie had been offered a lucrative lecture tour on the feline criminal mind, which she'd declined on the basis of not having enough time to do it justice; the truth, of course, was that she loathed being away from their small bedsitter at the back of the Butter sisters' bakery, where pies and pastries were on tap and the companionship of Tilly had proved vital to her well-being.

When Hettie first invited Tilly to share her small room, it was more out of sympathy for Tilly's plight as a homeless cat than the expectation that she would prove to be the most significant friendship in Hettie's life. Tilly was a homemaker, mainly because she'd never had one of her own. She had weathered many a storm on cold winter nights, taking advantage of scraps of cardboard and newspaper to keep herself warm. Now she was queen of her own fireplace, with an abundance of fleecy blankets and warm cardigans to make up for the years of battling the elements and, on occasions, the cruelty and violence of other cats more streetwise than she was. She loved the small day-to-day gifts that her new life offered, and although living and working with Hettie could prove difficult at times, thanks to her friend's rather extreme, bad-tempered views on life, Tilly possessed the patience and understanding needed to bring a peaceful harmony to their existence.

Today was different. Hettie had bustled out early that morning to attend what promised to be a fractious meeting between the town's cricket club and the parish entertainment committee. A civil war was brewing regarding the use of the recreation ground, which was home to the cricket pitch and to a calendar of other annual events; in a rare moment of community spirit, Hettie had stupidly agreed to mediate, leaving Tilly at home to face her own demons.

She sat at the desk that doubled as a table, staring at a radio script she'd prepared earlier and surrounded by tools of the trade, ready for 'a bit of a practice' as she'd put it to Hettie over their morning tea. To her left was the Dansette record player, newly acquired from her friend Jessie's charity shop; it had taken Tilly some time to remove the lid, as the catches were rusty, but now she was satisfied that she was ready for a 'run through', to use the correct term.

The headphones – or 'cans' – had proved to be a trial, as they were too big for her and kept slipping down over her eyes, and she couldn't quite remember what the difference was between a 'cue' and a 'back anno'. In fact, she'd discovered a whole new language since her recent conversation with Wilco Wonderfluff. Wilco – whose real name was George Tibbs – had come to Whisker FM as celebrity holiday relief for the station's late night 'Catchat' show when its fortunes were at rock bottom; within a month, he had injected some cash and transformed the town's local station into an eclectic sweep of music and speech-based programmes, designed to catch the ear of cats from every walk of life. He had made plenty of enemies among the tired, worn-out presenters and DJs who were used to waffling their way through the weekly diet of gardening phone-ins, pointless competitions and second-paw news stories grabbed from the *Daily Snout*, but the new blood he'd injected into the airwaves harnessed the genuine talent of local musicians, artists and writers, and even Morbid Balm – who worked for the local undertakers, Shroud and Trestle – had been persuaded to take part; her late night 'Good Goth' show was an instant success.

Tilly had been recommended to Wilco by Turner Page, the town's librarian, as an expert on crime fiction with a voracious appetite for all things Agatha Crispy. Wilco was instantly taken with Tilly's abundant enthusiasm for life. Instead of a weekly book-review spot, he'd convinced her to present a two-hour show on Thursdays between four and six, incorporating true crime, book reviews and lots of cheerful music. Tilly was flattered, but had underestimated the technical aspects of becoming a radio presenter. She had only recently come to terms with the concept of the telephone answering machine that lived in the staff sideboard, and still harboured a great mistrust of the kettle that switched itself off when it boiled; even the principle of the video machine that recorded their favourite TV shows when they were out on a case was beyond her. To be put behind a radio desk which resembled the control panel of a jumbo jet was probably more than any small, long-haired tabby could cope with, but Wilco had assured her that with 'a bit of a practice' all would be well.

She put the script down, feeling self-conscious at the prospect of talking to herself, a fear that most radio presenters shared. A stack of singles to her right drew her attention, and she decided to choose the piece of music which would start her imaginary show. Wilco had suggested that she concentrate on 'bubblegum pop' for her record selections, with the odd truck-driving, country tune for cats listening in on their car radios, and Hettie had helped her by delving into her own box of 45 rpms. Her understanding of music was a little more informed than Tilly's, whose favourite record was 'Nellie the Elephant'.

After much deliberation, she decided on 'Yummy, Yummy, Yummy' by the 1910 Fruitgum Company, mainly because she liked the name. She pulled the disc from its paper sleeve and pushed it down over the spindle on the Dansette. Lifting the arm into the centre to start the turntable, she placed the needle onto the record; due to the size of her paws, it was something of a crash landing, but the Fruitgum Company obliged her by coming in halfway through their 1960s hit. It wasn't exactly the start that Tilly had been hoping for, but she allowed the song to come to a natural conclusion before picking up her script. 'Hello, and welcome to "Tea Time with Tilly",' she said brightly, and was about to offer her fantasy listeners a list of things to look forward to in the show when Hettie flung the door open with a face as black as thunder.

'Don't even ask!' she said, making a beeline for her armchair and slumping down into it. 'What a complete waste of time. I don't know about community spirit – they were at each other's throats from the outset! They even reduced Bugs Anderton to tears, and she's used to calling the shots.'

Tilly abandoned her practice session and padded over to the kettle, hoping that a mug of sweet milky tea might stem the flow of vitriol coming from her friend, who had clearly had a difficult morning. Hettie had barely begun her critique. 'Bunty Basham put forward a perfectly good case for starting the cricket season early during the nice weather,' she continued, 'but then

Tarquin Flapjack came up with the idea of The great Easter bake off. Instantly the meeting was split into two camps, both wanting to use the recreation ground at the same time, and to make matters worse, Wilco Wonderfluff stuck his paw in and pointed out that Whisker FM wouldn't be moving out of its temporary home in the cricket pavilion any time soon, because Bunty had agreed that they could broadcast from there until the summer. Elsie Haddock tried to be the voice of reason by offering her famous sister, Fanny, as a judge for the bake off and agreeing to score for Bunty's cricket team, but of course they can't have two things happening at once on the same bit of bloody turf!'

'The great Easter bake off! That sounds exciting!' said Tilly, as she poured hot water onto the tea bags. 'I don't see the point of starting the cricket early, though. That just means the town will lose even more matches than usual, and with Poppa and Bruiser away on a bikers' holiday, they'll have no cats who can bat properly. Bunty does her best, but most of the team only turns up for a day in the sunshine. If it wasn't for Balti Dosh and her fast bowling, they'd never get anyone out, either.'

Hettie and Tilly had spent many a sunny afternoon snoozing in the sunshine as the town's nearly all-female cricket team was soundly beaten, not because they were fans of the sport, but because their landladies traditionally provided a jolly good cricket tea. 'I'm not sure how it's all going to turn out,' admitted Hettie. 'The plan is for everything to take place across the

Easter weekend, including the usual stuff – egg hunt, bonnet parade and an outdoor screening of *The Sound of* Sodding *Music* again! Just another chance to see Julie Android dragging her guitar up a bloody mountain. And with just over a week to go before Easter, I can't help thinking it's all a bit too late.'

'So how did you leave it?' asked Tilly, passing Hettie a ginger nut to dunk in her tea and narrowly avoiding a conversation on her friend's least favourite film.

'As fast as I could! The fur was about to fly, so I told them I had an urgent case to attend to and left them to it. The Methodists were arriving as I was on my way out, all armed with plastic boxes full of homebakes to reclaim their hall for the Wednesday lunch club, so by now all hell will have broken loose. Anyway, how are you getting on with your radio practice?'

Tilly shook her head. 'Not very well, I'm afraid. I wish I'd never agreed to do it. There are far too many knobs and switches, and I'm supposed to talk at the same time. I think I'll have to tell Wilco that I just can't manage it. I had a nightmare about it last night. I was in the studio and the record stopped, and I couldn't think of a thing to say or find another record to put on.'

'So what did you do?' asked Hettie, reaching for another ginger nut.

'I woke up crying, hugging my hot water bottle so tightly that I punctured it with my claws. It soaked through my fleecy blanket and my pyjamas.'

'Well, you'll have to sort something out – it's your first show tomorrow. What if I do the knobs and switches and you just talk until you get the hang of it? I'm sure Wilco wouldn't mind an extra pair of paws, and anyway, he's too busy fighting his corner over the cricket pavilion.'

Tilly beamed at Hettie. 'That would be lovely, and you can choose the music as well – you know much more about it than I do. Perhaps you should do the true crime bit, too?'

'OK, we'll muddle through together,' said Hettie. 'Now we've got that sorted, let's celebrate by having a slap-up lunch at Bloomers. My treat.'

Chapter Two

Molly Bloom's café had become the town's social centre as well as somewhere to enjoy tasty, affordable breakfasts, lunches and teas. Molly had entered into the community spirit by offering an evening home to the Caterwaulers Folk Club, The Stetson Slappers Line Dancing Group, and the monthly meetings of the cricket, ping-pong and Cluedo clubs. With the help of her flatmate, Dolly Scollop, Molly had created a business model that was instantly successful, and the combination of her Irish hospitality with Dolly's Cornish eccentricities drew customers from all over the town and beyond. Cats would while whole days away, lurching from one delicious meal to another in the warm and welcoming surroundings. Some customers brought books to read and tucked themselves into corners; others met up with friends to chew over the world's troubles while enjoying some of their favourite dishes from the blackboard behind the counter.

Bloomers had also recently become the unofficial registered office for Hettie and Tilly's detective business, just one of many perks earned from their successful cases. Molly had assigned a particular table to them, and occasionally they conducted interviews there as part of their investigations. Today, however, the two friends slid into their bench seats with nothing more taxing to investigate than the café's lunch menu. 'I'm going for the fish pie and the treacle suet pudding,' Hettie announced loudly, sharing her enthusiasm with the other diners.

'I might have the spaghetti Bolognese to start with,' Tilly said.

'Is that really a good idea? You're wearing your best spring cardigan, and last time you ordered spaghetti you had to be sponged down in Molly's kitchen.'

Tilly looked a little crestfallen; her eating habits left a lot to be desired, and her large paws were often more of a hindrance than a help in transporting food from plate to mouth. 'I suppose if I chopped it up and used a spoon it might be all right, but maybe I should stick to something simpler.'

Hettie had no doubt that Tilly would stick to whatever she ordered, but said nothing as Dolly approached to take their order.

'Now my dears, 'ave you decided? The Bolognese is off – well, not off off, if you get my meanin', but run out, to be precise, on account of there bein' a rush for it. We've a nice chicken curry with rice if you've a mind for foreign stuff, but all the traditionals are still available at present.'

'I'd like the fish pie and the treacle pudding,' said Hettie, as Tilly scoured the menu for an alternative that wouldn't put her spring cardigan in jeopardy.

'And I'll have the jumbo fish fingers and chips with extra tomato sauce, and a milk pudding with chocolate crispies to follow, please,' Tilly said eventually, as Dolly stood pencil poised.

The Cornish cat disappeared through the double doors that led to the kitchen, where Molly was cooking and plating up the orders. It was clear that the lunchtime rush was far from over, even before the door to the high street burst open again and Bunty Basham led the uprooted meeting into the café.

'Well, that's enough to put any cat off her lunch,' mumbled Hettie. 'Keep your head down and they might not notice us.'

Hettie's warning to Tilly came too late: Bunty spied them immediately and left the gaggle of cats she'd brought with her to find a table. 'Hello again,' she said, forcing her way through the crowd. 'I bring news! Hostilities have ceased for now, and we are in the process of bringing about a fragile but hopeful optimism to the Easter weekend.'

Tilly loved to hear Bunty Basham's public school accent. No one knew exactly where she'd come from, but her thigh-slapping demeanour had gained her many friends in the town as an organiser of sports and recreation. She was viewed by most as a jolly good sort: not only did she care for her ageing mother, but – for her sins – was the captain of the cricket team, ran a mean netball squad, and had even ventured into rugby as a winter diversion. Bunty was an all-rounder, both in stature and in life; a giant of a cat, and a formidable opponent on field and court – but not even her enthusiasm could alter the sad fact that the folk of the town were just plain lazy and showed little interest in winter or summer recreations. Winter was a time for snoozing by the fire, and summer offered patches of warm sunshine in which to sleep the day away.

Hettie tried to look interested as Bunty moved in on their table, forcing Tilly to shuffle along the bench. 'We've decided to share the recreation ground,' she continued. 'Tarquin's idea of a bake off competition is really too good to miss. As long as his marquee doesn't get in the way of my fielders, all will be well.'

'What about Whisker FM? Has Wilco agreed to find another place for his radio station?' asked Hettie.

'Ah, well, that is a bit of a sticking point at the moment because of the cricket teas. To be honest with you, that's the only reason half the team turns out at all.' Hettie shared a knowing look with Tilly as Bunty continued. 'It's my fault, really. When Wilco was looking for a temporary billet for his airwaves, I offered the pavilion, thinking that the cricket wouldn't start until the middle of June. By then, Wilco assured me that he would have found an alternative, but as all the Much-Purring villages have decided to start their cricket season early, I've had to comply with the majority; otherwise, we'd have no one to play against once the fixtures are set.'

Hettie was tempted to point out that that might have been the best plan. Bunty's team had only clocked up one win last summer, and that was due to Much-Purring-on-the-Rug being suspected of ball tampering, but she was diverted from the thought by the arrival of Molly Bloom, hot and flushed from her kitchen and carrying a tray of lunches.

'So, I hear there's to be a bake off competition planned for Easter?' she said, putting Hettie's fish pie in front of her. 'Tarquin's after borrowing some of my kitchen stuff for his contestants – mixing bowls and the like – and Elsie tells me that her sister, Fanny Haddock, is to be a judge. Between you and me, I'm not one for watching her *Cook Along with Fanny* show on the television. That cat will stuff a chicken with anything she finds lying around, so she will. Have you seen some of those colours she uses to paint her claws? And as for the lipstick, don't start me on that one.'

'Well, nothing has been nailed to the mast yet, so to speak,' responded Bunty, eyeing up Tilly's chips, 'but we are trying to accommodate Tarquin's bake off with an Easter cricket match. Wilco has offered a live broadcast of both if we don't turn him out of the pavilion, so we may need a separate tea tent. I'll have to smile nicely at the Butter sisters for that one.'

'Then there's the Easter bonnet parade and the egg hunt – how are you going to fit all that in?' asked Molly. 'You know what they're like round here – if the kittens have nothing to do, there'll be mischief, to be sure.'

'The egg hunt was a disaster last year,' chimed in Tilly, spearing a fish finger. 'Marmite Spratt forgot to hide them, and all the kittens screamed their heads off and ruined the outdoor screening of *The Sound of Music*.'

'You can only ruin something that's good to start with,' mumbled Hettie through a mouthful of fish pie.

Hettie's sarcasm was lost on Bunty, but Molly offered a giggle as she left them to their lunch and went over to take the newcomers' orders. Bunty rose to join her party. 'Good luck for tomorrow,' she said to Tilly. 'Wilco tells me it's your first radio show. I'll be listening.'

Tilly's stomach lurched at the very thought of her debut at Whisker FM. Suddenly she had no appetite, and Hettie was forced to mop up the remaining chips and fish fingers once she'd finished her own lunch. The puddings slid down more easily, though, and the two cats paid up and returned home to choose some music for Tilly's big day.

Chapter Three

Tilly woke to a plague of butterflies in her stomach. She had lain awake worrying for most of the night, with only Hettie's rhythmic snoring to keep her company. At the first sign of light filtering through their window, she had fallen into a fitful sleep in which her radio dream returned with a vengeance; now, as she struggled awake, she knew that, no matter how difficult it was going to be, she would have to face her demons.

She glanced across at Hettie, still fast asleep in her armchair, and took comfort from the fact that her friend would be there to assist her in what might turn out to be her darkest hour. Most cats, she supposed, would give their right paw to become a radio presenter, with the chance to show off, impose their musical taste on others, and generally talk about themselves; Tilly knew she would never fit that demographic. She had opinions, of course, but she rarely shared them and never put herself forward unless it was absolutely necessary, using Hettie as her personal shield against some of life's more troubling situations. Being part of The No. 2 Feline Detective Agency had given her confidence, but deep down she was still the mild-mannered, shy tabby she had always been. In her homeless days, much to her detriment, she was always the last to fall upon the scraps left out by more fortunate cats, and she would wait long into the night for a safe place to sleep, away from the streetwise cats who frightened and bullied her at the slightest opportunity.

Hettie had been her saviour. She'd been temporarily homeless herself and understood the perils of the outside world. Betty and Beryl Butter had rescued her and offered the store room at the back of their high street bakery for a small rent, which generously included coal for a fire and a daily choice of pies and pastries from their range of freshly baked delights. With the Butters' approval, Hettie had extended their offer to Tilly, and now the two long-haired tabbies had finally found a place they could call home. The detective agency had been one of Hettie's many enterprises: she was a cat who had reinvented herself several times over, with a moderately successful music career followed by a whole stream of odd ventures; inspired by Tilly's voracious appetite for crime fiction, she had finally hit upon a winner. Their sleuthing business was now much in demand, and – after a rather shambolic start – they had become the town's official Holmes and Watson.

Tilly threw off her blankets and filled the kettle, preparing two mugs for their morning tea and loading the toaster with two slices of bread. She peeled the foil off three cheese triangles and watched as the kettle boiled and switched itself off. Normally, the prospect of a new day filled her with joy, but even the spring sunshine now forcing its way into the room did little to lift her spirits. The spectre of Whisker FM hung in the air, and she wished over and over again that she had turned down Wilco's invitation.

She made the tea and spread the toast thickly with the cheese, absent-mindedly licking the knife when she'd finished. On cue, attracted by the familiar smell of breakfast, Hettie lifted her head, yawned, stretched, and sat up ready to receive her first meal of the day. Tilly responded by delivering a mug of tea and a slice of toast to the arm of Hettie's chair, taking her own breakfast back to her bed.

'You look a bit out of sorts,' observed Hettie, biting into her toast. 'It's your big day. You'll be a radio star by teatime.'

Tilly stared down at her toast and pushed it away. 'Actually, I think I might be sick in a minute. I might have to cry off and stay in bed today.'

'Nonsense,' said Hettie, rescuing Tilly's toast and claiming it as her own. 'You'll be fine once you get stuck in. It's just nerves. They'll disappear as soon as the red light comes on.'

Hettie's reassuring approach failed, and the very mention of an 'on-air' red light sent Tilly diving for the sink to relieve herself of the steak and kidney pie that she'd half-heartedly enjoyed the night before. Hettie helped her back to bed and, in an act of encouragement, switched on the radio. The not-so-dulcet tones of Branston Bean boomed out at them. He was one of the few survivors of Wilco's presenter reshuffle; surprisingly, the lisp that plagued him was actually more of an entertainment than a disability. 'You're lithening to Withker FM,' he announced before launching himself into the travel news. 'No reporths of any hold upths; trainths and buthes running on time; and no inthidenths or acthidenths to report.' Branston slammed in the travel jingle to end his not exactly informative message, and went straight to one of his classic music choices: 'Remember You're a Womble'.

'There you are,' said Hettie. 'I honestly don't know what you're worried about. You can knock Branston Bean's socks off any day. You've just got to believe in yourself.'

Tilly rested on her blanket, listening to Branston's dull little quips, punctuated by yet more awful music. By the time the eleven o'clock news bulletin arrived, she had convinced herself that 'Tea Time with Tilly' might even be worth listening to. Feeling much better, and hungry now, she sprang from her bed and spent some time choosing the right cardigan for her radio debut. They stored their clothes in the bottom drawer of their filing cabinet – an often tangled mess of jumpers, T-shirts, jackets, socks, hats and scarves, mostly bought from Tilly's friend, Jessie, who ran the local charity shop. Today, Tilly chose a royal blue cardigan with yellow buttons and trimmed pockets.

Hettie had busied herself in packing up the singles she'd chosen for Tilly's show. Now that her friend was up and about, she announced that it was time for a Butters' egg and bacon bap and a frothy coffee each and left Tilly to practise her cues while she joined the eager line of cats waiting to be served in the bakery.

Betty and Beryl Butter's queues were always good-natured, an opportunity for the townsfolk to catch up on community affairs and gossip. Today, as Hettie joined them, there seemed to be only one topic of conversation: Tarquin Flapjack's proposed Easter bake off was gathering momentum, and the added excitement of the TV cook Fanny Haddock being enlisted as a judge made the prospect even more special. Tarquin had papered the town overnight with application forms for would-be contestants, and now bake off madness was spreading amongst every cat who had ever wielded a rolling pin or pastry cutter. Hettie listened as recipes were discussed, methods compared and intimate details of Fanny Haddock herself passed up and down the queue. She was relieved finally to place her order with Beryl and have a brief conversation that wasn't about competitive baking. 'So it's Tilly's big day,' said Beryl, generously filling the baps with bacon and a fried egg from her portable griddle. 'Sister and me are shutting early so we can settle down to listen. We never thought we'd be sharing the bakery with a radio star.'

Betty joined in as she frothed the coffees, shouting to be heard above the machine. 'We never listened local till Wilco took over, but now we have their breakfast show and the teatime one on every day – although we're not that keen on Branston Bean, are we, sister?'

Beryl shook her head. 'No, we're not. I'm surprised Wilco kept him on after his revamp – awful music, silly competitions, and I can't understand a word he says, although I don't suppose that's his fault. It's just as well we're too busy to listen at this time of day or we might have to complain. Thank goodness he's been moved off the breakfast show, at least. We much prefer Tansy Flutter. She comes in for a pie and a cake most days after her early morning stint, and she does a lovely exercise session at a quarter to eight every morning. Sets us up for the day, it does. You and Tilly should try it.'

Hettie shrank back at the very thought: as far as she was concerned, there was no such thing as a quarter to eight in the morning, let alone any need for exercise. She paid for the baps and coffees and stepped out into the high street, and was about to enter the alleyway that ran down the side of the bakery to the back door when Tarquin Flapjack approached her and thrust one of his application leaflets into her paw. 'No time to waste,' he said. 'I'll be sifting through the applicants and running heats in the Methodist Hall. Fanny Haddock has agreed to attend as part of her judge's role, so if you want to be involved, you'd better look sharp.'

Hettie blinked at the intrusion and was about to tell the cat where to stick his leaflets, but he was gone before she could respond. Tarquin Flapjack had been one of Wilco's casualties. He had, for far too many years, been the Saturday night chat show host, too full of his own importance to care genuinely about his listeners. At that time of night, frail and elderly cats tuned in just to hear a reassuring voice until their medications surrendered them eventually to sleep. He encouraged his listeners to phone in and discuss their lives, hopes and fears, but his responses were abrupt and callous in delivery, and – whatever the subject or the needs of his callers – he would always manage to turn the conversation to his own attributes, making himself the centrepiece of the show. His ego stretched much further than his actual programme: he encouraged get-togethers amongst his on-air 'family', and charged them for the pleasure of taking tea with him en masse. Elderly and lonely cats flocked from every corner of the town to meet him, mistakenly thinking he cared, but behind closed doors he referred to his fans as a herd of 'geriatric fur balls', who were there to be exploited in as many ways as he could devise.

When Wilco sat down to reshape Whisker FM, Tarquin was the first to get his marching orders. Having listened to just one Saturday night performance, Wilco was in no doubt that this bigoted, self-opinionated, egotistical show-off didn't fit his criteria as the station's new manager. Tarquin's sacking brokered a few mild protests, mostly encouraged by the presenter himself, but Wilco soon boosted the listening figures by taking on the slot personally and establishing a 'memory lane' feel. Now, the seniors of the town happily reminisced on old times, shared their sometimes primitive poetry, and put the world back on its axis by offering wisdom earned from long lives and experience.

Tarquin took his ego with him when he left Whisker FM, and now nurtured his own importance by forcing himself onto any committee in the town that would have him. Some still treated him as a radio celebrity and welcomed his opinions and suggestions, rather naively thinking that he was all for the common good; others steered clear, seeing him for what he really was. Hettie was in the latter camp, not because of his reputation but because she simply couldn't stand him.

She was pleased to see that Tilly had cheered up when she returned with the breakfast baps. She'd been practising her book review for the show, and her choice was Nicolette Upstart's latest effort, *Sorry for the Bread*, a crime novel bursting with poisoned crusts, deadly greenhouses and illicit passion fruits. Nicolette was one of Tilly's favourite crime writers, and she had actually booked the author to appear at the town's literary festival a couple of years earlier. The festival itself became a book lover's nightmare when several murders occurred, which Hettie and Tilly successfully solved, but Nicolette was still standing by the end of it and the festival's notoriety had boosted her book sales beyond all measure.

Tilly put down her script and pounced on one of the baps. 'I'm starving,' she said, taking a large bite and allowing the egg yolk to cover her paws as it oozed out of the bread.

Hettie kept a safe distance between them, savouring the bacon and occasionally coming up for air for a sip of frothy coffee. Much licking and cleaning followed in companionable silence until the two friends were ready – and almost willing – to face the reality of Tilly's first radio show.

Chapter Four

The recreation ground was on the edge of town and served many purposes throughout the year, as well as offering a playing field to the local infant and senior schools. The pavilion and cricket pitch were the jewels in its crown, mainly because they were cared for by one of the town's retired sporting legends, Mr Edward Dexter. Dex, as he was known to the clientele at the Cat and Fiddle, had bowled many a maiden over in his time, and had, on his retirement from the game, settled in a cottage overlooking the cricket pitch. He lived on his own in peaceful isolation, surrounded by the trophies earned during his cricketing days, and his love for the game still informed his retirement: he'd renamed his cottage 'The Stumps', and had encased it with a fence made up entirely of old cricket bats. He was a cat who kept himself to himself, but always offered a cheerfully raised paw to passers-by, adopting his umpire response. No one had ever seen him dressed in anything but his now faded cricket whites; even in winter he sported the outfit, enhanced by several layers of cricket jumpers which gave him an odd, inflated look.

He was hard at work rolling the cricket pitch as Hettie and Tilly approached the pavilion, and he offered a joyful chirrup as they passed, his pipe jammed firmly in his mouth. Pausing briefly to adjust his cap against the spring sunshine, he pushed the giant roller on, leaving a velvet green sward of perfection behind him. 'I don't know why Mr Dexter spends so much time on that cricket pitch,' observed Tilly. 'Bunty's team will only dig it up once they start the season.'

'They certainly hit more turf than balls from what I've seen,' agreed Hettie, 'and Balti Dosh took out at least two wicketkeepers last season with the swing of her bat. Mouth guards are a necessity when she's in. If only Bunty could train them to hit the actual ball, we might fare better against the Much-Purrings.'

The cricket talk came to an abrupt conclusion as Hettie opened the door of the pavilion: suddenly they were in a different world. Whisker FM's small reception area – brightly painted in the station's colours of sunshine yellow and sea blue – was adorned with framed pictures of the presenters. Wilco Wonderfluff took centre stage, flanked by a slightly out-of-focus portrait of Branston Bean and a seriously airbrushed image of Tansy Flutter. In her glory days, Tansy had been crowned Miss Much-Purring-on-the-Mat twice, and had toured the Much-Purring villages on a golden throne mounted on a milk float. Morbid Balm looked suitably Goth-like as she stared down at them from the portrait gallery, but the best example of radio station personnel sat at the reception desk, painting her claws an exotic orange and chewing frantically on pink gum which she occasionally blew into a large bubble, allowing it to burst and stick to her whiskers.

Marzi Pan would never have been Wilco's first choice of receptionist, but she was his niece and he'd agreed somewhat grudgingly to take her on to give his sister a break. Most cats left home to seek their independence as soon as they could, but Marzi had grown accustomed to the comfortable home life that her mother provided although there was no love lost between them; she had, in fact, taken over the whole of the house with her fashions and fads until her mother was obliged to live in her bedroom just to get away from her teenage daughter. Her father, Peter Pan, had – like his namesake – flown away shortly after Marzi's birth. Now, with Marzi gainfully employed at her uncle's radio station, her mother was clawing back her small terraced house room by room, forcing her daughter's detritus into a manageable space and hoping that Marzi would finally get the message that it was time to spread her wings, just as her father had done.

'Hello and welcome to Whisker FM,' she said, reading from a card in front of her in the monotone voice reserved for those still mastering their letters. 'How may I help you today?'

Hettie pushed Tilly forward to announce herself. 'I'm Tilly Jenkins, and I'm here to present "Tea Time with Tilly" at four o'clock,' she said.

Marzi jammed the brush back in her nail varnish bottle and picked up a pencil. 'Can you say all that again? I'm supposed to write it down.'

Tilly sighed with frustration. The clock above the receptionist's head said a quarter past three, and the butterflies she'd woken up with were starting to flutter in her stomach again. 'I said, I'm Tilly Jen…'

'Hang on, hang on!' Marzi exclaimed. 'Is that Tilly with a "T"?'

Hettie couldn't resist, and waded in. 'I can't imagine how else you might spell it, but we are in a bit of a hurry to get to the studios. Wilco is expecting us, so if you could let him know that Tilly with a "T" is here, that would be really helpful.'

Marzi blinked at Hettie, unruffled by any sense of urgency, and reached across her desk, forcing one of her orange claws onto a button on her intercom system. 'Tilly with a "T" is in reception,' she shouted, not trusting the volume of the apparatus.

Mercifully, Wilco responded immediately and appeared through the door marked 'studios', offering a beaming smile of welcome to both Tilly and Hettie as he ushered them through to the radio station's inner sanctum and left Marzi to complete her varnishing in peace. 'I wasn't expecting a full complement from The No. 2 Feline Detective Agency,' he remarked.

Hettie responded on Tilly's behalf. 'If you don't mind, I'm here to help out. We thought it would be easier if Tilly did the talking and I did the technical stuff.'

'Good plan, and great to have you both on board. The more the merrier. It's my mission to harness as many talented cats as possible from the town and really put this radio station on the map. When I first got here, it was run by a load of keen amateurs who seemed to be doing it for a bit of fun or for their own gratification, and not giving a thought to who might be listening or what they might like to hear,' Wilco explained, as Branston Bean slunk past him on his way out to reception. 'I've still got some adjustments to make to the daytime shows, but all in good time.'

In front of them were two studios, both with large windows, one of them occupied by the afternoon show presenter. Gilbert Truffle was a master of the airwaves, having cut his teeth in choppy seas on pirate radio boats longer ago than anyone could remember. Gilbert was a very old cat, riddled with arthritis and a little hard of hearing unless he had his headphones on, but his voice was strong and engaging, and he had the knack of lifting his listeners' spirits through friendly, intelligent banter and an eclectic choice of music. Wilco had been delighted when Gilbert made the move from national radio, and now he'd become one of the most popular broadcasters on the new look and listen Whisker FM.

Wilco nodded towards Gilbert through the glass. 'That cat taught me everything I know about radio,' he said. 'If you're in any doubt about how you should sound, just listen to Gilbert.'

Tilly nodded shyly. Her butterflies deserted her, replaced now by a slight hint of excitement as Wilco flung open the door of the empty studio. She commented later that it smelt of hot carpet, and the stillness and soundproofing added to the effect. For Hettie, it was like coming home: she'd spent quite some time in studios during her music career, cutting six albums and several promotional singles, as well as doing many radio interviews.

Wilco wasted no time in demonstrating the radio desk. He pointed to the brightly coloured faders first. 'Red's for presenting, green and blue for guests, black ones are for the gram decks, two of them, and the purple ones are for tape-recorded interviews. Outside sources for telephone calls are on this unit here – you just have to flick them up and down like a telephone exchange. This bank of carts has all the jingles and ads you'll need: top of the hour, travel news, and a special presenter ident jingle – you should play that as often as you can to get the listeners used to a new voice. All the faders have pre-fades, so you can check your levels before it goes out.'

Hettie nodded, pleased to see that there was nothing in the set-up to worry her, but Tilly gulped and shrank back into a corner as far from the radio desk as possible. The radio jargon frightened her as much as the prospect of broadcasting, and the studio clock now informed her that it was half past three.

'If you're going to drive the show for Tilly, you should have a play with the desk,' Wilco suggested. 'I'll leave you to it, but I'll be back at four to get you started.'

He swept out of the studio, leaving Hettie and Tilly to get accustomed to their new surroundings. 'I don't think I'll ever get used to this,' Tilly cried, putting her paws over her eyes. 'It's just too frightening.'

Hettie decided to employ the tough-love tactic. 'Look, you were so pleased when Wilco invited you to do this. You went round talking to yourself for days to practise, and all our friends are really looking forward to your show. You can't let them down – you're better than that. Pull yourself together, sit in that chair, and stick those headphones on while I get a handle on these faders.'

Tilly was used to Hettie's rants and they were never aimed directly at her, but this time she felt the sharpness of her friend's tongue personally and it did the trick. She emerged from her corner, clambered onto the presenter's swivel chair and clamped the headphones firmly on her head. Satisfied that they were making progress, Hettie checked out the microphones and their corresponding faders. She then moved to the record decks. 'What would you like to start with?' she asked, moving one of Tilly's headphones away from her ear.

'I'd like the Fruitgum one to start, as it's jolly, and then "My Boy Lollipop". When do you want to do the true crime slot?'

Now she was seated at the helm of the radio desk, Tilly had taken on a whole new demeanour. It was as if she had been powered up by an unseen force, and Hettie smiled to herself; she was more than aware of the centre-stage effect from her music days, when she had commanded vast audiences at live gigs, becoming what they wanted her to be for the length of a performance. 'Well, as you now seem to be producing the show, I'll do my bit whenever it suits you,' she said, cueing up Tilly's choice of starters.

Tilly's new sense of purpose encouraged her to read through the scripts she'd prepared as Hettie put the discs she planned to play in order. Before they knew it, Wilco was back in the studio to oversee the transition from Gilbert Truffle to 'Tea Time with Tilly'. 'Gilbert has agreed to read the four o'clock news and the sport,' he explained, 'but you'll have to take control while he's doing it by opening this fader and pressing the big red button. As soon as he plays his out jingle, you're on. Play in your ident and away you go.'

There seemed to be so much to remember, and even Hettie was starting to feel nervous, but Tilly looked strangely calm as Gilbert Truffle said his goodbyes and launched himself into the four o'clock news bulletin. Under the watchful eye of Wilco, Hettie pressed the red button, sealing Tilly's fate. There was no going back now.

The news was brief, mostly highlighting plans and events for the Easter holidays, with a brief clip of Tarquin Flapjack announcing his bake off competition. The sports bulletins were also short and to the point, confirming that the town's cricket season would start earlier than usual. Gilbert slammed in his final jingle and Hettie pushed the button on Tilly's ident. Suddenly the studio was filled with the sound of the Caterwaulers Folk Club, announcing to the listeners in tuneful harmony that it was now 'Tea Time with Tilly' that they were listening to. Wilco had enlisted the town's purveyors of ballads and folky tales to record 'the station sound', as he put it, and they had generally made a good paw of it, although Hartley Battenberg had recorded a spoof ident for Branston Bean, including a lisp in his first name. As well as being the best act the folk club could offer, Hartley was a stand-up comedian and Wilco was sorely tempted to go with his alternative version, but thought better of it; instead, he invited Hartley to use his comedic talents on a daily chuckle hour show on weekday evenings at six.

Hearing her own jingle almost put Tilly off – she would say later that it was just too lovely – but Hettie nudged her into her introduction by opening her presenter fader and revealing the 'on-air' red light for the first time. Tilly rose to the challenge – a little dry-mouthed, perhaps, but clear and precise. 'Hello, and welcome to "Tea Time with Tilly" – two hours of lovely things, including the latest book from Nicolette Upstart, a true crime tale from Hettie Bagshot, and some very nice music.' She nodded to Hettie, and the 1910 Fruitgum Company launched into 'Yummy, Yummy, Yummy'. Pleased with his new recruits, Wilco gave them the claws-up and retired to his small office to listen to the rest of the show.

To fill in between records, Tilly had – at Wilco's suggestion – prepared some interesting facts and celebrity birthdays to share with her listeners. She enthralled them with the fact that the town's department store, Malkin and Sprinkle, was sixty years old this month, and that Lavender Stamp's post office used to be a chop house during the Regency period.

Her star birthdays included the famous cat burglar, Archibald Ruffles, and the heavyweight tomcat champion boxer, 'Gloves off' O'Riley. Hettie kept the music coming, moving from Millie Small and her 'Boy Lollipop' to The Monkees' 'Daydream Believer'.

The two cats were doing remarkably well until the sultry figure of Marzi Pan appeared in the studio, waving a piece of paper at Tilly. 'This is your travel news and weather. I've had a ring round, but to be honest I can't find any. Oh, and you've had a complaint from a listener who wants to know why Tarquin Flapjack isn't on any more. The same listener phones six times a day, so I shouldn't worry. We all know it's Tarquin making the calls and disguising his voice.'

Marzi left the studio and Tilly stared at the piece of paper she'd left behind, which looked like an inebriated spider had crawled across the page. Clearly Marzi had problems forming her letters as well as reading them. 'I've stuck your travel and weather jingle in ready to play,' said Hettie, trying to be helpful. 'You've got about a minute left on this record.'

Tilly looked up from the note and started to panic. 'I just can't read this, so what shall I say?'

'Oh, just make it up,' suggested Hettie. 'I've never heard an accurate travel or weather bulletin on the radio, so why should we start now? We know it's sunny outside today. Ten seconds and you're on!'

Tilly gulped and cleared her throat, ready to do her first travel bulletin. Hettie played in the jingle and Tilly responded as it faded away underneath her. 'No reports of anything nasty happening out there,' she began, 'and the cars and buses are all running smoothly, except when they have to stop for traffic lights at the junction of Cheapcuts Lane and the High Street – there's always a queue there. The weather is lovely at the moment, but it will be a bit colder later tonight.' Tilly nodded to Hettie, making it clear that she had nothing else to say. Hettie responded by hitting the button on the 'travel out' jingle and playing The Hollies' hit 'Bus Stop', trying to keep things topical.

Hartley Battenberg had arrived in the studio next door, ready for his show at six, and he gave Tilly a cheerful wave and a claws-up. She was pleased to see that he, too, was practising his script, which made her feel a little more confident of her own shaky beginning.

It was mutually decided that Tilly should do her book review next. For her, it was the only bit of solid ground in the whole programme; she was more than used to discussing novels at Turner Page's library book group, and never short of something to say. Hettie counted her in as The Hollies faded away, adding Tilly's ident jingle for an extra flourish. She was having a wonderful time with the studio's technical kit, and was in her element. Tilly was being brave, eyeing up the wastepaper bin on occasions in case she had to be sick.

Her book review was comprehensive, extolling the virtues of Nicolette Upstart's writing style, her murderous plots, and the gardening and baking skills which she had harnessed in her latest book, *Sorry for the Bread*. Tilly went on to recommend other books by the author, including *The Death of Lucy Cat*, a particular favourite of hers, and finished her review by announcing that the author herself would be doing an event at the town's library later that summer.

Hettie followed up the review with Stevie Nips' 'Hedge of Seventeen', giving Tilly a breather with a track that was five minutes long. Sadly, there was no time to put her paws up: Marzi Pan burst into the studio again, this time with Tarquin Flapjack in tow. 'He needs to put out a message!' she said, exiting as quickly as she'd arrived.

Tilly stared blankly at Tarquin across the radio desk and waited for him to speak. He responded to her lack of welcome by making himself comfortable in front of one of the guest microphones, waiting for Miss Nips to finish her song, but Hettie decided to intervene on Tilly's behalf. 'I'm sorry, Mr Flapjack, but we weren't expecting you. Is your message urgent? Has someone died?'

Tarquin stretched his neck, assuming an authority he no longer had. 'After all my years of service to this station, I don't think I need an excuse to broadcast. Judging by what I've heard this afternoon, the sooner

I'm back on the airwaves, the better the listeners will like it.'

Hettie's hackles rose as Tilly felt the insult. 'My understanding is that you were sacked from here for that awful Saturday night show you used to do,' she said, moving in for the kill. 'Maybe we should ask Wilco if he's happy to let you give out your message at all?'

On cue, Wilco appeared at the door and Tarquin stood up like a cat caught in the act. 'How many times do I have to tell you that I don't want you anywhere near a microphone on this radio station?' Wilco began, taking the cat by the arm and steering him out of the studio. Tarquin protested, but Wilco manoeuvred him into the corridor, and Hettie and Tilly watched through the glass as the two cats measured up to each other. The spat was short-lived, as Wilco forced the unwanted presenter back through reception and out onto the playing field along with the wad of bake off leaflets that he'd deposited with Marzi. The leaflets scattered in the wind, a bit like Tarquin's broadcasting career. Edward Dexter watched as the snowstorm of paper swirled in the air, making sure that none of it landed on his sacred turf, and ever ready to make a catch if required.

Tarquin Flapjack turned reluctantly on his heel, thwarted in yet another bid to make his radio comeback. He'd hoped that his faithful listeners would rise up and demand he be reinstated if they heard him again, under the illusion that they still cared; sadly, they were having a much better time with Wilco on Saturday nights and had quite forgotten about the previous presenter.

After making it clear to Marzi that Tarquin was not to be allowed into the studios again, Wilco called in on Tilly just as Hettie was presenting her true crime feature. She'd chosen to highlight the Furcross case, the very first No. 2 Feline Detective Agency job that she and Tilly had taken on, set in a home for slightly older cats. Hettie laid out the suspects, gave details of the actual investigation and demonstrated their skills at solving the mystery that had haunted the town several years before. Wilco was fascinated, and even Tilly – who'd helped to solve the case – listened as if she'd never heard of it before.

After completing her presentation, Hettie turned to Sonny and Cher for some light musical relief, giving Wilco a few moments to heap praise on his new recruits. 'It's a great listen,' he said. 'Good music, strong subjects, entertaining and informative, with just the right amount of edge to it. I'm sorry about Tarquin Flapjack trying to hijack the microphone. He thinks he's God's gift to broadcasting, but he's so out of touch with what we're trying to do here. You two make a brilliant double act, though. I don't suppose you'd be willing to take on the mid-morning show between you? There may be a vacancy soon?'

Before Tilly could answer, Hettie leapt in. 'We'd love to,' she said, 'but we have cases coming out of our ears at the moment, and the next murder could be just around the corner.'

Wilco accepted defeat and Tilly was relieved, but Hettie's prophecy was all too soon to come true.

Chapter Five

The bakery was shut up for the day when Hettie and Tilly made their way to the back door, but Betty and Beryl were waiting for them by the bread ovens in the hallway. 'There's been a disaster at Molly Bloom's café!' Beryl said, buttoning her coat.

'You'd better look sharp and get round there,' Betty added. 'No time to waste. Your services are required.'

Tilly felt a little disappointed, as there had been no mention of her triumphant show and both Butter sisters had promised to listen. She'd skipped out of the radio station, buoyed up by Wilco's praise, and had even taken a short cut across the cricket pitch, much to Edward Dexter's dismay. Arriving home to trouble was not what she was looking for, even if it did mean helping Molly Bloom out.

Hettie was equally annoyed, as she'd been looking forward to a Butters' pie, a nice cake, and a pipe or two of catnip. It had been a stressful day, and she'd planned to celebrate Tilly's success in front of their own fire, but they were bundled back out by their landladies and marched down the high street to Bloomers. The café looked closed when they got there, and Hettie was about to turn round and head for home when Beryl gave her a sharp shove in the back, forcing her to open the café door.

All was quiet. The tables were laid up with cutlery and condiments, and looked as they always did except that there were no customers. 'So where is everybody?' asked Tilly to no one in particular.

'We're here!' came the response, as two dozen heads popped up from under the tables. Molly Bloom bustled through from her kitchen with a giant three-tiered chocolate cake in the shape of a radio desk, complete with multi-coloured buttercream faders, biscuit record decks, and coiled liquorice circles that looked remarkably like tiny 45 rpm singles. In the centre of the desk sat a chocolate model of a cat wearing headphones. 'Is that me?' squealed Tilly, delighted with her surprise.

'Well, who else could it be?' said Molly. 'To be sure, you are the radio star of the day.'

A cheer of agreement went up from around the café, and Tilly took in all the cats who'd come to celebrate. Most of the high street's residents had turned out for her: Lavender Stamp, the town's postmistress; Dorcas Ink, the printer; Hilda Dabbit, who ran the dry cleaners; and Elsie Haddock, who'd closed her fish and chip shop early to attend the party. There were new friends, too, as Wilco had gathered together some of his presenters to celebrate their new recruit. Gilbert Truffle, Tansy Flutter and a rather sulky looking Marzi Pan had all made the effort, with a promise that Hartley Battenberg would be joining them when he finished his show at seven. Morbid Balm ticked boxes in both camps, being a friend and business associate: she was often called in to help when Hettie and Tilly were dealing with dead bodies, and now she was also one of Wilco's specialised music presenters. Bloomers was packed with well-wishers, and more and more of the town's residents piled into the café to celebrate Tilly's triumph.

Everyone agreed that the cake was magnificent. The Butter sisters had been up late into the night decorating it, and Beryl had crept out before the sun was up to deliver it to a bleary eyed Dolly Scollop, who'd set her alarm accordingly. It was the centrepiece of the party, but Molly and Dolly made several trips from the kitchen with plates of meat-paste sandwiches, bowls of crisps, and an abundance of the Butters' savoury pastries – sausage rolls, miniature pasties, and egg and bacon quiche squares, a particular favourite of Tilly's.

When the central table was groaning with food, Wilco stepped forward to say a few words. Like a true broadcaster, he cleared his throat and began. 'Friends, we are here to celebrate Miss Tilly Jenkins' first foray into the magical world of radio, and what a magnificent paw she made of it! We should also acknowledge her technical support, delivered by Miss Hettie Bagshot. I know how well-loved these ladies are in this town, and how much safer we all feel as they go about their work at The No. 2 Feline Detective Agency, and I promise you all that Whisker FM is here to support the community at large, with cats like Tilly and Hettie who make our lives richer and more informed through their broadcasts. I would now like to invite Tilly to cut her cake.'

Tilly stepped forward, her ears pink with embarrassment. Taking the cake slice proffered by Dolly Scollop, she cut into the sponge to an energetic round of applause. Wilco stepped forward once again with a large rectangle wrapped in brown paper. 'And this is for you,' he said, forcing the parcel into Tilly's arms. She staggered under its size and weight, and Hettie came to the rescue, holding it while Tilly stripped the paper off with her claws and found herself staring down at her own image. The shock on her face made everyone laugh. She'd only ever seen snaps of herself before, mostly in the local paper when a case that she and Hettie had solved hit the headlines; now she was staring at a life-size picture, framed and sporting her name in bold capitals like the portraits she'd seen earlier in Whisker FM's reception.

Wilco followed up with another, much smaller parcel, which Tilly eagerly opened. It was a stack of presenter cards, all bearing the same photo, the station logo and phone number, and 'Tea Time with Tilly' printed across the bottom. 'We send these out to listeners so they can see what you look like,' he said. 'They like them to be signed.'

'Well, I'll have one of those right now,' said Betty, scrabbling in her shoulder bag for a biro. Before anyone could have so much as a sandwich, the cats formed an orderly queue and Tilly signed away her first batch of presenter cards.

Hettie watched her friend bathe in her well-earned glory, although the cynical side of her felt that the party was really a marvellous marketing opportunity for Wilco's radio station. It wasn't all smiles. Later she noticed Tarquin Flapjack and Branston Bean staring in through the window from the high street. They appeared to exchange a brief conversation before moving off in opposite directions, the old guard being replaced by the new, and Hettie suddenly felt uneasy, although she couldn't say why.

The party continued well into the evening, with champagne and alcoholic ginger beer being drunk in equal measure. Lavender Stamp was the first to wobble home to her post office, much to the relief of many of the other cats; Lavender was disliked for her rather unfriendly customer service, and enjoyed making her patrons feel uncomfortable at the slightest excuse. Tilly received more and more compliments as the evening progressed, but it was Gilbert Truffle who made the biggest impression on her, showering her with praise and adding some non-patronising broadcast tips. Tansy Flutter had been very welcoming, too; the cats discovered a shared appreciation for the crime novels of Agatha Crispy, and Tilly was able to impress Tansy by telling her that she'd actually met the author on a trip to Devon.

Hettie, Tilly and the Butters were the last to leave Bloomers, having helped Molly and Dolly to tidy the café ready for breakfast the next day. In contrast to the night before, Tilly fell asleep the moment she crawled into her blankets. Hettie treated herself to a pipe of catnip, enjoying the peace that had finally come after such a hectic day. She pulled her dressing gown up to her chin and settled in her armchair, where she was soon dead to the world.

The telephone, which lived in the staff sideboard, began to ring half an hour later. It was Tilly's job to answer it, as Hettie felt her privacy was being invaded every time it rang, and usually she was delighted to engage with the outside world; now, as she abandoned her warm blankets to crawl into the sideboard, she felt less enthusiastic about who might be breaking in on her sleep. Dragging the phone out of the cupboard, she pulled the receiver off the hook while Hettie scowled from her armchair. 'The No. 2 Feline Detective Agency, Tilly speaking. How may I help? Oh hello, Wilco. What can we do for you?'

Wilco's message was brief and to the point, and Tilly's facial expressions told Hettie that something was seriously wrong. Tilly replaced the receiver and pushed the phone back into the sideboard. 'It's Hartley Battenberg!' she said. 'He's been murdered at the radio station, strangled with his own headphones while he was eating a steak and kidney pie!'

Chapter Six

St Kipper's church clock struck midnight as Hettie and Tilly arrived at the recreation ground. The blaze of lights coming from the pavilion steered them across the grass to where Wilco waited anxiously, hopping from one paw to another. He'd fled the studio after his terrible discovery, stopping in reception to call for help before stepping out into the night air, hoping it would blow away the image of Hartley Battenberg's lifeless body.

'I'm sorry to call so late,' he said, 'but I just didn't know what to do. It was such a shock. I've never seen a dead cat before, and he's such a mess. Steak and kidney and pastry everywhere – all over the radio desk. He must have been eating his supper, which is strictly against the rules as the crumbs bung up the faders. And his eyes! I just can't get it out of my head.'

Hettie could see that Wilco was going to be very little help at the moment, and she needed to see the crime scene for herself. 'Take care of Wilco and I'll look in the studio,' she said to Tilly, pulling the door open. 'Perhaps a cup of sweet, milky tea might help with the shock?'

Tilly nodded and steered the station manager to a seat in his own reception before availing herself of the tea-making facilities behind Marzi Pan's desk. In spite of why she was there, she noticed with delight that the portrait she'd been presented with earlier was now hanging on the wall with the rest of the presenter photos. As she busied herself making three mugs of tea, she felt an overwhelming sense of pride at being part of Whisker FM, and was in no hurry to spoil it by viewing what lay beyond the door of studio 1A.

Hettie stood for a moment outside, staring through the glass at the horrific image before her. It was almost like a stage set, with several of the studio's spotlights trained on the figure who sat in his chair behind the radio desk, head to one side and eyes bulging. Hettie pushed the door open and moved in for a closer look. Hartley Battenberg, still clinging to his last broadcast script, had indeed been strangled with his own headphones; they were unplugged but still clamped over his ears, and the lead had been wrapped several times around the cat's neck before being tied to the headrest at the back of the swivel chair. What was left of a steak and kidney pie hung precariously from his purple, protruding tongue. Hettie looked more closely at his paws; his pads and claws showed no sign of pastry, and there was nothing on the script to suggest that he'd been eating before the killer had struck; it was clear to her that the pie had been forced into Hartley's mouth while he was struggling for life, or very soon after his death. She looked around for the wastepaper bin and found it kicked over near the door. Carefully, she searched through the contents – screwed up bits of weather and travel news, an abandoned banana skin and an empty crisp packet – but there was no sign of a pie wrapper. Returning to the body, she looked at the carpet immediately around the presenter's chair, but there were only a few pastry crumbs and the tiniest chunk of steak. Then she found what she was looking for – the rest of the pie, bulging from one of Hartley's trouser pockets.

Since forming the detective business, she had always tried to shield Tilly from the worst aspects of their work. Dead bodies came with the territory, but they were usually her department and she left Tilly to draw up lists of suspects and make copious notes during interrogations; this time, though, Tilly's eye for detail was needed at the coalface. Hettie made her way back to reception to find Wilco huddled over a mug of tea. Four sugars had helped to steady his nerves, but the haunted look on his face was still very much in evidence. Tilly had done her best to distract him, but had run out of conversation and was obviously pleased to see her.

'I'm afraid I can't spare you this one,' Hettie said, gratefully accepting a mug of tea and a custard cream that Tilly found in a tin marked 'Marzi's'. 'I need you, your notebook and your descriptive powers in the studio, and it really isn't a pretty sight.'

Tilly gulped her tea down, brushed the biscuit crumbs off her whiskers, and pulled a notebook and pencil out of her mac pocket. Wilco said nothing, and continued to stare at the dregs in his mug. Hettie hesitated, wondering if he should be left on his own, but rationalised that the evidence should come first and led Tilly into the studio corridor. 'I want you to jot down anything you think is interesting,' she said, as her friend stared open-mouthed at the body on the other side of the glass. 'Pay special attention to the pie.'

Tilly always paid special attention to pies, especially when she was about to eat them, but Hettie's instruction was a strange one and it encouraged her to venture into the studio for a closer look. It was the second time in several hours that she had found herself taking a deep breath in the studios of Whisker FM, and this was a lot more disturbing than reading the travel news. She began to scribble in her notebook as soon as she reached the body, noting – as she put it later – the nasty bits first. She wrote down a detailed description, including the fact that Hartley was wearing a Muddy Fryer T-shirt, bought from the singer's merchandise stall when she last appeared at the folk club. Tilly sniffed at the visible remains of the pie and agreed with the general consensus that it was steak and kidney, then turned to the victim's pocket, noting down the crimping of the crust and drawing a small diagram of it.

While Tilly continued to make her notes, Hettie removed the script from the dead cat's paws, folded it up and put it in her mac pocket. She then looked in more detail at the radio desk, trying to assess whether the killing had taken place during or after his broadcast. The faders were all closed and the 'on-air' button was off. According to the meter levels in front of her, the station seemed to be broadcasting something so she pulled up one of the outside source faders and was rewarded with the Feline World Service, an option that all local radio stations turned to when their broadcasting day came to an end. FWS broadcast twenty-four hours a day, with correspondents from around the globe. 'Looks to me like Hartley had finished his show before the killer struck,' Hettie said, closing the fader on a reporter from Columbia who was bemoaning a bad harvest of high grade catnip, 'unless it was someone who knew how the radio desk works and was capable of leaving it on autopilot.'

'But why would Hartley stop to eat a pie when he knew he was going on to Bloomers for a party after his show?' said Tilly.

'My thoughts exactly – but he clearly didn't eat it. Most of it's still jammed in his pocket. I think the pie might have arrived with his killer, and it's probably the best clue we have.'

'Shall we bag it as evidence?' Tilly suggested, using a phrase she'd heard on *Starsky and Hutch*.

'I suppose we should.' Hettie reached for a piece of scrap paper out of the litter bin and folded it into a cone, then carefully pulled the pie out of the dead cat's pocket and slid it into her makeshift evidence bag. 'We'd better give Morbid Balm a ring,' she said. 'She'll have to come and collect him, and there may be other clues once she's got him back to her preparation room at Shroud and Trestle. If you've finished with your notes in here, we'd better have a word with Wilco.'

Hettie and Tilly made their way back to reception, where Wilco had hardly moved. Tilly sat by him while Hettie dialled the undertakers. She was in luck, as the call was diverted to the 'on duty' number and Morbid Balm answered in a sleepy but businesslike fashion.

Morbid sat up in her black fleecy blankets when she recognised Hettie's voice, knowing that the call-out was bound to be interesting. The Goth cat had been a real asset to The No. 2 FDA during their murder cases, and she never shied away from a violent death. Her respect for the cats who ended up on her mortuary slab was immeasurable, and she was keen to make sure that the deceased went to their graves looking the best they could: glossy fur, polished teeth, straightened whiskers and clipped claws were all part of the service.

Morbid was shocked to hear that the 'removal' was from Whisker FM, but she promised to be there within the hour, leaving Hettie time to question

Wilco. 'I know you're still in shock,' she began, 'but there are a few things I need to ask.' Wilco nodded slowly as Tilly chose a clean page in her notebook and wrote 'Wilco' in big letters across the top. 'I have a few security questions first. What made you come back to the radio station after the party, and how did you find it when you got here?'

Wilco lifted his head and pointed to the portraits on the wall. 'I wanted to get Tilly's picture up in reception to save me taking it home and bringing it back again tomorrow. When I got here, everything looked normal. There was a safety light on over the reception desk, and I went to the drawers to find a hammer and some picture hooks. I checked the answer machine while I was there, and there were two calls – both of them complaining about Tarquin Flapjack losing his show, and both of them from Tarquin himself. He bombards us every day, pretending he's an irate listener, but we've all learnt to ignore his made-up voices. I was about to leave when I noticed some crumbs on the floor, which made me cross because Marzi is supposed to hoover and dust reception each day before she goes home. I went back to the desk for the brush and dust pan, and noticed that the crumbs led from the door through to the studios. I don't know what made me check, but I decided to investigate further and that's when I found poor Hartley in 1A.'

'So there was no sign of a break in?' Hettie asked. Wilco shook his head. 'And what about when Marzi

59

goes home? Is reception locked then, or can anyone just walk in and gain access to the studios?'

'No, we're very hot on that one,' said Wilco. 'If there's no receptionist, the main door is locked and the only way you can get in is with a key. Otherwise, the on-air presenter would be a sitting duck after hours.'

'And who holds keys to the radio station?' Hettie continued.

'Just about everybody,' said Wilco. 'Branston Bean, Gilbert Truffle, Tansy Flutter, Morbid Balm, Marzi – although she claims she's lost hers – and Hartley, of course. Most presenters need access, as they have to edit interviews and record things, often out of hours. And then there are the sports cats, as it's really their pavilion. Bunty Basham has a set, and Edward Dexter. I think that Betty and Beryl Butter might have a key as well for when they do the cricket teas.'

'What about past presenters like Tarquin Flapjack?'

'I got him to hand his key in, but I suppose he could have had another one cut before he gave it up.'

Hettie's frustration began to show; it would seem that she should have asked who didn't have a key to the pavilion; Wilco's answer would have been much shorter. 'What do you know about Hartley Battenberg?' Hettie asked, moving on.

'I've seen him play at the folk club. He's a good musician with a great voice, and he's very funny, too. I mean – he was funny. He had a sarcastic sense of humour and he sent himself up, mostly, but you wouldn't want to be the butt of one of his jokes. I loved his take on life. There was an edge to it, a breath of fresh air – just what Whisker FM needed.'

Hettie sensed another puff for the radio station coming, and decided to divert it by asking a few practical questions. 'Hartley presented a comedy hour between six and seven. What happens after that?'

'We go straight to FWS. We only broadcast from seven a.m. to seven p.m. weekdays at the moment. The weekends are a bit different. I do a late night show on Saturdays and Morbid has her late show on Sundays, but I'm hoping to expand the hours with some new presenters in future. I'm looking for suitable premises first, though, so we have a permanent base before getting any bigger. I promised Bunty we'd be out by the summer so that the cricket and rugby teams could have their pavilion back.'

'And what about Tarquin Flapjack?' asked Hettie. 'He doesn't seem to want to lie down quietly after being sacked. Could he have killed Hartley to get back at you?'

Wilco thought for a moment before answering. 'No more than any of the other cats I've had to get rid of. I'm afraid it's the name of the game in radio. When I worked on national stations, we all used to hold our breath around February each year in hopes that our contracts would be renewed when the March schedules were announced. You could never take anything for granted. Something as simple as not being asked to attend a photo session for the new presenter cards or calendars was enough to make us suicidal – that was a clear sign you were on your way out. I feel Tarquin's pain, but I'm afraid the listeners come first. Without them, we're nothing.'

Hettie pressed the point. 'Can you think of any other cats who might want to sabotage Whisker FM?'

'Well, I had a difficult conversation with Branston Bean earlier today over his choice of music. I told him I thought he'd be better suited to a weekend show, where he could explore the more light-hearted nature of pop culture. I suggested he could do something like the old Kittens' Favourites show that Uncle Mac used to put out.'

'How did he take that?'

'Not very well, really. Most presenters who get moved to weekends feel that it's the kiss of death, but I'm afraid in Branston's case it's weekends or nothing. He really isn't up to a show like mid-morning. It isn't even the speech impediment that bothers me; it's the fact that all he does is play records – he's little more than a disc jockey, and there's no substance to the show. At that time of day, cats should be phoning in, engaging with us and the live guests in the studio. I gave him a couple of weeks to make up his mind while I look around for a replacement.'

Hettie was fascinated by the cut-throat radio business, but she was getting nowhere with the murder of Hartley Battenberg. She knew that Hartley's death could easily be personal and have nothing to do with Whisker FM, but it was important to build up a suspects list as quickly as possible. 'Leaving the presenters to one side, are there any other cats who may have issues with the radio station?'

Wilco shook his head from side to side, pondering the question before answering. 'When we first moved in to the pavilion, some of the sports cats were a bit miffed, but Bunty smoothed things over with them and I do pay rent into the cricket and rugby fund. Edward Dexter was a bit difficult – I had one or two run-ins with him. He's very protective of the recreation ground. The slightest blade of grass out of place and he's on it, if you know what I mean, but lately he's been much happier about us being here. A lot of that's got to do with Tansy Flutter. She's made it her mission to befriend him. She pops into The Stumps most days after her show to have a cup of tea – a bit like pouring Darjeeling over troubled turf, if you like.'

Hettie appreciated the analogy and Tilly wrote it down word for word in her notebook, as she thought it was clever. The conversation was brought to an abrupt conclusion by Morbid Balm's appearance at the door, and Hettie rose from her chair to let her in. 'I'll have a look at the job before I bring my stuff in,' the mortician said, getting down to business immediately.

Hettie responded by leading her through to the studios, where Hartley Battenberg was centre stage.

'Someone's done a good job there,' Morbid said, taking a close look at the body. 'Have you finished with him? Rigor is setting in big time, so I need to straighten him out as soon as possible.'

'Tilly's made lots of notes, so I think we can hand him over to you now,' said Hettie. 'We think he was killed at around seven o'clock, after his show.'

'That figures,' said Morbid. 'Another couple of hours and he'll be as stiff as a board, so I'd better get to work. He was obviously strangled, but the pastry is a bit odd.'

'We removed the rest of a pie from his pocket,' Hettie explained.

'Well, that is interesting! Steak and kidney, isn't it, judging by what's hanging out of his mouth?'

'Why is that interesting?' asked Hettie, keen to pick up on any wisdom the Goth cat had to offer.

'Because he was one of those vegan cats, all vegetables and tofu! He invited me back for supper one night after the folk club – they were doing a special evening on death poetry, so I went along. The poetry was awful and so was the supper, sadly. He lived in one of those high-rise posh flats at the back of Sheba Gardens. Nearly burst my lungs climbing those stairs, and with only a lettuce leaf and some pulverised soya curd to show for it! I was on my way after a weak cup of peppermint tea. Lovely flat, though – full of musical instruments. He was quite a talented cat, and his radio show was hilarious.'

Hettie was interested to learn a little more about the victim. Morbid had given life to the body in front of them, but there was still no explanation as to why that life had ended so violently. 'Would you say he was popular at the folk club?'

'Oh yes, definitely. It was a bit of a rowdy night. Like I said, the poetry was awful and cats were getting bored and not listening until Hartley stepped up and delivered a thirty-verse murder ballad. You could have heard a pin drop. He was their star turn, all right. Anyway, I must fetch my gurney and get him shifted.'

Morbid bustled out into reception and Hettie followed. Tilly sat on her own, writing up her notes, while Wilco paced up and down outside the pavilion, taking in deep breaths of air. Morbid's van was parked discreetly at the back of the building and Hettie watched as she flung open the back doors and pulled out a collapsible stretcher on wheels. She pushed the trolley across the grass and into the pavilion, and Tilly stood to open the studio door, ready for Morbid and her gurney to go about their work. Minutes later, Hartley Battenberg left the radio station for the last time on his journey to Shroud and Trestle.

For decency's sake, Wilco put a 'temporarily out of order' sign on studio 1A, locked up the station and rode home across the recreation ground on his bicycle, promising to pay Hettie whatever it cost to catch Hartley's murderer and to call her if anything further occurred to him.

The church clock at St Kipper's struck two as Hettie and Tilly made their way across the cricket pitch, hoping to salvage some sleep before their investigations gathered speed the following day. Their departure had not gone unnoticed, as Edward Dexter watched from his sitting room window.

Chapter Seven

Hettie woke with a thumping head, mainly due to her lack of sleep: no sooner had she settled down in her armchair than the Butter sisters were firing up their bread ovens, ready to bake the bread, cakes, pastries and pies that filled their shop six days a week. It was the only drawback to renting a room in the bakery: most of the hard work had to be done in the very early hours to supply the many cats who travelled from miles around to secure their favourites from Betty and Beryl's extensive range of delights. Hettie was a late sleeper, and her mood and temperament relied on a good ten hours each night. Normally, she was completely unaware of her landladies' crack-of-dawn activities, but after their nocturnal visit to Whisker FM, she and Tilly had fallen into a light, troubled sleep, open to any outside disturbance. The roar of the bread ovens – just outside their door in the back hallway – could be very annoying, especially when accompanied by cheerful renditions of songs from popular musicals. Betty had recently favoured a selection from *Hair*, the show that Beryl took her to see as a late Christmas present. Betty had been very much taken with 'The Age of Aquarius', and had even toyed with the idea of having her long white fur braided and beaded; after a concerned conversation with her sister, she'd settled for belting out 'Good Morning Starshine' as she crimped her crusts and beat the meringues. In solidarity, Beryl often joined in, adding harmonies and conducting with her pastry fork.

Hettie had tried very hard to sleep through that Friday morning's cacophony, and even Tilly – who loved greeting a new day – was resisting the very thought of struggling from her blankets, but both cats knew that the day would be a full one. They had a murder case on their paws, and a list of suspects as long as one of Beryl's jumbo baguettes.

Life looked a little less bleak after Tilly had delivered the morning tea, and with the promise of some hot buttered toast to follow, Hettie's headache began to transform itself from a blinding tsunami into a dull throb. 'I suppose we'd better get stuck in,' said Tilly, loading the toaster. 'There are a lot of suspects to talk to, and with Poppa and Bruiser away with Miss Scarlet, we're on foot.'

Hettie sighed at the prospect. Their friend, Bruiser, was a very important part of The No. 2 Feline Detective Agency; he was the muscle of their operation, and more importantly he drove Miss Scarlet, their motorbike and sidecar. Hettie had never quite got the hang of their only mode of transport, and when Bruiser was invited to take up residency in a purpose-built shed at the bottom of the Butters' garden, he was the obvious choice for chauffeur. Poppa was an equally important part of Hettie's team. He'd been her roadie during her music days, and now – as well as being the town's plumber – he supplied an extra pair of paws when needed. 'Well, I suppose they're allowed one holiday a year,' she grumbled. 'Sod's law, really – we've had months of easy jobs, and now we've got a murder on our paws and we're really up against it. If we've got to rely on Clippy Lean's bus service, we're sunk before we leave the bakery.'

Like most things in the town, the public transport system was run on an ad hoc basis: there was a bus timetable, but no one had seen it for years, and Clippy Lean, the town's award-winning bus conductress, was so well liked that no one dare complain if her bus was late or didn't turn up at all. Tilly knew that the day was going to be a difficult one, and compensated by spreading the butter extra thickly on their toast. They sat contentedly enjoying their breakfast, savouring a few peaceful moments before – as Hettie would comment later – 'the pastry hit the fan'.

'I think we should start with your notes,' said Hettie, licking the butter off her paws. 'We need to draw up a list of suspects, then decide who to talk to first. We'll have to take a look at Hartley Battenberg's flat as well, in case there's anything that points to his murder.'

Tilly responded by grabbing her notepad and flicking to a clean page. She wrote 'Suspects' at the top of it, underlining it three times. It was one of her favourite moments during a case, and it always started the sifting process which was vital at the beginning of any investigation. 'Shall I write them down in order of nasty to nice cats, with the top suspects first?'

Hettie thought for a moment before replying. 'I think we should write them down in the order we're going to interview them, with the most likely candidates first. That will save time. Hopefully this murder is a one-off, and we can wrap it up before Easter.'

'I think Tarquin Flapjack should be at the top of the list. He's a bit nasty, and he's cross about losing his radio show.'

'Good idea,' agreed Hettie, 'and stick Branston Bean down next, followed by Wilco.'

'Wilco?' questioned Tilly. 'But he has an alibi. He was at my party when Hartley was murdered, so he couldn't have done it.'

'I know, but he's up to his neck in this radio business, and he's made a few enemies along the way. We were packed into Bloomers like sardines last night – anyone could have left the party and come back later, and it's only five minutes from Bloomers to the recreation ground. Come to think of it, Wilco set up the party in the first place, so he could have done it as an elaborate alibi for himself.'

Tilly gave in to Hettie's logic and made Wilco Wonderfluff number three on her list. 'If we're including the cats who were at my party, shall I add the rest of the radio presenters?' she asked.

'Yes, and you might as well stick everyone down who has a key to the pavilion,' said Hettie, pulling on her business slacks and one of her much treasured Clannad T-shirts. 'They all had opportunity, if not motive.'

Tilly read through her notes, adding more and more suspects to her list until she was sure she hadn't missed anyone. 'Shall I read them out?' she said at last.

Hettie nodded and sat back in her armchair to consider the names as Tilly listed them. 'Tarquin Flapjack, Branston Bean, Wilco Wonderfluff, Gilbert Truffle, Tansy Flutter, Edward Dexter, Bunty Basham, and Marzi Pan, although Wilco said she's lost her key. I haven't included Morbid or Betty and Beryl. I can't honestly see them strangling anyone.'

'No, and I think we've got more than enough there to go on,' said Hettie. 'We'd better start at the top of the list with Mr Flapjack, heaven help us. I'd like to get him out of the way as soon as possible. Do you have one of his leaflets handy? I think his phone number is on it.'

Tilly found the bake off leaflet, which she'd been using as a bookmark in Nicolette's latest offering. 'There's the number,' she said, 'but look – it's the heats for the bake off at the Methodist Hall today. It says all applicants should bring their signature dishes to be judged between ten and three. Fanny Haddock is going to be there, evidently.'

'Perfect. We'll start there, but first I need to ask the Butters if they'll store this pie in their fridge. It's the best bit of evidence we have at the moment.' Hettie picked up the remains of the pie she'd rescued from Hartley Battenberg's pocket and was about to leave the room with it when a knock came at the door.

Betty and Beryl stood on the threshold bearing gifts. 'Sister has inadvertently burnt this batch of sausage rolls, on account of her getting carried away with her upward arm swings. Our old mother used to say when they're brown they're done and when they're black they're buggered,' Beryl said, pushing a tray of only slightly overbaked pastry at Hettie.

'I blame Tansy Flutter and her breakfast show, she's far too interesting,' Betty said in her own defence. 'What with the murder last night, I'm surprised she had time to fit her exercise slot in this morning. We had all the lurid details. That poor cat – she said he'd been eating a steak and kidney pie at the time. I just hope it wasn't one of ours.'

Hettie passed the tray of sausage rolls to Tilly and pushed the remains of Hartley's pie under Betty's nose. 'This was the pie. We found most of it in his pocket. It would be helpful if you could store it for us in your fridge.'

Betty took the pie and sniffed it, allowing her sister a closer look. 'Thank goodness!' she said. 'Nothing to do with us, is it, sister?'

Beryl shook her head. 'No, that's definitely not one of ours. Home-baked by the look of it.'

'What makes you say that?' Hettie asked, marvelling at the sisters' knowledge of pastry.

'Well, it's all down to the crimping of the crust,' said Beryl. 'See here – it's not a proper job. There's been seepage, and every pie maker has their own style of crimping, don't they, sister?'

Betty took up the discussion on pies, while Hettie and Tilly each made short work of a sausage roll off the tray. 'The thing about pie making is it's personal. No pastry is the same, and crimping is like signing your name. This pie has an inferior crimp. It's too thick. They've used too much egg glaze, and there's too much pastry for too little filling. I agree with sister: it's home-baked, and a poor effort.'

Hettie was beginning to wonder why the Butter sisters hadn't been asked to judge the bake off competition instead of Fanny Haddock, but she said nothing. She was still digesting the revelations gleaned from Betty and Beryl's inspection of the evidence. It was hard to believe that the killer had baked a pie, taken it to the radio station, strangled Hartley Battenberg and left the pie as a calling card. 'I suppose we'd better get stuck in to this case, although it's going to be difficult without transport,' she said, posting another sausage roll into her mouth.

'Sister or me would be happy to run you about in the Morris,' Betty offered. 'As long as one of us is in the shop, that should be fine.'

Hettie seized the moment, grateful for the help. 'We have to go to the Methodist Hall this morning, as they're having the heats for the Easter bake off. There are one or two cats we need to talk to there. Maybe you could drop us off, if it's not too much trouble?'

'We've got to deliver some flans and pies to Malkin and Sprinkle in half an hour, so if you don't mind bunching up a bit in the front, sister could drop you off then.'

Hettie accepted their offer enthusiastically, and the Butters went about their business. Hettie and Tilly ate another sausage roll, then gathered up the things they needed for the day. Tilly made a point of wrapping the remaining pastries in greaseproof paper and adding them to her business satchel along with her notepad and two sharpened pencils, just in case the lead broke on one of them. Hettie, who always travelled light, grabbed her mac, and the two cats emerged into the spring sunshine.

The high street was quite peaceful for a Friday, and Betty and Beryl's Morris Minor convertible was the only car in sight. The two white cats were pushing and shoving several of their bakery trays, piled high with some of Malkin and Sprinkle's most popular lines, onto the back seat. When the Butter sisters first arrived in the town from Lancashire and purchased a somewhat run-down bakery, Mr Malkin and Mr Sprinkle were unconcerned about the prospect of a high street trade war. Within a few short weeks, they'd changed their minds, as Betty and Beryl's pies and pastries took the townsfolk by storm. It was in fact Hettie who had pointed out to Mr Malkin that the pies in his food hall were inferior to those she enjoyed in the Butters' bakery. He was a fair-minded cat and made a point of sampling the goods for himself, coming to the conclusion that he needed to stock a range of the sisters' delights in order to keep his own in-house bakery afloat. The deal had proved lucrative for all concerned, and in the department store's food hall, the Butters' franchise was known as 'The Extra Lovely Range'. Mr Sprinkle had arranged a special fixture to display the pies and pastries to their best advantage, and was rewarded by empty shelves each day by lunchtime. Disappointed cats would make the journey up the high street to the bakery itself, where Betty and Beryl did a roaring trade, invariably selling out by three in the afternoon. As Hettie had played no small part in the Butters' booming business fortunes, she had been rewarded with a place to live under Betty and Beryl's roof – a safe harbour for her, and now for Tilly.

Betty waved them into the front passenger seat. 'It's a bit of a squash, but the pastries have priority,' she said, starting up the engine. Tilly resorted to sitting almost on top of Hettie as Betty yanked the gear lever into first and pulled away from the kerb, intent on doing a three-point turn in the lay-by outside the post office. The reverse gear proved elusive, giving Hettie the opportunity to read Lavender Stamp's hurriedly scribbled message on the post office door: 'Closed until Monday'. Lavender was a law unto herself, and – as she was the only post office in town – she decided when and if she opened; today, she obviously had bigger fish to fry than postal orders and registered letters.

The three-point turn was completed in six moves, several expletives used only by cats born in Lancashire, and some helpful advice shouted across the street by Beryl. At last the Morris was pointing in the right direction and Betty put her foot down, moving from first to fourth gear with nothing in between. The hood was up to protect the pies from a possible sudden shower of rain but, as the Morris sped down the high street, it converted itself into an open top car, much to Tilly's surprise when a sudden rush of wind threatened to bucket her onto the back seat, endangering the perfectly baked and crimped pies. She hung on to the dashboard for the rest of the trip, grateful to arrive unscathed at the Methodist Hall, where she and Hettie quite literally fell out of the passenger seat and onto the pavement.

With a wave and a toot of her horn, Betty continued on her way to Malkin and Sprinkle, leaving Hettie and Tilly to gather up the dignity that had been lost in their ungainly exit from the Morris Minor. To their great embarrassment, it appeared that half the cats in the town witnessed their arrival: a very long queue had formed outside the Methodist Hall. The cats were all clutching their signature dishes, ready to impress Fanny Haddock and all hopeful of a place in Tarquin Flapjack's Easter bake off competition.

Chapter Eight

Tilly's friend Jessie ran the charity shop opposite the Methodist Hall. Jessie loved news, and – seeing Hettie and Tilly's arrival – she was quick to poke her nose out of her shop door. 'Hello you two,' she said, keen to catch up on any gossip. 'What brings you to Cheapcuts Lane? You're surely not entering the bake off, are you?'

Tilly shook her head. 'No, we're investigating a murder and one of the suspects is in there,' she said, waving her paw in the direction of the hall.

'Not Hartley Battenberg's murder!' squealed Jessie, unable to contain her excitement. 'It was all over the radio this morning. I was glued.'

'I'm afraid so,' said Hettie. 'Did you know him?'

'Not exactly, but I've seen him at the folk club a few times. I listened to his show last night as it came straight after "Tea Time with Tilly". What a star you are! I was sorry not to make your party.' Jessie pointed down at one of her paws, which was encased in plaster. 'The sooner I get rid of this, the better. That'll teach me to stand back to admire my own window display, and who'd have thought falling off the pavement could cause such chaos? Nurse Featherstone Clump says I'm stuck with this for another two weeks, which means I'll miss the first cricket match of the season now that Bunty's decided to start early. I couldn't keep wicket with this thing on, anyway. Slow walking is all I'm good for at the moment. I thought I might have a bash at the bake off with my apple and gooseberry pie, but the queue's too long and I ate half of it last night, so there's not much left to show Fanny Haddock. You should have seen the fuss when she arrived earlier – big black limo, and that awful Flapjack cat fawning all over her. She looked a piece of work, to be honest – much older than she comes across on TV. I'm not sure I'd want her digging her spoon into one of my pies, really, not with all that claw varnish!'

Jessie was clearly in the mood for a chat, but Hettie was keen to interview as many cats as possible on Tilly's list. 'I think we'd better get on,' she said, before Jessie could introduce another subject. 'We'll pop in later if you fancy putting the kettle on?'

Jessie clapped her paws together at the thought of an update on the murder, and promised sardines on toast to go with a milky tea before waving her friends off. As she had said, the queue of cats hopeful of a place in the bake off competition seemed never-ending. It appeared that half the town had turned out, clutching their plastic boxes of home-made cakes, buns and pies to be scrutinised by TV's cook of the moment. Getting into the Methodist Hall proved the first obstacle, but Hettie decided to use her own celebrity. 'Excuse me,' she said, pushing her way to the front of the queue as Tilly clung to the belt of her mac. 'We have urgent business – we're investigating a murder.'

It did the trick: the crowd parted as if Moses had asked, and Hettie and Tilly entered the hall, leaving the cats outside to ponder who might have been murdered. Those who listened to Whisker FM were able to inform the folk around them of the finer details of Hartley Battenberg's demise, and the queue shuffled along happily now that they had something interesting to talk about.

Inside, the queue continued towards a central trestle table, where Fanny Haddock sat flanked by Tarquin Flapjack and Bugs Anderton, the town's Friendship Club president. Bugs was big in all things community, and spearheaded most of the recreational pursuits that involved senior cats and stay at home mothers with kittens. Her Scottish roots and the fact that she was a short-haired ginger cat made her quite formidable, but Hettie and Tilly had seen a very different side to her during several of their past cases, and they now regarded her as a friend and confidante.

Hettie approached the table, nodding to Bugs but making a beeline for Tarquin Flapjack, and leaving Tilly to assess whether any more of their suspects were in the queue. Balti Dosh, the town's convenience store owner, was in the middle of a somewhat clinical appraisal of her samosa pie. Balti was a true crime fan and was always pleased to pass the time of day with Hettie or Tilly over her counter in Whisker Terrace, but today she only had eyes for Fanny Haddock as the TV cat delved into the centre of her samosa.

'The thing is, one has to take into account the texture,' Fanny said, forcing a bright red claw into the centre of the pie. 'There's plenty of filling, but it's loose – do you see?' The claw had managed to scoop most of the filling out onto the plate, spoiling what had been perfect when Balti pulled it from her oven earlier in the day. Fanny licked her claw and continued. 'You've got your flavours right, though – just the right amount of spices, and I suppose what you've done here is a bit different so we'll give you a try. Miss Anderton will take your details, and we'll see if we can make a cook of you yet.'

Balti was delighted, but she didn't take kindly to Fanny Haddock's own technique of patronising her dish. Balti's store was renowned for its excellent selection of home-cooked Indian foods, and she wasn't terribly happy about the TV cook teaching her to suck eggs.

Bugs took up her clipboard and included Balti in the first 'cook off'. 'You'll need to come back tomorrow at two p.m. for the lattice pie challenge,' she said, issuing Balti with a pink ticket.

'And do I need to bring anything with me?' Balti asked.

'No, it's the technical challenge. All contestants will be making the same pie, and the ingredients will be here waiting for you. Good luck.'

Balti moved on quickly with her pink ticket, mainly because the cat behind was forcing his granola tray bake into her back, keen to have it assessed by Fanny Haddock. As things turned out, he wouldn't be invited to the technical challenge: Fanny had a coughing fit at her first bite, and declared that the mix of cranberry and nuts was only fit for lining a hamster cage. Hettie was fascinated, both by Fanny herself and more especially by the keenness and desperation of the would-be contestants. The tray-bake cat seemed devastated as he walked away from the table, and spent some time sobbing on the wall outside the hall, such was his disappointment.

There was a lull in the proceedings as a mop and bucket was fetched to clear away a strawberry meringue that had made a bid for freedom. Hettie took advantage of the break to engage Tarquin Flapjack, and there was no beating about the bush. 'If you don't mind, I'd like to talk to you about the murder of Hartley Battenberg,' she said, loud enough for the cats at the front of the queue to hear.

Tarquin adopted a dismissive tone and played to his audience. 'Would you indeed? Why do you think I could be of the slightest help in that matter?

You may not have noticed, but I am rather busy at present.'

'I'm sure that Miss Haddock and Miss Anderton could manage without you for a few minutes – unless you'd rather I question you here, in front of them?' Hettie retorted, enjoying the spectacle she was creating.

Bugs secretly wanted to applaud Hettie's boldness. She had never been a fan of Tarquin's, and was delighted to see him squirm so publicly; Fanny, pleased with the opportunity to come up for air, took out her compact and plastered her nose in powder, then added another layer of bright red lipstick to her lips which bled across her teeth, perfectly matching her claws.

Tarquin shuffled off his chair and moved to the side of the hall, away from his audience. Hettie followed him, and was joined by Tilly and her notebook. 'Could you tell me where you were between six and midnight last night?' Hettie began.

'I don't see why I should, but, since you ask, I met up with Branston Bean and we had supper at the Cat and Fiddle.'

'Where and at what time did you meet up with him?' pressed Hettie.

'It was outside the radio station, actually,' said Tarquin. 'As you are aware, Wilco had just shown me the door and I noticed Branston sitting on one of the benches. I went over to pass the time of day, and found him distraught. He told me that Wilco had threatened him with the sack unless he took on a weekend show. He was so upset that I suggested we meet for supper later.'

'And what time did you get to the Cat and Fiddle?'

'I got there at about seven-thirty. Branston arrived fifteen minutes later.'

'So what were you doing between leaving the radio station and getting to the Cat and Fiddle?'

'Nothing much. I exchanged a few words with Edward Dexter, who was clipping his front hedge, and then I went home. I picked up a jacket and went to meet Branston.'

'And where did Branston Bean go after you'd spoken to him at the radio station?'

'I've really no idea. You'll have to ask him that. Now, if you don't mind, I need to get back to organising the bake off heats. We have far too many cats in the queue, and we need to get through them by the end of today or the whole schedule will be disrupted. If you'd let me put out my message on your so-called radio show yesterday, we wouldn't be in this mess.'

Tarquin's words were aimed at Tilly, but it was Hettie who responded. 'What was the message you were so keen to get across?'

'I wanted to say that the competition was closed to stop any more cats applying. Now we have a queue snaking halfway round the town with cakes, pies and pastries, and I almost wish I'd never suggested it.'

'Before you return to whatever it is you're doing, do you like cooking?' asked Hettie, offering the question as a wild card.

Tarquin was taken aback by such a change of direction, and gave a somewhat flustered answer. 'Well, I do cook, obviously, but I find your question more than a little impertinent and I don't see what my domestic arrangements have to do with your enquiries.'

'Nothing really,' lied Hettie. 'I just wondered if your interest in having a bake off competition came from a love of cookery, that's all.'

'If that's the case, then yes – since leaving the radio station, I have taken an interest in cookery, although I wouldn't regard myself as an expert in that field. Now, I really must get on.'

'Just one more question. After supper, where did you go?'

For the first time in the conversation, Tarquin looked visibly disturbed and it was several seconds before he responded. 'We walked and talked as far as I can remember. Branston was still very upset. We both went home at about eleven, I suppose, and that's really all I have to say. Now, if you'll excuse me, I promised to provide refreshments for Miss Haddock and Miss Anderton.'

As Tarquin Flapjack headed for the small kitchen, a rumble of thunder rang out ominously around the hall, signalling that several days of unseasonably warm sunshine were about to end in a downpour. 'What do you make of him?' asked Tilly. 'He seems just as nasty as we thought.'

'Yes, but he's hiding something, and I think it's to do with Branston Bean. We need to speak to him next. How did you get on with the queue – any more suspects in it?'

Tilly turned to another page in her notebook. 'I think we're in luck with several of them. I spotted Branston Bean, Tansy Flutter, Bunty Basham and Gilbert Truffle – he wasn't in the queue, but he was interviewing cats who were. Oh, Cherry and Hilary Fudge are there as well.'

'What have Cherry and Hilary Fudge got to do with Hartley Battenberg's murder?' Hettie asked, somewhat bemused.

'Nothing,' replied Tilly, 'but I thought I'd mention it because we like them.'

Hettie allowed her eyes to lift themselves briefly to the heavens, accepting and rejoicing in the fact that Tilly lived in a slightly different world to everyone else. The rumble of thunder grew louder, and suddenly the queue inside the hall fragmented as a surge of cats all pushed in from outside to avoid the rain that had begun to land in giant splashes on the pavements. The trestle table was engulfed by cats and their homebakes, and Fanny Haddock was nearly knocked off her chair by a beef Wellington that had travelled some distance through the air. Bugs Anderton, who was more than used to crowd management, hauled herself up onto the table and called for calm, suggesting that everyone sat quietly on the floor until the impending storm had passed.

Hettie surveyed the chaotic scene, trying to locate some of Tilly's suspects, but she thought better of it as more and more cats poured into the hall, now soaked from the deluge that raged outside. 'I think this would be a good time for sardines on toast at Jessie's!' she shouted, propelling Tilly towards the door.

Outside, Cheapcuts Lane was running with water. The storm was almost biblical in its intensity, and the queue was gone, replaced by lake-sized puddles and a few abandoned plastic boxes floating on the surface. It was, of course, a known fact that cats and water only mixed in extreme circumstances – annual baths, sticky situations and the occasional washing of clothes – so it was no surprise to Hettie and Tilly to find the street deserted as the rain bucketed down from the sky. They waded across to Jessie's shop just as the storm came to an abrupt end: the black clouds parted to reveal a deep blue sky, allowing the sun to resume its dominance, silvering the puddles with an almost blinding light. Hettie pushed hard on Jessie's shop door but it resisted. Staring through the glass, she realised that the shop was packed to the gills with cats who'd run for shelter from the tail end of the queue.

Realising that the rain had now stopped and keen to regain their places, Jessie's door was flung open by a stampede of cats, all making a bid for freedom amidst a sea of umbrellas, baskets, cake tins and boxes. Tilly was knocked for six by Bunty Basham and landed in a deep puddle. Bunty offered a mumbled apology as she fought her way towards the Methodist Hall, hoping to improve her position in the queue. Hettie helped Tilly to her feet, and the two friends stood back as more and more cats tumbled out of the charity shop.

Eventually Jessie herself came to the door, looking flustered and more than a little concerned for her own safety. She was relieved to see Hettie and Tilly and beckoned them in. 'Right!' she said, with some conviction. 'That's it for today. I'm closing up – my rails are in tatters, my bric-a-brac is almost unsalable, and my floor's soaking wet from dripping macs and umbrellas. I wouldn't mind, but I haven't taken a penny all morning except for Edward's cricket bat and I've never known the shop to be so full. I usually pray for rainy days as they're good for business, but I resent being used as a glorified bus shelter.'

Jessie had every reason to be cross. Tilly, who often looked after the shop while her friend was out on a buying trip, was horrified as she surveyed the scene. Puddles on the floor, clothes trampled, jigsaws spilling out of their boxes, a bargain basket of mittens, hats and scarves – left over from the winter – tipped upside down. 'I'm so sorry,' she said, patting Jessie's paw. 'I'll help you tidy up. I'm sure it's not as bad as it looks.'

There was no denying that Jessie needed some help, but Hettie was keen to further her murder investigations and came up with a plan. 'Look,' she said, 'how about Tilly and me clean up a bit while you stick the kettle on – and did you mention sardines on toast?'

Jessie cheered up immediately. 'I most certainly did, and thank you both for coming to my rescue. Sardines on toast and milky teas coming up.' Jessie disappeared through to her kitchen at the back of the shop, and Hettie and Tilly set about bringing some order to the mess. Tilly began by clawing jigsaw pieces back into their box and Hettie collected up the clothes to return them to the rails – but suddenly she froze.

Behind the clothes rails sat Gilbert Truffle, his head bent forward onto his chest. Gilbert had clearly presented his last radio show, because Gilbert was dead.

Chapter Nine

There was no response from Whisker FM as Hettie dialled the number repeatedly on Jessie's telephone. She knew very little about Gilbert Truffle, and Wilco Wonderfluff was the obvious cat to contact. 'I'm having no luck,' she said, putting the receiver down. 'Goodness knows where Marzi Pan is. Hardly a great advert for your accessible local radio.'

Tilly glanced at a clock in Jessie's bric-a-brac section. 'Gilbert should be on in an hour. He starts his show at one o'clock. We'll have to get a message through somehow.'

Jessie switched on the small transistor radio behind her counter. Pussy Parton was coming to the end of 'Jolene', and the three cats waited to see who was presenting the show. Wilco's voice came across loud and clear, promising a packed afternoon of fun with Gilbert Truffle.

'He'll be lucky,' commented Hettie, 'unless they're offering an outside broadcast live from Shroud and Trestle.' Her words were more than a little off colour, but Jessie and Tilly appreciated the joke and it lightened their spirits sufficiently to enjoy a round of sardines on toast as they waited for Gilbert Truffle to be collected by the local undertakers.

'I've just thought of something,' said Tilly, licking tomato sauce off her paws. 'Branston Bean should be on at the moment, but I saw him in the queue for the bake off earlier. I wonder why he wasn't doing his show today?'

'Well, according to Tarquin Flapjack, he was pretty fed up after Wilco's chat with him yesterday. Maybe he decided to stand himself down. He was terrible, anyway,' said Hettie.

'I for one wouldn't miss him,' chimed in Jessie. 'Half the time he talks absolute nonsense, and his music is awful – but I'm very sad that I won't hear Gilbert again. I loved his afternoon show. Whatever's happening? First Hartley Battenberg and now Gilbert Truffle.'

'One thing's for sure,' responded Hettie. 'These murders are all about Wilco's radio station. I'm beginning to wonder who's going to be next?'

Her deliberations were interrupted by the arrival of Morbid Balm in her van. Those still in the queue for the Methodist Hall all turned their heads as one as the Goth cat prepared to go about her business. 'You seem to be making a habit of dead radio presenters,' she said, taking a close look at the body still propped up by Jessie's clothes rails. 'Perhaps I'd better finalise my will.'

Hettie laughed nervously as Morbid inspected a wound in Gilbert's chest. Tilly grabbed her notepad ready to jot down Morbid's observations, keen to include every minute detail. 'Nice and clean. One good thrust straight into the heart. I doubt he knew anything about it before hitting the floor. Slid down the wall, by the looks of it.' Morbid gently pulled at Gilbert's legs until he was lying flat, and the bulge in his trouser pocket became obvious. She investigated further, and rescued an almost perfect pie; she sniffed it, broke a section off, and concluded that it was of the mince beef and onion persuasion. Pulling a polythene bag from her own pocket, she placed the pie in it and handed it to Hettie. 'There you are – another one for your collection. I'd better get him tucked up in a freezer as we've a funeral at three. I'll take a closer look at him later, but I would say that the cause of death is obvious and it probably happened less than an hour ago. He's barely cold. I'll call you if anything else shows up in my prep room once I've got him on the slab. I'd say you're looking for a sharp, long-bladed knife, if that helps?'

Hettie marvelled at how Morbid was able to treat a violent death no differently from a visit to the supermarket. She was methodical, unflappable, and – as many of her bereaved families said – kind. 'Before you go,' said Hettie, 'you said you visited Hartley Battenberg's flat. I don't suppose you have his address?'

'I do indeed,' said Morbid. 'I never forget an address – you never know when you might have to do a removal. It's flat 26, Pawsome Mansions, just down from the library. I think it's the fifth floor, but there's a janitor so you can check that. Anyway, we'd better get Gilbert shifted. Time's ticking on and that freshly dug grave at St Kipper's won't wait.'

Hettie helped to load the body into Morbid's van, causing a great deal of consternation amongst the cats outside the hall. Gilbert was covered in a sheet to maintain his dignity as he was stretchered out of Jessie's shop, and there was much conversation about who might be under the makeshift shroud. The very presence of Hettie and Tilly suggested that the death had not been a natural one, probably due to the fact that the murder of Hartley Battenberg was still fresh in their minds.

Jessie made another round of milky teas, wanting to keep Hettie and Tilly with her for as long as possible; she loved hearing about their latest cases, but this one was far too close for comfort. The full impact of Gilbert Truffle's murder was only now beginning to register, and the thought of being on her own in the place where it had happened filled her with dread.

Hettie read her thoughts, noticing how often Jessie glanced at the space by her clothes rails where Gilbert had breathed his last. 'I tell you what,' she said, employing a distracting tactic, 'we're up to our necks in it at the moment, and with Bruiser away, everything is going to take much longer. If your foot will hold up, would you do us a huge favour and go to Whisker FM to tell Wilco what's happened? We just don't have time to wait for Marzi Pan to turn up and answer the phone.'

Jessie brightened immediately; a mission was just what she needed. 'I'd love to,' she said, moving towards her window display. 'Nurse Featherstone Clump says I need to do some gentle walking, and I can deliver this to Mr Dexter at the same time. He couldn't carry it this morning when he popped in to buy it – it'll save him coming back tomorrow.' Jessie reached into the window and pulled out a cricket bat. She was quite famous for her window dressing, and always seemed to catch the mood of the town. The current display, which she'd only finished that morning, was a celebration of the Easter weekend to come. The window was full of bunting, bonnets, cardboard Easter eggs, assorted bakeware, and a dummy dressed in cricket whites, surrounded by bats, balls and a set of stumps.

'Did you say that Edward Dexter was here this morning?' Hettie asked.

'Yes. He loves a browse and he's got money to spend, which is my sort of customer.'

'And what time was this?'

Jessie thought for a moment before replying. 'Well, he was still in the shop when the rain started, talking to Bunty Basham – she'd popped in to tell me about nets at the weekend, and I had to tell her to count me out because of my foot. It all got a bit frantic after that.'

'So you've no idea when he left the shop?'

Jessie shook her head. 'No. It was such a crush, and cats were coming and going. Some made a run for it, others pushed their way in and stayed until the rain stopped. Why? Surely you don't think he had anything to do with Gilbert's murder, do you?'

'Right now, except for the three of us, anyone in the vicinity could have done it,' said Hettie. 'The whole thing is a bloody nightmare!'

'Well, there's one piece of good news – maybe even two,' said Tilly, rearranging the clothes rails to cover up where Gilbert had died. 'Tarquin and Gilbert can both come off my list of suspects. Gilbert is dead, and Tarquin was still in the Methodist Hall at the time of his murder.'

'That's providing the murders are connected,' Hettie pointed out. 'One could have caused the other. Tarquin or Gilbert could have murdered Hartley Battenberg last night. It seems it's all about crushes and opportunities.'

'What do you mean?' asked Tilly, knowing that Hettie was about to make an important point.

'That it's much easier to remain anonymous in a crowd. We've already said that anyone could have left your party last night, killed Hartley, and returned without being noticed, and it's the same here: any cat jammed into Jessie's shop could easily have stabbed Gilbert and disappeared before the body was discovered. Macs and umbrellas are perfect disguises during a rain storm.'

Tilly was a little crestfallen at Hettie's logic, but knew she was right: it was clearly too early in their investigations to cross anyone off her list. 'So what's next?' she asked, putting the pie that had so recently lodged in Gilbert Truffle's pocket into her satchel.

'I think we should set up some interviews at Bloomers for tomorrow, and take a closer look at the victims today,' said Hettie, trying to be decisive. 'If we get a move on, we should catch several of your suspects in the bake off queue. We'll give them a time for tomorrow, then strike out for Pawsome Mansions. After that, we need to find out more about Gilbert from Wilco.'

'Shall I tell him you want to talk to him?' asked Jessie.

'Yes, we'll call in at the radio station later, but don't say too much about the murder. He just needs to know that Gilbert is dead for the moment. Tell him we'll explain more when we see him, and if by any chance you find a bloodstained knife on your travels, give us a shout.'

The three cats stepped out into Cheapcuts Lane. Jessie locked up her shop and limped away towards the high street, feeling proud and a little excited at being part of Hettie's team. She had long admired the work of The No. 2 Feline Detective Agency, mainly because of the insider titbits that Tilly fed her on a regular basis, but now she was genuinely involved, carrying an important message as part of a murder investigation. The pain in her broken foot almost disappeared as she put it through its paces, making good progress towards the recreation ground and using Edward Dexter's cricket bat as support.

Hettie and Tilly decided to save time by splitting up to locate the cats they wanted to question in the queue. 'I'll work from the front, inside the hall, if you take on the ones outside,' Hettie suggested. 'Let's check the list to see who we're looking for.'

Tilly read out the names. 'Bunty Basham, Tansy Flutter and Branston Bean – that's all I spotted in the queue, besides Gilbert. We still need to talk to Marzi Pan and Edward Dexter, but I didn't see them here.'

'Well, we'll keep our eyes peeled just in case they joined the queue later. The more cats we can talk to at Bloomers tomorrow, the better. It'll save us a lot of footwork and, looking on the bright side, it's mixed grill Saturday. Molly and Dolly's frying pans will be in overdrive.'

Tilly clapped her paws at the thought of a Bloomers mixed grill, and set out across the road to locate some of her suspects. Hettie was in luck and found Tansy Flutter at the front of the queue, offering up her butterfly buns to the scrutiny of Fanny Haddock. The

TV cat was impressed with the buttercream, but felt that the sponge was overbaked. Tansy hopped from one foot to another, nervously waiting for a verdict and eyeing up the pink tickets that sat in front of Bugs Anderton. Hettie noticed that Tarquin Flapjack was now conspicuous by his absence.

Tansy Flutter had led a colourful life before becoming a broadcaster. She was barely out of kitten pants before she was snapped up by a TV advertising company to promote Cloddah's Clotted Cream, quickly followed by Captain Cat's Fish Fingers and a summer season of Bill's Barbeque Bits. Her advertising days floundered when it was discovered that she'd been moonlighting for *Play Cat*, a magazine kept on the top shelves of newsagents and only bought by a certain sort of tomcat. A brief dalliance with Wilco Wonderfluff had bucketed her into mainstream broadcasting, and she had welcomed his invitation with both front paws. At Whisker FM, she had finally found what she was looking for: a steady job, an appreciative audience, and – as her stunningly long glossy grey fur grew a little ragged with middle age – a profession that relied on a pleasing voice rather than a pretty face.

Tansy held her breath as Fanny took another bite of the bun, chewing slowly before swallowing. 'If this is your signature dish, I'm a little concerned that you may struggle further on in the competition. You've chosen something so simple that I wonder if you can cook at all, but the buttercream is one of the best I've ever tasted – besides mine, of course – and so I've decided to put you through for tomorrow's cook off.'

Tansy couldn't believe her luck and punched the air as Bugs Anderton added her name to her clipboard, issuing a much sought-after pink ticket. Hettie moved in swiftly to invite Tansy to Bloomers for 'a little chat', as she put it. Tansy readily agreed to fit Hettie in between her breakfast show and the cook off, and skipped out of the Methodist Hall with the remainder of her butterfly buns, euphoric at her triumph.

Hettie spotted Bunty Basham halfway down the queue and pounced while the going was good. Bunty resisted at first, pointing out that nets had to be her first priority and that she needed the afternoon in case she was chosen for the cook off. Hettie argued that she needed to eliminate her from the enquiries, and the two cats eventually agreed to a quick morning coffee at Bloomers, leaving Edward Dexter briefly in charge of the cricket team. It hadn't escaped Hettie's notice that the plastic box Bunty held tightly in her paws contained several small pies, and she couldn't resist asking the obvious question. 'Those pies look lovely. What have you filled them with?'

'Mince beef and onion,' Bunty replied. 'My old mother's recipe, actually, but don't tell anyone. There were six but someone made off with one of them during that storm. I only put the box down for a minute to put my brolly up.'

An altercation at the front of the queue interrupted Hettie's train of thought. It was a voice she knew well, and she moved towards it in time to appreciate the full blast of sentiments. The town's postmistress, Lavender Stamp, was excelling herself on the finer points of becoming a TV cook, retaliating for the culinary slap she'd just received from Fanny Haddock.

'How dare you suggest that my toffee and pecan pie is shop bought!' Lavender screeched. 'Let me point out that we never see you doing any cooking on your show. We all know you have a legion of helpers who do the work, and that poor cat who assists you is run ragged with your insults. When did you last cook a pie of any sort from scratch? And you sit there playing God, brought in to pass judgement and making wild and unfounded accusations.'

Fanny held her ground and refused to rise to the bait. She leaned forward, confronting Lavender nose to nose. Only a few cats were close enough to hear the few words the cook uttered. 'It still has the price on it.'

Lavender stared down at the label tucked underneath the foil tray that the pie was encased in; it clearly said 'Butters' Bakery', with the price she'd paid for it yesterday afternoon.

Hettie tried to resist the smirk that was spreading across her face as Lavender blew out of the Methodist Hall clutching her shop-bought pie. It was a rare sight to see the harridan of the town wrongfooted in such a public way. Hettie was grateful that neither she nor

Tilly had any reason to visit the post office in the next week, as Lavender would surely take her humiliation out on her unsuspecting customers in the vilest of ways.

There were no other suspects to be found in the hall, so Hettie joined Tilly outside, where she had had moderate success. 'Branston Bean says he'll try and come to Bloomers, but he's having a meeting at the radio station tomorrow evidently,' said Tilly. 'I'm afraid I pretended I liked his show and asked him why he wasn't on this morning. He said he'd been given the day off, so he decided to enter the baking competition, which seems reasonable, I suppose. Guess what his signature dish is?'

'Would it have anything to do with pastry?' suggested Hettie.

'Yes, it would. He had four steak and kidney pies in a tin – three, actually, as he was eating one of them when I moved on down the queue.'

'I had a similar experience with Bunty Basham, except her pie filling was mince beef and onion. She says there's one missing, but the big news is that Lavender Stamp has been caught cheating with a shop-bought pie.' Hettie was pleased to be the bearer of such sensational gossip.

Tilly giggled. 'So that's why she flew past me just now, looking like she'd caught her tail in a lawnmower!'

It was Hettie's turn to laugh at Tilly's apt description of the postmistress undone, but the day was getting away from them and the walk to Pawsome Mansions was a long one. She was keen to take a look at Hartley Battenberg's flat before having further discussions with Wilco about the rising death toll of his radio presenters.

Chapter Ten

Pawsome Mansions stood out as being a bit of a mistake amongst the neatly arranged semi-detached houses and bungalows. The town's leafy suburb housed the more well-to-do cats who'd earned and spent their money wisely, took joy in creating perfect gardens, and fiercely protected their peaceful way of life. When the Mansions were built to replace a rather shabby enclave of prefabs, the flats were supposed to provide an opportunity for older cats to downsize and live out their remaining days in secure and luxurious splendour; as soon as the first one appeared on the market, a stampede of young professional cats arrived, eager to get their paws on the property market, and, as the demand grew, so did the prices. The community at large took a dim view of their ordered lives being constantly shattered by the roaring of fast cars, expensive motorbikes and youthful exuberance. The newcomers were cats who lived life in the fast lane in every sense of the word, and paid little attention to their surrounding neighbourhood.

Footsore and flustered with the building heat of the day, Hettie and Tilly arrived at the Mansions an hour after they'd left Cheapcuts Lane. The walk had given the two cats the time to assess where their investigations had got them so far, and Hettie was the first to admit that it was probably nowhere. The high-rise block of flats shone in the afternoon sun as they approached, the glass and steel structure dominating what had once been an open sky. 'I wouldn't want to live here,' said Tilly. 'It looks like one of those multistorey car parks. Just look at all those horrid little boxes – how could any cat in their right mind want to call one of them home?'

Hettie agreed but could see the sense in no-stress luxury living. 'If you've got the money and you don't mind being hissed and spat at by the house dwellers as you climb into your Aston Martin, it's probably not a bad life, but I'd love to know how a folk singer and stand-up comedian could afford to live here.'

***

Albert Fritter was paid to be nosy. His title was head of security, but his role was little more than a glorified door opener because that's what he did all day. It was a far cry from his military service, and only the medals pinned to his jacket and the fact that one of his sleeves was empty testified to a more glorious past. He was content with his lot and especially liked the luxury ground floor flat that came with the job. Mrs Fritter was particularly pleased with the aspect, as it opened onto a small, private courtyard garden, where she sunned herself and potted up the odd geranium.

Albert didn't wait for Hettie and Tilly to approach his reception desk, but met them at the door. 'Can I be of assistance?' he asked. 'You look a bit lost, and I should point out that these flats are private.'

He put Hettie's back up immediately, and she decided to dispense with any prepared niceties and cut to the chase. 'We are here on official business, investigating the murder of one of the residents of this building. We need to gain access to his flat, and I assume you hold keys to all the apartments?'

'I do indeed,' Albert responded, raising himself up to his full height and swinging back on his heels to establish his authority. 'I don't just hand out keys like catnip drops, though. The security of this building is paramount, and I assure you no one gets past Albert Fritter.'

'Well, Mr Fritter, there's a first time for everything,' said Hettie. 'I see by your medals that you are a brave and honourable cat, and I'm sure you wouldn't want a murderer to go free because you refused to cooperate with our enquiries, would you?'

'Be that as it may, my orders are to let no cat pass this point unless I have prior notice, and to contact the flat in question by the telephone here on my desk.'

Hettie tried desperately to contain her anger. She was tired and hot, and in no mood to be treated like some rooky recruit on a parade ground. 'That's all very well,' she said, 'but we do need to search Mr Battenberg's flat.'

Albert Fritter hesitated, not entirely grasping the situation. 'I thought you said you were investigating a murder? I'm sure Mr Battenberg has nothing to do with it.'

'He has everything to do with it,' snapped Hettie, raising her voice in frustration, 'because he's dead – killed, murdered, or any other way you'd like to describe it – and we are trying to find out who might have done it. There may be evidence in his flat that will lead us to his killer. So will you please hand over the key to his flat and stop holding up our investigations!'

Albert Fritter stared blankly at Hettie, then began to shake uncontrollably, with tears running down his face. It was Mrs Fritter who came to the rescue. Hearing raised voices, she'd abandoned her crochet to see what was happening and wasted no time in locating Hartley's spare key from a board behind the reception desk. 'Come on, Albert – let these folks get on with their job,' she said, putting the key in Hettie's paw. 'I'll make you a nice cup of tea and a bacon sandwich.' Looking across the desk, she offered an apology. 'He can't cope with shouting – it's the shell shock, you see. He'll be in tears for the rest of the day now. He's not as strong as he looks. I'll sort him out, though – just leave the key on reception when you're done.'

Hettie was grateful for the explanation and felt slightly guilty about her treatment of the old soldier. 'I really didn't mean to upset him, but it's imperative that we take a look round Mr Battenberg's flat. Did you know him?'

'Only in passing the time of day. He kept himself to himself. We had a few complaints about him playing his music too loud, but nothing serious. Nice young cat, really – had an eye for the girl cats, too, but we were so sorry to hear he'd died, weren't we, Albert?'

Albert continued to stare into space, allowing his tears to soak through his medal ribbons and giving Hettie an excuse to head to the stairs with Tilly, leaving Mrs Fritter to cope with the fallout she'd unwittingly created.

'Why aren't we using the lift?' asked Tilly.

'Because I don't trust them, and I wouldn't want to rely on the Fritters to rescue us if the thing got stuck.'

Morbid had been right to say that the flat was on the fifth floor, and both cats were out of breath by the time they reached Hartley's door. The apartments were deceptive from the outside and, as the two friends stepped into Hartley Battenberg's life, Tilly's description of 'horrid little boxes' had to be revised immediately. The door opened into a large living room, full of sunshine and musical instruments which Hettie spent some time admiring. 'There's no doubt about the fact that Hartley wasn't short of money,' she said, picking up one of three Gibson guitars and strumming it. 'Perfectly in tune, of course, and I bet the others are, too. And just look at his stereo set-up – you could put on a concert with those speakers. They must have cost a small fortune.'

Tilly appreciated the guitars and the stereo, but her eye was caught by the opulent comfort of the giant white sofa littered with Turkish cushions that took up the whole of one wall. She was particularly taken with the ornate hubble-bubble pipe of blue patterned glass which sat on an oak coffee table and glinted in the sun, throwing patterns across the white walls. A decorative box, inlaid with mother of pearl, was next to the pipe and Tilly couldn't resist lifting the lid. The smell of catnip was unmistakable, and drew Hettie away from her inspection of Hartley's video and record collection.

'High grade catnip, classic guitars and a stereo system to die for – I can't help but feel that Hartley Battenberg wasn't quite what he seemed,' said Hettie, helping herself to a pawful of catnip, which she forced into the pocket of her business slacks. 'Waste not want not, as Betty Butter says.'

'Maybe you should take it all,' suggested Tilly. 'We don't want the Fritters getting their paws on it. I'm not sure it would suit Mr Fritter, although it might help to cure his shell shock, poor cat.'

'Strictly speaking, all this stuff belongs to his next of kin,' said Hettie, 'but as we have no idea at present who that might be, I'll fill my other pocket as well.'

Tilly giggled as Hettie helped herself to more of her favourite treat before moving to one of the closed doors off the living room. It opened into a small fitted kitchen, neatly set out with a breakfast bar, floor and wall cupboards, a sink, cooker and a very tall fridge. The kitchen was spotless, and the only obvious sign of habitation was a plate, bowl and set of cutlery left to dry on the draining board. 'I assume those are from his last supper,' Hettie remarked, as she began to investigate some of the cupboards. 'It's all a bit sterile for a bachelor cat. Everywhere is just so clean and tidy, with everything in its place, and there's no real sense of him here. It's like someone has cleaned up before we got here.'

Tilly agreed but was keen to investigate the fridge. She only just managed to reach the handle on her tiptoes, and hauled the door open to reveal an ice box of delights. 'Well, if someone has been in, they didn't clear the fridge,' she said, taking in the treats before her. 'Just look at all this! Prawns, chicken, lovely cheeses, half an apple pie and lots of pots of strange beans and yoghurts.'

'I thought Morbid said he was a vegan?' said Hettie, joining Tilly at the fridge. 'Vegans don't eat prawns or chicken. I'm beginning to think we're in the wrong flat.' She pulled open several of the kitchen drawers, which revealed nothing more exciting than cutlery and every day cooking utensils. 'Let's take a look in his bedroom,' she suggested, moving back into the living room and choosing one of the two remaining closed doors.

Hartley Battenberg's bedroom was the same as the rest of his flat. A perfectly made bed dominated the small room, which was made to seem larger by the reflection of mirrored sliding doors on two of the walls. Hettie slid one of them across to reveal a selection of day, evening and leisure wear, all beautifully laundered and ready to be worn. 'He obviously didn't buy his clothes from Jessie's charity shop,' she remarked, delving into Hartley's pockets and finding nothing more significant than a plectrum and a guitar capo in a jacket which he'd probably worn at the folk club.

The clothes seemed to be set out in two sections: the everyday wear was casual, unassuming and plain, while the other half was made up of high quality, made to measure outfits and designer gear, bought by someone who had no concern for the price tag. 'It's as if there are two cats living here,' observed Hettie, 'a vegan folk singer and a high-powered elitist rolling in money.'

'Maybe his family has money,' suggested Tilly. 'Perhaps the folk singing vegan thing was a sort of rebellion against the status. Everyone we've spoken to so far seems to have liked him and accepted him as an ordinary sort of cat, rubbing along like the rest of us.'

'Well, clearly someone saw a different side to him to want to get him permanently out of the way,' said Hettie, closing the wardrobe door on Hartley's two personas.

Tilly tugged at the sliding door opposite, which resisted. 'This won't open,' she said, giving it another tug.

Hettie crossed the room to help but the door wouldn't budge. She looked around for an implement to force it with and suddenly remembered something she'd seen on a TV advert. Getting down on to the floor, she ran her paw along the bottom of the sliding door until she found what she was looking for. With a click of the catch, the door was released and Hettie slid the mirrored glass back to reveal an innovative home office. 'Just look at this for a set-up,' she said in admiration, 'Built-in desk, TV and video, filing cabinets, typewriter, and even one of those fax machines they've got in Turner Page's library.'

Tilly's eyes nearly popped out of her head. 'It's just like something from one of those James Blond films. I wish our office looked like that, although I wouldn't want a fact machine.'

'Fax!' corrected Hettie, starting her search of the filing cabinet. The top drawer revealed nothing but stand-up comedy scripts, meticulously dated with when and where they had been performed. The second held a stack of utility bills, all marked 'paid' in impeccable order of month and year. Hettie took a closer look at the paperwork regarding the flat, noting that Hartley had paid cash for it three years before, when the flats were built. There was proof of another, more modestly priced property in Southwool, and a rent book which suggested that Hartley was also a landlord. Interestingly, the name on the rent book was 'Miss T. Flutter'.

'That's a turn-up for the book,' Hettie said, pushing the find under Tilly's nose. 'I assume that this is Tansy Flutter's rent book, but she seems to be paying a king's ransom for a place to live. Those houses are round the back of the fish canning factory on the north beach, and hardly worth what he's been charging.'

Southwool was the closest seaside to the town and boasted a theatre, two pleasure beaches, a very old, ornate pier, and a fish canning industry that employed most of the cats who didn't work in the holiday trade.

'I didn't realise that Tansy travelled in every day to the radio station,' observed Tilly. 'She must have to get up in the middle of the night to do the breakfast show.'

'Yes, I agree – living outside the town isn't ideal, and why would she want to pay such a high rent? She could afford one of those luxury chalets with a sea view for the price she's paying Hartley for one of those poor old workers' cottages.'

'Maybe she likes the smell of fish?' offered Tilly.

'Whatever the reason, I think we'll hang on to the rent book for now. We'll see what she has to say when we meet her at Bloomers tomorrow.' Hettie moved on to the bottom drawer, which had been set aside for radio station business. There was an envelope full of Hartley's presenter cards, several pages of schedule notes going back as far as the year before, a collection of old editions of *Radio Times*, and – right at the back of the drawer – a scrapbook which Hettie pulled out and passed to Tilly. 'Take a look at this while I have a root through these desk drawers.'

Tilly pounced on the scrapbook, keen to turn up something of interest, but was a little disappointed to find that it was just a series of press cuttings covering the radio station's various triumphs – charity auctions, open days and the arrival of new presenters. Wilco's takeover bid was recorded across several pages, and a rather lacklustre campaign by Tarquin Flapjack's followers took up a few single paragraph cuttings, including an unfortunate picture of Tarquin with his paw in his mouth. Tansy Flutter featured in several cuttings, usually posed in leotard, leg warmers and headband, ready for her radio exercise classes. Gilbert Truffle clocked up most column inches: poached from a national station to join Whisker Radio, his arrival in the town was seen as a very big story and a real coup for Wilco Wonderfluff. He was pictured in the radio station's reception, holding up his presenter portrait, and Tilly smiled as she noticed Marzi Pan sitting at her desk in the background, oblivious to the camera and painting her claws. She scanned the article on Gilbert to see if she could find anything personal about him, and was quickly rewarded. 'Guess where Gilbert Truffle lived?' she squealed, delighted with her discovery.

'In Hartley Battenberg's fridge?' offered Hettie, rummaging through a top drawer of paperclips, assorted pens and glue sticks.

'That's just too silly,' said Tilly. 'According to this newspaper article, he only lives in the town during the week, as he has a family home that he shares with his sister. It's in the Fens, and she grows celery, evidently. That's not the interesting bit though – it says here that he lodged with Hilary and Cherry Fudge. He's quoted as saying that they've provided him with a home from home.'

'You're joking!' said Hettie, starting her search of the second drawer in the desk. 'I'd have thought they'd had enough of lodgers after the Mystery Paws case. Now another of their clients has hit the deck.'

Hilary and Cherry Fudge ran a modest guest house in the town. The mother and daughter cats were community driven, and were often enlisted as first aiders by Bugs Anderton, as an important part of her event health and safety management structure. They had, on occasions, actually saved lives with their textbook approach to first aid, and Cherry had gone on to qualify as an ambulance driver, making her mother a very proud cat indeed. The lowest moment for the Fudges came when a young musician was murdered in one of their guest house bedrooms, a case which Hettie and Tilly had solved successfully. Now it was clear that – once again – they would hit the headlines, putting their five star status in jeopardy.

'Bugger!' exclaimed Tilly. 'I could have booked them for a chat at Bloomers tomorrow if I'd known Gilbert was their lodger. I told you I'd seen them in the bake off queue.'

'And you'd better add them to your suspects list, as they could have stabbed Gilbert in Jessie's shop,' said Hettie playfully. 'It wouldn't be the first time a landlady has bumped off a lodger – and they are a bit strange.'

Tilly liked the Fudges, but had to agree that their outlook on life verged on limited and obsessive. Cherry lived very much under her mother's paw. Like Marzi Pan, she should have flown the nest long ago, but Hilary's determination to create a cat in her own image had succeeded, and now Cherry inhabited her mother's world with no wish to become independent in any way.

'Now this looks a bit more promising,' she said, pulling a stack of documents out of the bottom drawer for Tilly to sort through. 'Bank statements and savings books, and just look at this!' The removal of the paperwork revealed a stack of bank notes, tied up in an elastic band at the back of the drawer. 'There must be hundreds of pounds here!' said Hettie, flicking through the bundle of notes. 'Why would you keep this much money around in cash?'

'Maybe he didn't have time to put it in the bank,' suggested Tilly. 'According to this savings book, he's got loads of money stashed away, and look – the latest bank statement is the same. He was worth thousands.'

'I think we need to take all this away with us, and the scrapbook, too. For a fairly new recruit to Wilco's radio station, he seemed very keen on what the other presenters were doing. It looks like he's been collecting those cuttings for months.'

Hettie checked the time. 'We'd better get a move on. We still have Wilco to deal with. Sadly, we'll have to leave all this cash where we found it. We don't know if he had any family, but if he did, I suppose it belongs to them. I hoped we'd find a will, but there's nothing like that here. In fact there's nothing very personal here at all.'

Hettie pushed the cash back into the drawer and closed it. She was about to pull the sliding door across on Hartley's home office when her attention was drawn to the neat row of videos lined up above the TV. 'I wonder why he kept these particular videos here?' she said, reaching for one of them and forcing it into the video machine. She switched the TV on and pressed play. It was a home movie of sorts, showing the high street in the town. The camera slowly moved past Elsie Haddock's fish and chip shop, Hilda Dabbit's dry cleaners and Meridian Hambone's hardware store, lingering briefly on Bloomers before picking up on a queue outside Lavender Stamp's post office, zooming in to focus on some of the cats.

'Oh look!' cried Tilly. 'There's Molly Bloom and Bugs Anderton, and that's Tarquin Flapjack, isn't it? And Bunty Basham – she's just going into the post office.' The video cut out, and Hettie hit the fast forward button to see if there was anything else on the tape, but the rest of it appeared to be blank.

'That's all a bit odd,' said Hettie. 'Not exactly high-end viewing. Admittedly the fact that Lavender Stamp allows her post office queue to spill out onto the pavement might be interesting to some cats, but why would you want to video it?'

'Maybe he was making a documentary about the high street and the shops?' suggested Tilly.

'Maybe, but why miss out on filming the Butters' bakery if that was the case? I think we should take all these videos away with us. There's no time to look at them now, and to be honest I'm starving. Jessie's sardines on toast went nowhere.'

'I've just remembered!' said Tilly. 'We've still got sausage rolls in my satchel.'

'Well, break them out!' said Hettie, pulling the rest of the videos down onto the floor.

Tilly fetched her satchel from the living room. Perched on the edge of Hartley's bed, she carefully removed the pie they'd found in Gilbert Truffle's pocket and put it to one side, concentrating on the sausage rolls that the Butters had given them earlier. The two cats sat and chewed their way through the remaining pastries, taking care to eat every crumb. Tilly then put the evidence pie, as she called it, back into the satchel, along with Hartley's bank statements and savings book.

Feeling much better after their impromptu picnic, Hettie disappeared into Hartley's kitchen, returning minutes later with a black dustbin bag. 'I'll stick the videos and the scrapbook in here,' she said. 'We'll have to drop it off at home on our way to the radio station. We'd better start making tracks – it's a long walk back, and we need to talk to Wilco about Gilbert before we go any further. I also think we should call in on the Fudges to see what they made of him, but that will have to wait until tomorrow.'

Hettie threw caution to the wind and allowed them a ride down in the lift. The descent was without incident, and they were safely delivered to the ground floor. Mrs Fritter had installed herself on reception, with no sign of Albert. 'We're taking a few items away that may help with our investigations,' Hettie said, drawing attention to the dustbin bag. 'We'll return them when we've finished. Do you know if Mr Battenberg had a cleaner for his flat?'

Mrs Fritter blinked before answering. 'Well, we do offer a daily cleaning service, but Mr Battenberg didn't require it. He liked to work from home, and he said having a daily cat would disrupt his concentration.'

'And do you know what sort of work he did from home?' Hettie asked.

'I'm not sure, but I think he was a writer. He did comedy shows, and I think he might have even written songs.'

'Did he have many visitors – friends or family, perhaps?'

'He brought cats back with him from time to time – mostly girls and not really very often. As for family, I'm not sure that he had any. He came across as a bit of a loner. Some days he was so dressed up I hardly recognised him – posh suits and dark glasses; other days, he looked almost scruffy, if you know what I mean?'

Hettie nodded, thinking back to the contrast she'd found in Hartley's wardrobe. It was becoming clear to her that he had led a double life; the question was which one of those lives had turned him into a murder victim? And what, if anything, had he got in common with Gilbert Truffle?

Chapter Eleven

Exhausted from their walk, Hettie and Tilly left the items they'd taken from Hartley Battenberg's flat on their doorstep, ordered an egg and bacon quiche and two cream horns from the Butters for their supper, and struck out for Whisker FM. Wilco was on air when they arrived at the pavilion, and they had to wait for him to let them in during a record. There was no sign of Marzi and, as he made his way back to the studio, Wilco cursed the fact that he had become a one-cat band. Hettie and Tilly followed him, and Wilco made short work of a link into the next record, setting up another track to follow so that he would at least have time to start a conversation with his visitors.

'Thank you for sending a message about Gilbert,' he began. 'I just can't get my head around it. First Hartley, and now this. I don't understand what's happening. I thought that having to cover for Branston this morning was the worst of my worries, but then Marzi wanted the day off, and now the news of Gilbert's death. It's all too much. I feel like I'm in the middle of a bad dream. I've been sitting here all day, playing one record after another and talking rubbish into this microphone while all hell is breaking loose.'

'Shall I make us a nice cup of tea?' offered Tilly, trying to dilute the misery and self-pity that Wilco seemed to be immersed in.

'That's an excellent idea,' said Hettie, summoning up more enthusiasm than she actually possessed. Tilly left the studio leaving Hettie to deal with the forlorn presenter.

Wilco sat hunched in his swivel chair, watching the needle progress across the latest hit from Cat Stevens. Hettie waited until the record had finished and Wilco had faded in the next one; it was a perfect segue, but the presenter showed no satisfaction in the manoeuvre. 'Wouldn't it be better to make your apologies and plug into FWS?' Hettie suggested. 'We do need to talk to you as a matter of urgency, and I'm not sure any of us can concentrate while you're still trying to present a show.'

Wilco nodded slowly, seeing the sense in what Hettie had suggested. As the record came to an end, he sat up and delivered an upbeat goodbye, explaining that – for technical reasons – they would now be joining the Feline World Service, and that Tansy Flutter would be with them bright and early on the breakfast show from seven a.m. tomorrow. He punched the off-air button, and FWS took over, offering a report on a cat flu outbreak in Bermuda.

Wilco took off his headphones, wound the lead around them, and threw them into a drawer under the radio desk as if he couldn't stand the sight of them. 'Shall we go and talk in reception?' he suggested. 'I'm sick of the sight of these four walls today. The way I feel at the moment, I wouldn't care if I never presented another show.'

Hettie said nothing. She was trying to decide whether Wilco was mourning the loss of two presenters, or worrying about the damage it might do to Whisker FM. It was clear that the cat was hugely ambitious for the radio station to succeed, and she wondered how far he would be willing to go to get what he wanted. The news of Hartley Battenberg's murder would surely have increased listeners to Tansy's breakfast show, and the death of the station's most popular and well-known star might easily turn into manna from heaven. It was a known fact that in times of trouble local cats turned to local news, and it was an absolute gift that the deaths were so closely connected to the radio station itself.

Tilly had busied herself in reception, and by the time Hettie and Wilco joined her, she had even managed to find a packet of lemon puffs lurking in Marzi's in-tray. Wilco gratefully accepted the tea, but waved the biscuit away and slumped down on one of the chairs. Tilly saw instantly that this wasn't the best time for a lemon puff, and put them back where she'd found them. Settling herself into Marzi's chair behind the desk, she pulled her notepad out of her satchel and waited for Hettie to start her questioning.

'I'm sure Gilbert's death has come as a tremendous shock to you,' she began, 'but we need to know more about him – and Hartley, for that matter; it's clear that these murders revolve around the radio station but we have to look at the motivation behind them so that we can identify the killer.'

'But I thought Gilbert had just died?' Wilco protested, 'You say he's been murdered?'

'Yes I'm afraid that's the case,' said Hettie, noting Wilco's reaction. 'What can you tell us about Gilbert?'

Wilco looked up at Gilbert's portrait on the wall, as if willing him to speak. He was obviously trying to compose a satisfactory response to Hettie's question, and eventually he found some words. 'He was the ultimate professional, and he made it all look so easy. He never flapped, he was always in control and generous with his time – just a good sort.'

Hettie felt that the eulogy was rather too perfect and decided to probe a little deeper. 'He was obviously a huge asset to Whisker FM, but how did you convince him to give up his national radio work to come and broadcast from a cricket pavilion? It's not exactly what he's been used to, is it?'

'He just phoned me out of the blue and said he'd like to get involved,' Wilco explained. 'I first met him when he was hosting a radio training course. He did them as a sideline to his shows. He was really encouraging, and we sort of kept in touch. To be honest, I think he fancied a change. He wanted to get back to basics as far as broadcasting was concerned, and when he read in the *Broadcast* journal that I was taking this on, he jumped ship to come and join us.'

'I understand that he only lodged in the town during the week, and lived with his sister in the Fens. Do you know why he chose to do that?'

Wilco shook his head. 'Not really. When he quit his job, I suppose he fancied a complete change of scenery, and I believe his sister inherited their family's smallholding in the country. It must have made sense to him for some reason to lodge in the town instead of commuting. Maybe he planned to retire to the Fens eventually; he was getting on a bit.'

Hettie couldn't decide whether Wilco was being deliberately vague or hardly knew Gilbert Truffle at all, and she decided to change the subject. 'What about you? What made you want to take all this on? It seems like a very expensive hobby.'

'It is, but until today I thought it was worth it. Before I took it on, I'd been out of broadcasting for a bit. I'd hopped round a few stations to keep my paw in after leaving the national service, but I'd become disillusioned with the whole business – too much shoving and pushing from managers who had never presented a programme in their lives. The heart had dropped out of it for me. Then I got a call to come and do a holiday relief show here, and my creative juices began to flow again. It was a bit of a shaky start, as the station was on its beam end. I'd got some rainy-day cash put by, so I suggested that I boosted the coffers. Before I knew it, most of the old guard had left and I found myself running the whole thing.'

'And did the old guard, as you put it, mind your takeover bid?'

'Not at all. I think they were pleased to hand it over. Tarquin was difficult right from the start and dug his heels in, but it was clear to me that he was only in it for himself and had completely forgotten his responsibilities toward the listeners. Quite simply, he had to go.'

'You mean he wasn't part of your personal vision?' suggested Hettie.

Wilco chose not to acknowledge her rather cutting remark, so Hettie moved on to Hartley Battenberg. 'We visited Hartley's flat today, and it would appear that he was a bit of a mystery. Most cats we've spoken to, including you, knew him as a folk singing, stand-up comedian. It's clear from some of the things we found in his flat that he was also a very different cat, with almost a split personality. Did you get any sense of that?'

'What sort of things?' Wilco asked, showing a little more interest.

'I'm afraid we're not at liberty to say at this point, but I can tell you that he was a very rich cat and I'm not sure the sort of money we're talking about came from folk singing and being funny.'

'Well I really don't know what to say. It just goes to show how little you know about anyone, really.' Wilco rose to his feet. 'It's been a long day, and I need to get some rest and have a think about what to do next. I've got hardly any presenters. I gave Branston the day off to think about his future – he may or may not be back on Monday, and it looks like I'll have to go cap in paw to Tarquin Flapjack and beg him to return just to keep the station on the air. Thank goodness for Tansy. At least I can rely on her.'

'Before you leave,' said Hettie, keen to ask another question, 'how did you and Tansy meet?'

Wilco was cautious in his answer. 'We walked out together for a bit. Nothing serious, but we shared a love of radio, so when I took over here, I got in touch and invited her to do the breakfast show.'

'And do you know why she chooses to live in Southwool and commute every day?' asked Hettie. 'It can't be easy, getting up at that time every morning.'

'Goes with the territory in broadcasting, and I think she just likes to live by the sea,' said Wilco, crossing over to the reception desk. 'I almost forgot – as things are a bit unsettled at the moment, I'll give you a key. You might need it when you come in to do your next show.'

Wilco gave the key to Tilly and walked towards the door, signalling that the interview was over. Tilly gathered up her notepad and pencil and slid the key into her cardigan pocket. The three cats left the pavilion, and Wilco locked up behind him. 'I don't suppose you two would like to take on a few more shows?' he said, unlocking his bicycle.

Hettie and Tilly shook their heads in unison. 'I'm afraid we have our paws full at the moment, but thank you for asking,' Tilly said.

Wilco shrugged and rode away across the cricket pitch, much to the annoyance of Edward Dexter, who'd been busy putting the nets up for Bunty Basham's Saturday practice session.

Hettie watched as Wilco and his bicycle left the recreation ground and disappeared into the maze of closes and crescents which made up one of the town's smaller housing estates. She looked across to The Stumps, where Edward Dexter now stood motionless at his gate. 'I suppose we should go and talk to him next,' she sighed wearily.

'Maybe we'll have some time tomorrow,' suggested Tilly. 'Things might be a bit clearer by then. He's not exactly at the top of our suspect list, so I think he'll save for another day.'

Hettie agreed and the two cats trudged homeward, looking forward to their supper and some mindless TV. By the time they reached the bakery, it had turned cold. The day had been a mixture of hot sunshine and stormy downpours, and now – as the temperature plummeted – there was a nip in the air that made

Tilly head for their small fireplace the moment they were over the threshold. Hettie dragged the dustbin bag they'd dropped off earlier into the room and put it under their desk, while Tilly busied herself with kindling and firelighters.

Within minutes, a cheerful blaze danced in the grate and the room became instantly warm. Hettie halved the quiche onto two plates, adding a bag of crisps to each, and Tilly wasted no time in pulling on her pyjamas. 'Shall we have tea or fiery ginger beer with supper?' she asked, switching on the television.

'I think we should have ginger beer,' said Hettie, decanting Hartley Battenberg's catnip into her own tobacco pouch from the pockets of her business slacks.

Tilly pulled open the door to the staff sideboard, which was very much her domain. With limited storage space in their room, the sideboard had become a Tardis, crammed with everyday essentials that only she could put her paws on. It took her no time at all to find the bottle of ginger beer, but when she emerged from the cupboard, she brought the telephone and answer machine with her. 'It looks like we've got a message! It's flashing.'

Hettie rescued the ginger beer from Tilly's paws as the telephone and answer machine clattered to the floor. 'Are you sure you haven't left another of your messages?' she asked, knowing that Tilly often left messages for herself when they were out, just for the sheer joy of hearing her own voice when they got home.

Tilly looked indignant. 'I don't do that any more,' she protested. 'It was only when we first got it. It was so exciting, and I was just trying it out really.'

'What about that holiday we went on? You left messages every day for yourself. It took ages to go through them when we got home.'

Tilly pretended that she hadn't heard Hettie's last remark, and put the machine into rewind. The two cats moved closer to the small speaker, and Tilly pressed the play button. 'Hello, Gilbert Truffle here. I have some information regarding Hartley Battenberg's murder. The thing is, I know who did it. I'm staying with Cherry and Hilary Fudge if you'd like to call me back on 262034, or you can get me at the radio station this afternoon.'

Hettie rewound and played the message again before commenting. 'Well, looking on the bright side, I think we have a clear motive for Gilbert's murder,' she said. 'He quite simply knew too much and had to be silenced.'

Tilly checked the machine, noting that the call had come in at ten that morning. 'That's such a shame,' she said. 'We must have only just missed him. We left here just before ten this morning. But why would he ask us to call him and then go out to do interviews in the bake off queue?'

'Did he see you when you were looking for suspects?' asked Hettie.

'No, I don't think he did. He looked busy, and I only went up and down the line. If he'd seen me, he would have said something, I'm sure – especially if he knew who the murderer was.'

'Well, he obviously didn't think he was in any danger to be out there so publicly doing interviews. It just goes to show how wrong you can be.'

'I wonder what happened to his tape recorder?' Tilly said. 'There was no sign of it in Jessie's shop. Maybe the murderer took it?'

'I think one thing's for sure,' said Hettie, taking a large bite out of her quiche. 'No one is safe while this killer is out there, and clearly he or she will stop at nothing to cover their tracks.'

Chapter Twelve

Tilly woke early. She loved Saturdays, especially as it was the day when she and Hettie always lunched out at Bloomers. Molly Bloom's mixed grill was invariably on the specials board, and it was their treat of the week. She busied herself with the morning tea and delivered a mug of it to Hettie's armchair. Hettie stretched and yawned, feeling refreshed after a dreamless sleep, mainly brought about by a pipe of Hartley Battenberg's catnip. She sat up, trying to engage mentally with the day's prospects, and allowed the events of the previous day to come flooding back to her.

Tilly followed up the tea with a slice of toast, liberally spread with a cheese triangle. Hettie devoured hers before setting out the plans for the day. 'So,' she began, 'we've got Tansy, Branston and Bunty to interview this morning, followed by a mixed grill, and then I think we should pay a call on Edward Dexter.'

'What about Cherry and Hilary Fudge?' asked Tilly. 'They might be able to tell us more about Gilbert.'

'Yes, that's a good point, but they might be involved in this bake off thing this afternoon, so let's leave them till later. We could give them a call to see when they're free.'

Tilly wiped her paws on her pyjamas and pulled the telephone out of the sideboard. She played back Gilbert Truffle's message again and jotted down the number he'd left. Hilary Fudge answered immediately, and wasted no time in telling Tilly that Cherry had been chosen to attempt the bake off's lattice pie challenge that afternoon, and had been up most of the night practising. Eventually, Tilly managed to interrupt long enough to ask if they could spare some time to talk about Gilbert. Hilary pointed out that Gilbert always went to his sister's at the weekends and wouldn't be back until Monday morning, completely misunderstanding the question. Tilly looked across at Hettie and put her paw over the receiver. 'She doesn't know he's dead,' she whispered. 'What shall I tell her? She thinks he's at his sister's.'

'She obviously doesn't listen to Whisker FM. I bet Gilbert's death is all over the airwaves this morning,' said Hettie. 'You'd better tell her.'

Tilly broke the news as gently as she possibly could, arranging to call in on them in a day or two. She left Hilary sobbing loudly on the other end of the phone, with Cherry wailing in the background. 'Well, I'm glad that's over,' she said, pushing the telephone back into the sideboard.

Hettie glanced at the clock and got up to switch the radio on. 'It's nearly time for the ten o'clock news. Let's see what Whisker FM is saying about Gilbert.'

Tansy Flutter was coming to the end of her show, announcing the winners to her mystery voice competition, followed by the news jingle. It was Wilco's voice that came up next as he launched into the bulletin. He announced that investigations were continuing into the death of Hartley Battenberg, then followed up with an expansive update on the bake off competition and a clip of Fanny Haddock saying how high the standard of baking was in the town. Next came a story about a bicycle thief, and finally a fairly random stab at a weather forecast. The news out jingle crashed in, followed by Wilco's ident, and he was off on another marathon of broadcasting.

'How very strange,' said Hettie, switching the radio off. 'No mention of Gilbert at all, and it's such a big story. You'd think he'd want to make capital of a double murder, especially a cat as well known as Gilbert Truffle.'

'Maybe he's hoping for more information before he puts the story out,' Tilly suggested.

'Aren't we all,' said Hettie, pulling her business slacks on. 'We'd better get to Bloomers before your suspects start to arrive. We could fit in a bacon bap if we get a move on.'

Hettie left Tilly choosing a cardigan for the day, and made her way round to the bakery to order their supper and deliver the 'evidence' mince beef and onion pie to the Butters' substantial fridge. Beryl cast her eye across it and agreed that it was home-made, but not by the same cat as the steak and kidney pie; the crimping was very different.

Bloomers was busy with cats keen to secure a full breakfast before Dolly Scollop wiped down the specials board to put up the lunch menu. Hettie and Tilly arrived just in time to order a bacon bap, and made their way to their table to prepare for the first interview. Tilly had barely wiped the tomato sauce from her whiskers before Tansy Flutter turned up and headed straight for them. 'I hope I'm not late,' she said, a little out of breath, 'but I was delayed by Wilco telling me about poor Gilbert. I just can't believe it.'

'We were surprised that you weren't reporting it in your news bulletins as it's such a big story,' said Hettie.

'Wilco has decided to keep it quiet until he can get hold of Gilbert's sister,' said Tansy, as Dolly approached with her order pad. 'He said he didn't want her to hear about it on the radio. I'm just so shocked – first Hartley and now Gilbert. It makes you wonder who's going to be next.'

Tansy ordered a fruit scone and a pot of tea, and Hettie added two frothy coffees before getting down to business. 'There are some questions we need to ask you about Hartley Battenberg,' she began. 'How well did you know him?'

Tansy thought carefully before answering. 'I didn't really know him very well at all. He was around and about, and I suppose I saw more of him when he got his show. He often came into the radio station to record stuff while I was on air – bit of an early bird, really. He hated doing things live, and he even liked to pre-record his comedy sketches.'

'And you never saw him away from work?' Hettie asked.

'Only if there was a station get-together. Wilco is keen on us being a team, but I had very little to do with Hartley.'

'That's odd, considering you rented your house from him in Southwool.' Tansy's ears reddened through her grey fur. Hettie sat back, satisfied that the presenter had been caught in a lie. 'Shall we start again?' she suggested.

Tansy looked down at her feet, allowing a tear to escape and splash onto her bomber jacket. 'I know I shouldn't be glad he's dead, but I could have danced for joy when I heard the news. He was really quite nasty, and to be honest I was frightened of him.'

Dolly delivered their order, giving Tansy an opportunity to blow her nose and compose herself. 'We need you to tell us everything you know about Hartley Battenberg, and I promise whatever you tell us will go no further unless you actually murdered him,' said Hettie trying to be reassuring.

'Murdered him!' repeated Tansy. 'No, of course I didn't! I could never kill anyone – but if I could, Hartley would have been at the top of my list.'

'Why?' prompted Hettie.

'Because he was the sort of cat that everyone liked, but underneath it all he was a vile predator. I've done some stupid things in my life. I've got involved in situations I'm not proud of just to pay the bills, and Hartley pretended to be kind and understanding until I told him everything – then he turned it all against me and started asking for money to keep his silence.'

'You mean he was blackmailing you?' chipped in Tilly, as she scribbled frantically in her notebook.

Tansy nodded. 'Yes, I suppose that's what you'd call it, but it was more than that. As soon as I'd told him about my past, he seemed to take over my life, telling me where to live and who to see. When I moved into his horrible house in Southwool, he used me to entertain his friends. I had to host parties with other girl cats he'd brought in. It was horrible, and he made me pay a ridiculous rent for the house. My only joy was the radio job, and I couldn't tell anyone what was happening because he threatened me. Anyway, no one would have believed me. Wilco thought Hartley was the best thing since chicken drumsticks, but he never saw him the way I did. I'm just pleased that it's over and I can start to live my life again.'

'Do you think Hartley was blackmailing anyone else?' Hettie asked.

'I really couldn't say, but it wouldn't surprise me. He was always pretending that he was broke, putting on the poor, starving folk singer routine, but I paid him a fortune to keep his mouth shut so I knew him for what he was – and those flats off Sheba Gardens don't come cheap. The trouble was, he was the sort of cat you trusted. He listened and said all the right things, and he was funny. I think it was his sense of humour that made cats like him.'

'Did you ever visit him at his flat?'

'Not very often. I hosted a couple of parties there for some of his equally nasty friends, all up from London in their fast cars. He didn't look like a folk singer on those occasions.'

'I understand that he was a vegan – did you know that?'

'Vegan my front paw!' said Tansy. 'All that stuff was about his image at the folk club – baggy jumpers, fruit teas and pretend mince. No, he served the best steak and sausages at his parties, and he ate plenty of it himself.'

'Do you have any idea who might have killed him?'

Tansy shook her head. 'No, but whoever it was, I'd like to shake their paw. He was ruining my life, and the world is a better place without him.'

'What about Gilbert Truffle?' asked Hettie. 'How did you get on with him?'

'Oh he was lovely, a real gentle cat. I can't believe he's gone, and stabbed to death in a charity shop. I must have been only yards away at the time with my butterfly buns; it's just so surreal: why would anyone want to kill Gilbert?'

'That's something we need to find out,' said Hettie, noticing that Branston Bean had just arrived. 'If you think of anything else that might be helpful, please don't hesitate to get in touch.'

Tilly responded by pulling a business card out of her cardigan pocket and sliding it across the table. Hettie was impressed, as they so rarely remembered to carry them. 'Good luck with the bake off!' Tilly shouted as Tansy headed for the door, nodding a greeting to Branston.

Hettie clawed Tansy's untouched fruit scone to her side of the table, not wanting to waste it. 'Do sit down, Mr Bean, and thank you for coming.' Tilly said, patting the seat next to her.

Branston sat down and Hettie pounced immediately. 'Could you tell me where you were on Thursday night between six and midnight?'

Branston was taken aback at Hettie's directness, and decided to protest his innocence before any more questions were fired at him. 'If thith ith about Hartleeth's murder, I had nothing to do with it. I wath out for the evening with a friend, and thatth really all I have to thay.'

'We know that you met up with Tarquin Flapjack at the radio station, and later at the Cat and Fiddle, but where did you go in between?' Hettie countered.

'I jutht walked around a bit,' Branston responded. 'I'd had a very upthetting day.'

'And why was that?' asked Hettie, pretending she knew nothing about Wilco's ultimatum.

'Jutht thome trouble with Wilco over my show. He wanted to move me to weekendths, and it was all too upthetting. He'd already moved me off breakfatht to make way for Tanthy, and I'd only just got uthed to mid-morningth, but iths all OK now heth changed hith mind and I'm back on Monday.'

'I'm pleased to hear it,' Hettie lied, 'but I have to tell you that you were in the vicinity of two deaths within twenty-four hours, the first one at the radio station where Hartley Battenberg was killed and then yesterday morning in the charity shop, close to the Methodist Hall, where Gilbert Truffle died. I call that a bit of a coincidence to put it mildly.'

Branston fidgeted nervously before mounting a defence of sorts. 'I work at the radio thtation, and I wath one of hundredth of catth queuing outthide the Methodith Hall. Why would I want to murder Hartley or Gilbert?'

'You tell me,' said Hettie. 'Let's start with Hartley. What did he have on you? Something from your past perhaps?'

Branston stood up and started to walk away, but Hettie caught his arm and pulled him back to the table. 'No need to run away,' she said, 'there's a killer on the loose targeting radio presenters and you could be next. I repeat did Hartley Battenberg have something on you?'

'If he did, I wouldn't dithcuth it with you,' Branston said defiantly. 'All you need to know ith I didn't kill either of them and now if you'll excuthe me I have to prepare for the lattithe pie challenge.'

'Ah, so your steak and kidney pies caught the eye of Fanny Haddock, did they?' taunted Hettie. 'It's a shame about the one that choked Hartley Battenberg. Not a great crimp, I gather.'

Branston decided not to rise to the bait and this time he made sure of his exit, pushing Molly Bloom and a tray full of toasted sandwiches out of his way to reach the door.

'Well, that was enlightening,' said Hettie, absent-mindedly taking a bite out of Tansy's fruit scone. 'There's no doubt he's hiding something, and I wouldn't want to take him off your suspects list, but I'm not sure he's a killer, although he seemed to take the deaths of two of his fellow presenters in his stride.'

'What about Tansy?' asked Tilly. 'It sounds like she had plenty of reasons for killing Hartley, and she could easily have stabbed Gilbert in that rainstorm.'

'I agree, but she was very honest with us – although she could be double bluffing to cover her tracks. She did confirm our suspicions about Hartley, though. He clearly led a double life. I'm just wondering who else he was blackmailing. I think Branston is a safe bet, and we're just about to find out if Bunty Basham fits into the jigsaw. Here she comes.'

Bunty could always be relied upon to make an entrance: the larger than life cat was formidable in everyday clothes, but in her cricket whites she stood out like a giant moving edifice, barging her way across the café and coming to rest on the seat that Branston Bean had so recently vacated. 'I hope I haven't kept you both waiting. I'm in such an awful fix with the team. They all seem to think that nets are optional, and this damned bake off has suddenly become a priority. I'm afraid I've rather lost interest after my pies were rejected by that ghastly TV cook, but if I don't have eleven good cats and true to face Much-Purring-on-the-Rug, then I might as well knock it on the head now.'

Hettie tried to interrupt Bunty's diatribe on the state of the town's cricket team, or lack of it, but she batted on regardless. 'I mean, all one asks is a few hours a week. They've been in front of their fires all winter, and you'd think they'd want to get out in the fresh air and blow the cobwebs off their whiskers. But no. It's excuse after excuse – can't find my bat, my whites have turned green, I've broken my glasses and can't see to bowl. I've had the lot this morning. I don't suppose either of you is available?'

At last Hettie was able to take control of the conversation, and she jumped in with both paws. 'Normally we would love to help, but we're in the middle of a murder investigation – which is why we wanted to speak to you.'

Bunty shot a look at Tilly as she found a clean page in her notepad and wrote 'Bunty Basham' at the top, underlining it three times. 'Crikey! This all looks a bit official. Am I a suspect? How exciting!'

'I'm afraid everyone who knew Hartley Battenberg and Gilbert Truffle are suspects until we've eliminated them from our enquiries.'

'So it's true, then? Gilbert's dead as well as Hartley? There was much speculation in the bake off queue yesterday. One cat was convinced that it was Tarquin Flapjack who was loaded into Morbid's van, and we were all expecting the bake off to be cancelled as it was his venture – but we spotted him strutting about later. Fancy it all kicking off in Jessie's shop! I had no idea there was a body in there while I was sheltering from the downpour. It's all a bit creepy, really.'

Hettie could see that she would have to take a firmer paw to the proceedings before Bunty took over the interview entirely. 'I really want to start by talking about Hartley Battenberg,' she said. 'How well did you know him?'

'I didn't really know him at all. I'd seen him at the folk club and listened to his show on the radio a couple of times, but I wouldn't say I knew him.'

'Can you tell me where you were between six and the time you arrived at Tilly's party on Thursday night?' Hettie asked.

'Ah, that's an easy one. I was putting Ma to bed. She needs help with everything these days, and I wanted her settled before I went out.'

'And did you leave the party at any stage during the evening?'

'I think I stepped out for some air at one point. It was stifling in Bloomers, but it would only have been for a few minutes. Not long enough to murder Hartley, anyway, if that's what you're getting at.'

'And were you aware that he'd filmed you?' Hettie asked, playing a wild card.

Bunty suddenly looked fearful. 'Doing what?' she said, threatening to lose her composure.

'We found a video in his flat showing several cats queuing at Lavender Stamp's post office. You were at the front of the queue. Do you have any idea why he would do that?'

Bunty looked flustered and shook her head. 'Like I said, I really didn't know him, and I certainly wasn't aware of him doing any filming. I call that a damned cheek.'

'It's come to our attention that Hartley Battenberg was a blackmailer, which could explain why he was filming some of the cats in the town, but it's puzzling as to why he would home in on the post office?'

'I agree, that is a puzzle – but I'd never have had him down as a blackmailer,' Bunty responded, glancing at her sports watch. 'Now, if you've finished with me I really must get back to nets. I've left Edward Dexter in charge and he can get a bit over the top. I can't afford to lose any more players.'

'Just a couple more questions before you go,' insisted Hettie. 'Can you think of any reason why Hartley might have wanted to blackmail you?'

'Why? Have you found something I should know about?' demanded Bunty, getting agitated. 'I'm beginning to feel a bit intimidated by all these questions. I'm sure everyone has a skeleton or two in their cupboards, but – before you ask – I didn't kill Hartley Battenberg, and on reflection I don't know why I've been hauled off the cricket pitch to face this inquisition. I'm finding it very upsetting.'

'I'm sorry you feel that way,' said Hettie, softening her approach, 'but it would seem that Hartley Battenberg made a lot of enemies by preying on cats who were keen to bury their past. I just wanted to make sure that you weren't one of his victims.'

'Me, a victim?' Bunty said, clawing back a little of her confidence. 'Not on your life! I'm a motivator and a doer, so don't waste any time worrying about me, not when there are murderers to catch. Anyway, I really must get on. I promised Ma I would cook her a decent lunch after nets. She'll be fretting if I'm late. The joys of being a carer! I wouldn't recommend it.'

With that, Bunty Basham left Hettie and Tilly to their deliberations and headed back to the cricket pitch, where Edward Dexter was giving a masterclass to what was left of her team. 'Well, I think we rattled her cage,' said Hettie, as soon as Bunty was out of earshot. 'We got a similar reaction to Branston's – as soon as I mentioned blackmail, she couldn't wait to get out of here.'

Tilly thought for a moment before offering an opinion. 'I think the problem with blackmail is that no one wants to own up to their past. It has to be something really serious to pay for silence, and all the cats we've spoken to so far have settled lives now. They have too much to lose, and they're not about to tell us in case it all comes out.'

'At least Tansy was honest eventually. Wild horses wouldn't get Branston to give up his secrets, but Bunty is different; unlike the other two, she still seems frightened of something. It might have nothing to do with Hartley or Gilbert for that matter, but there's more going on in her life than a no-show cricket team, and it's probably none of our business.'

'What's next?' asked Tilly, draining her coffee cup and licking the froth from the rim.

'I think we should both interview two of Molly Bloom's mixed grills, then strike out for the recreation ground to have a chat with Mr Edward Dexter.'

Tilly clapped her paws with delight as Dolly Scollop advanced with her order pad. 'Don't tell me,' said Dolly, raising her paw. 'Two mixed grills with everything but the black pudding, and an extra serviette for Tilly.'

'Ooh, yes please, Dolly, but could you just say what's in it as it's all so lovely?' requested Tilly.

'All right, then – 'ere goes.' Dolly took a deep breath before giving the full details of the Saturday mixed grill. 'Sausage, liver, lamb chop, kidney, steak medallion, baked tomato, peas, fried mushrooms, battered onion rings and chips!' A round of applause rang out across the café as Dolly took a bow and Tilly squealed with pleasure. Even Molly poked her head out of the kitchen to delight in the effect that her mixed grill was having on her customers.

It took the best part of an hour for Hettie and Tilly to wade through their lunch, leaving only the bone that had once belonged to a lamb chop on their plates. The two friends waved Dolly away when she approached with the pudding menu, and hauled themselves into the high street, grateful for the walk to the recreation ground.

Chapter Thirteen

Edward Dexter enjoyed a frugal lunch, as his preference was for a cricket tea in the middle of the afternoon, regardless of the time of year or the weather. He'd become adept at the baking of scones, and the removal of crusts from cucumber sandwiches was a daily delight, as was his monthly jam-making day – an event which he regarded as vital to the success of a perfect cricket tea. The miniature pork pies came from the Butters' bakery, as Edward felt that the making of cold water pastry was a culinary adventure too far, but the rest of his daily indulgence was home-grown, even down to the strawberries and raspberries that went into his jam.

Edward's morning had been fraught with the lacklustre performance from Bunty Basham's cricketers – although 'cricketers' would not be an apt description of the motley selection of cats who turned up to practise their non-existent batting and bowling skills. Edward loved the cricket pitch; for him, it was hallowed ground, and to see a band of marauding cats trampling all over it and making wild swings with bat on ball was almost too much. He appreciated Bunty's enthusiasm for wanting to put a team together, and she had shown great promise herself with the bat, but one decent player does not a cricket team make.

He washed up his cup, plate and knife, leaving them to dry on the draining board, and settled to planting a new row of gooseberries in the garden at the back of his cottage. When Hettie and Tilly knocked on his front door, he chose to ignore the unwelcome distraction until the noise became more persistent. Grumbling, he came through his back gate to see who had decided to disturb his afternoon.

'Ah, Mr Dexter,' Hettie began, 'I'm Hettie Bagshot and this is Tilly Jenkins. We're from The No. 2 Feline Detective Agency, and we're investigating the murder of Hartley Battenberg. I wondered if you could spare some time to help us with our enquiries?'

'I see. Well, you'd better come in. No sense in discussing folk's business out here. I'll go round and let you in.'

Edward disappeared through the back gate and Tilly giggled. 'I wasn't expecting him to talk like that,' she said.

'He's from Porkshire – Brontë country, I think. It's where all the cats who play cricket come from, evidently.'

Tilly marvelled at Hettie's cricket knowledge and was about to say so when the front door of The Stumps was thrown open. 'Come in and sit thyselves down. Will you take a cup of Porkshire tea?' Edward asked, ushering them inside.

'That's kind of you, but no thank you,' said Hettie, fighting back a serious bout of indigestion.

'Well, if you'll excuse me, I'll just give me paws a rinse. I'll not be a minute.'

Edward left Hettie and Tilly to stare in awe at his cricketing triumphs, which filled the small parlour. A china cabinet and Welsh dresser were both packed with trophies, and the walls bore testament to his long and successful sporting career, picturing him proudly leaning on his bat or sitting in the centre of his team. There was a hatstand in the corner, decorated with caps of different colours; some were faded from the sun, but all bore badges from the triumphant victories that Edward had been part of.

'Now then,' said Edward, returning from his ablutions. 'I don't know what help I can be, but fire away and we'll see where it teks us.'

He sat in his chair by the fireplace and started to fill his pipe from a tobacco pouch while Tilly started a clean page in her notepad. Hettie chose to begin with the coming of the radio station. 'How did you feel about Whisker FM moving into the cricket pavilion?'

'I thought it was ridiculous,' responded Edward. 'I thought it would attract all the wrong sort of cats – those DJ types who run noisy discos and play all that loud pop music. I had several run-ins with Wilco, until he made me sit down and listen to Tansy Flutter. It takes a deal more than a pretty face to impress me, but I had to admit the lass talked a bit of sense, and I gradually changed my mind about what they were doing over there. I still say they have no business in the pavilion, and it's high time they shifted themselves to somewhere more suitable, but we've come to an understanding, and as long as they respect the grounds and the wicket with all their comings and goings, that'll do for me.'

'I'm sure you're aware that two of Wilco's presenters have died in the last couple of days,' Hettie continued. 'I wonder if you could cast your mind back to Thursday evening first? Did you see or speak to anyone from the radio station, say between six and midnight?'

Edward made much of lighting his pipe, using several matches before answering. 'Well, there was a bit of a to-do with Wilco and that Tarquin character outside the pavilion just before six. I was cross because they were chucking these leaflets all over the pitch.' Edward leaned forward to show Hettie the contents of his litter bin, which was overflowing with bake off propaganda. 'Wilco left Tarquin looking none too happy. Next thing, he was having a chat with that Branston Bean – he'd been hanging around outside the pavilion for some time. I saw you two leaving just after six, then Gilbert Truffle turned up and went into the pavilion. He came out a few minutes later with Wilco's niece.'

'You mean Marzi Pan?'

'Yes, that's the one – two puddings short of a beef dinner if you ask me. Anyway, Tarquin was passing the time of day with me by then, so I was a bit distracted. He was going on about his radio show, and how he hoped it would be back on the air very soon. I'm not sure why he thought I'd be interested. I always have me cricket videos on Saturday nights, and judging by the row he'd just had with Wilco, I thought he was being a bit optimistic. He cleared off, and at about half past six Wilco came out of the radio station, got on his bike and pedalled off towards the high street.'

'And did you see where Branston Bean went?' asked Hettie.

Edward shook his head. 'No, I'm afraid not. I assumed he went on his way after talking to Tarquin.'

'Did you notice anything later that evening?'

'It was dark by about seven-thirty, and I was watching *One Cat and a Dog*, as it came from the Porkshire Dales this week. Then I caught up on my correspondence. I was sat here at me desk by the window when I saw a light come on in the pavilion – that was about ten-thirty. I couldn't see anyone, but a while later I noticed you two going in.'

'I thought you said it was dark. How did you know it was us?'

'When that light comes on in the reception, it lights up the veranda – and I have to admit to having these handy,' Edward added, pointing towards a set of binoculars perched on his desk. 'I knew there was some bother going on when I saw the Shroud and Trestle van turn up. A bad business, really.'

'And did you know Hartley Battenberg?'

'No – not to put a name to, anyway. I only listen to Tansy Flutter, and she was full of it on her breakfast show on Friday. That's how I knew who'd died. Never heard of the lad till then.'

'And what about Gilbert Truffle – did you know him?'

'I knew of him before he came here, as he occasionally did a bit of commentary on the national service. Nice voice, no nonsense, lovely diction. I was pleased to meet him when he joined Whisker FM. He occasionally shared a cricket tea with me here at The Stumps. I can't think why anyone would want to kill him, he was a genuinely nice cat.'

'When did you find out that he'd died?'

'This morning at nets, Bunty Basham was full of it after her meeting with you.'

'And how well do you get on with Bunty?' Hettie asked.

'She's a good sort. I'm not one for encouraging girl cats to play cricket – I'd rather they stuck to baking and serving teas – but she's not a bad player, as I said, and I think the sport makes up for what she has to deal with at home.'

'What do you mean?'

'Well, I gather her mother has been a trial to her. Old Mrs Basham taught at that posh school in Southwool before she retired. She sent Bunty there, and I think she had a rough time of it. I get the feeling that there's very little love lost between her and her mother, and now of course Bunty has to do everything for her. I think she uses her sport as an escape. I just wish the rest of her cricket team were as keen as she is – we might even win the occasional match.'

'I believe you were in the charity shop in Cheapcuts Lane yesterday, around the time that Gilbert Truffle died,' said Hettie moving the conversation on. 'Did you see him there or notice anything out of the ordinary?'

'I saw him earlier, talking to some of the cats in the queue outside the Methodist Hall. He had his tape recorder with him. I had a fancy for one of the cricket bats that Jessie had in her window, so I was keen to secure it and I didn't take a deal of notice of anything else. Then the heavens opened and Jessie's shop filled with cats, all clamouring to get out of the rain. It was such a crush I couldn't wait to get out of there. I told Jessie I'd pick the bat up in a day or two and made a run for it.' Edward picked up the bat in question. 'Here it is. Jessie was kind enough to drop it off yesterday afternoon to save me a trip. She's a beauty – vintage Waller Warsop 1955. I'll not be adding this to me fence any time soon.'

Hettie decided not to engage on the merits of vintage cricket bats or novelty fencing, and bowled another question. 'Did you see Bunty in Jessie's shop yesterday?'

'Yes, but only briefly when I was on my way out. I said I'd see her at nets. I ran straight into Tarquin Flapjack on my way out of the shop, actually. He looked like a drowned rat.'

Hettie sat up, suddenly remembering that Tarquin had been missing when she'd returned to the Methodist Hall after the discovery of Gilbert's body. 'So are you saying that Tarquin Flapjack was going into the charity shop during the storm?'

'Definitely. He pushed past me to get out of the rain.'

It always amazed Hettie that the smallest piece of information could easily turn an investigation on its head. She and Tilly had spent all day listening to the accounts of witnesses and potential suspects; there had been revelations, twists and turns, possible lies and prevarications – but the fact that Tarquin Flapjack had been in close proximity to Gilbert Truffle when he died might well prove to be the most significant information they had gleaned so far. It was time to sift the evidence and narrow down the suspect list.

'I'm most grateful for your time,' Hettie said, 'and I have one more question before we leave you in peace. Have you, or anyone you know, ever received blackmail notes or threats of any kind?'

For the first time in their conversation, Edward Dexter was thrown off guard. He made much of knocking his pipe out on the fender before responding. 'I'll tell you this,' he said, leaning forward and lowering his voice, 'that lass on the breakfast show is being bullied. She's not said anything too plainly to me, but we often share a morning coffee and I can tell that she's fearful of someone. If I was you, I'd keep a special eye on her. She needs protecting.'

'Have you any idea who might be making her unhappy?' asked Hettie.

'No, but if I find out, I'll tek me bat to them. Now then, will you take a cricket tea with me before you go?'

'I honestly don't think we can put you to any more trouble,' Hettie said, still feeling the effects of Molly Bloom's mixed grill.

'It's no trouble at all,' Edward protested, rising from his chair. 'I'll not tek no for an answer. Scones are ready to be creamed and jammed, and it'll only tek a minute to cut some sandwiches.'

Edward headed for his kitchen leaving Hettie and Tilly with no choice but to wait for his laden tea trolley to come rattling into the parlour. The cricket tea was exceptional, and they played their part both with the salmon and cucumber sandwiches and the scones. Tilly managed hers without too much cream escaping onto her cardigan, and Hettie obliged Edward by accepting the last sandwich. He waved them off at his gate, offering an open invitation to call in on him at any time, and the two friends wended their weary way home to sift and sort through the building pile of evidence.

Chapter Fourteen

The Butters had left Hettie and Tilly's supper outside the door to their room, with a note to say that they'd been called to a meeting to discuss cricket teas for Easter Sunday. Hettie's stomach did an unpleasant somersault at the very mention of a cricket tea. It was a rare thing for her to distance herself from food but, as Tilly dragged the bag containing their supper into the room, she had to admit that currently she couldn't contemplate ever eating again. She was full to the very top of her long-haired tabby head, and Edward's excellent tea had probably been a scone too far.

Tilly felt the same, and pushed the supper to one side on the table before lighting the fire. Hettie switched on the TV in time to catch the six o'clock news. The headlines were boring – fish quotas and a new flea treatment – but the 'and finally' centred on the death of Gilbert Truffle and featured a look back at his distinguished career, starting with archive footage of him broadcasting on one of the pirate radio boats, and moving on to his national radio work and recent foray into local radio. The cat presenting the rather scrambled obituary gave no information about how Gilbert had died; there was a brief clip of his sister tearfully singing her brother's praises, but no mention of murder or even suspicious death.

'That's all a bit strange,' said Hettie. 'I wonder where they got the story from. I'd have thought the fact that he was murdered should have been a headline; instead we got a watered-down tribute at the end of the news.'

'Maybe they got their information from Wilco and he didn't want to own up to a second murder until the killer is found?' suggested Tilly.

'Well, one thing's for sure: he won't be pleased with the coverage – there was no mention of Whisker FM. I gather the use of the words "local radio" conjures up a vision of a load of would-be broadcasters making it up as they go along and misguidedly thinking that they're much more famous than they really are.'

'That's a perfect description of Branston Bean and Tarquin Flapjack,' Tilly pointed out, 'but that pirate radio film looked interesting. I'd love to do a programme on a boat.'

'I think you already do,' said Hettie. 'It seems to me that Whisker FM is starting to sink without trace. Anyway, I videoed the news in case we didn't get back in time, so you can watch the pirate bit again whenever you want to. Now I think we should get on with the stuff we've learnt today, and see if we're any further on with either murder. Let's start with who was present in the vicinity of both murders and had opportunity and motive.'

Tilly settled on her blanket by the fire and turned to the list of suspects in her notepad, beginning with Tarquin Flapjack. 'Tarquin was definitely on the recreation ground on Thursday evening. We know he had a row with Wilco before six, and after that he spoke with Branston Bean and Edward Dexter. We also know, according to his statement, that he arrived at the Cat and Fiddle at seven-thirty to meet Branston, and we saw him later looking in at Bloomers' window with Branston, although he didn't mention it. That must have been between ten-thirty and eleven; he told us that they both went home at eleven. We also now know that he was in Jessie's shop at the time of Gilbert's murder, as Edward said he collided with him at the shop door during the storm.'

'Yes, that was a real revelation. We wrongly assumed that he was still in the Methodist Hall where we left him, but there's a back door that leads from the kitchen into a yard – he must have left the building that way. The question is – why? Was it something that came up while I was questioning him, or did he plan to kill Gilbert anyway?' Hettie thought for a moment. 'We also need to consider why he might have murdered Hartley. Jealousy is an obvious reason after his sacking from the radio, but we now know that Hartley might have been blackmailing him. We also know that he's the sort who might have had his own key cut to the pavilion, and at a brisk walk he could have murdered Hartley at seven and got to the Cat and Fiddle by seven-thirty, using Branston Bean as an alibi. Edward Dexter might have missed him doubling back to the radio station, although he doesn't seem to miss much. The pies found on the bodies point to him as well, because of this bake off nonsense, but that might be a bit obvious and it could point to someone else trying to incriminate him. Let's look at Branston Bean next.'

Tilly turned to the page she'd allotted to Branston Bean, and started by reading her basic notes on the presenter. 'I've put that his shows are awful, and that his music is terrible,' she began. 'According to Wilco, he had a meeting with him on Thursday and told him that he was being moved to weekends, which Branston wasn't happy about. Tarquin spoke to him on the recreation ground around six o'clock and arranged to meet for supper. Edward saw them together, but didn't notice where Branston went after that. Tarquin said that Branston arrived at the Cat and Fiddle at about seven forty-five. But we've no idea what he was doing in between those times. When we spoke to him, he corroborated what Tarquin had told us about their meeting up, but refused to be questioned on the possibility of Hartley blackmailing him. I also made a note about Hartley recording a jingle poking fun at Branston and his lisp. Branston was in the bake off queue at the Methodist Hall on Saturday, and his signature dish was steak and kidney pie. That's all I've got on him.'

Hettie sat for a moment, digesting the information on Branston Bean. 'When you spotted him in the queue and arranged the meeting at Bloomers, was he wet or dry?'

'He was dry – why?'

'Because that suggests he sheltered in Jessie's shop, which means that he could easily have stabbed Gilbert Truffle and then taken his place in the queue after the rain stopped. And he has a key to the pavilion, so he could have murdered Hartley and still met up with Tarquin for supper. He seemed very agitated when we mentioned blackmail, too, so he's definitely covering something up. He's a strong candidate for our killer, along with Tarquin.'

'Maybe they're in it together,' suggested Tilly. 'They've both been sidelined by Wilco, and Hartley Battenberg did seem to be flavour of the month as far as the radio station is concerned.'

'Let's look at Tansy Flutter next. We do at least know that she had a really good reason for killing Hartley, but so far she's the only suspect who's opened up to us,' said Hettie.

'There's no evidence to suggest that she was anywhere near the radio station on Thursday night, but I suppose she could have slipped away from my party,' said Tilly, looking through her notes. 'She said she was pleased that Hartley was dead, and she seemed quite sad about Gilbert. She claimed that she didn't know Gilbert had died until after her breakfast show this morning, and that Wilco told her and said he wanted to keep it quiet until he could tell Gilbert's sister.'

'She was right at the front of the bake off queue when I arranged to question her and she was dry so she didn't get caught outside in the rain. I don't think she had the chance or opportunity to kill Gilbert in Jessie's shop,' Hettie added. 'She's definitely a victim in all of this, but I doubt she's a murderer – and if Edward is to be believed, she was vulnerable and needed protecting, and probably still does.'

'So shall I remove her from my list?' asked Tilly.

'Let's put her right at the bottom and take a look at Wilco next.'

Tilly had made copious notes on Wilco Wonderfluff and spent a few moments putting the information in order before delivering her thoughts. 'I'll start with Thursday,' she said. 'We got his call at about eleven-thirty, telling us that Hartley was dead. We arrived at the radio station just after midnight, and he told us he was there to put my picture up and noticed some crumbs coming from the studio. He went to investigate, and found Hartley dead in studio 1A. He talked a lot about the radio station and how he had made enemies when he took it over – like Tarquin, whom he'd sacked, and Edward, who wasn't happy about him using the cricket pavilion. He said that Tansy had helped to smooth things over with Edward – she'd "poured Darjeeling over troubled turf", to be exact. He also said he'd had words with Branston about moving him to weekends. He admired Hartley's sense of humour, and thought he was a breath of fresh air to the radio station. He'd seen him play at the folk club, too.'

'That's all fairly straightforward,' said Hettie. 'I seem to remember he gave a good account of radio politics and the rise and fall of presenters at the time, but I suppose we have to allow for his being in shock. He did rattle on a bit, but he was keen to offer money to have the case solved, which has got to be a plus as far as we're concerned. Let's take a look at the second interview after Gilbert's death. I think that was a bit more interesting.'

Tilly flicked over the page and delivered her notes on their second conversation with Wilco. 'I've put that he seemed very upset and shocked, and he was out of sorts because he'd been broadcasting all day. Marzi and Branston had the day off, and we know that Branston was down at the Methodist

Hall. He assumed that Gilbert had just died and seemed surprised about him being murdered. Wilco talked about Gilbert; he'd met him years ago when Gilbert trained him, and they kept in touch. He told us that Gilbert had seen an ad about Whisker FM and had given his job up on national radio to come and join him. He was a bit vague about Gilbert's choice to lodge in the town and go to his sister's at the weekends. Then he talked about his own career, saying that he'd hopped from one station to another, slightly disillusioned, until coming here to do holiday relief. He's ploughed his savings into the radio station, eventually taking over from the old guard, as he called them. He talked about sacking Tarquin because he'd forgotten his responsibilities towards the listeners.'

Tilly took a breath and continued. 'When you got on to Hartley and told him about his flat and his money, he seemed surprised, but he was suddenly keen to get off home. You asked him about Tansy and he was a bit dismissive; he said they'd walked out together, nothing serious, and then he'd invited her to do the breakfast show. He also said that he thought she liked living by the sea. Then he asked if we'd like to do more shows and gave me a key to the radio station. He was considering reinstating Tarquin, as he was running out of presenters. That's it.'

Hettie reached for her catnip pouch while she pondered Tilly's notes on Wilco. She filled her pipe and lit it, blowing a perfect smoke ring before offering some thoughts of her own. 'As far as I can see, Wilco had no real motive for killing Hartley or Gilbert. They were both an important part of his radio station, so why would he shoot himself in the foot? I'm puzzled by a couple of things, though. He didn't ask how Gilbert had died, and I assume Jessie didn't tell him as we asked her not to – but we can check that with her. I think we have to rule him out of Gilbert's murder, as he was on the radio at the time, but according to Edward Dexter, Wilco was the last to leave the radio station on the night of your party. Hartley would have been doing his show by then, so why did Wilco hang back and not leave with everyone else? We also know from Edward that Gilbert popped in just after six and left a bit later with Marzi Pan; maybe he saw something that he later connected with Hartley's murder. It makes you wonder what was going on during that time. Why so many comings and goings? Had Wilco called a meeting? And, if so, why didn't he mention it to us?'

'Maybe they were just gathering for my party?' suggested Tilly.

'Possibly, but when you come to think of it, with the exception of Tansy Flutter, all Wilco's presenters were in the vicinity of the radio station when Hartley was on air on Thursday evening. That's a bit of a coincidence.'

'Perhaps they all did it, like in one of Miss Crispy's books?' offered Tilly. 'If Hartley was blackmailing them, perhaps they all got together to shut him up for good.'

'That's a perfectly reasonable solution except for one thing – they were all at Bloomers by seven, and Hartley didn't finish his show until then. They couldn't be in two places at once, unless Edward popped over to the pavilion and bumped Hartley off for them. I think we're getting a bit bogged down with radio presenters. How about taking a look at Bunty Basham? I find her quite interesting.'

'According to my notes, she had plenty of opportunity to bump Gilbert off,' said Tilly. 'We met her coming out of Jessie's shop when she knocked me into a puddle, and she seemed in a terrible hurry.'

Hettie agreed. 'And we shouldn't forget that she claims to have had a mince beef pie taken while she was putting her umbrella up in the queue – that could easily have been a cover-up. But I don't think she was anywhere near the radio station on Thursday evening, and she was very present at your party.'

Tilly checked her notes. 'Yes, that's right – but she did say she'd popped out for some air. I suppose it's possible that she could have had time to get to the radio station and back to Bloomers without anyone noticing.'

'The thing that bothers me about all this popping in and out is that we were told that Hartley planned to come to Bloomers as soon as he finished his show at seven. We arrived around seven, and everyone was there by then, so none of our suspects could have murdered him at the end of his show,' Hettie pointed out.

'Not unless Hartley stayed on to do something and had mentioned that to someone. Maybe he was recording some more jingles before coming on to the party? Or he could have arranged to meet up with someone.'

'Based on that, the field is wide open and we shouldn't assume that the killer is on the suspects list at all. It seems to me that Hartley's double life would have made him quite a few enemies. There are all these so-called friends from London that he threw parties for. Tansy painted them as being an unpleasant lot, but they wouldn't have access to the radio station unless Hartley let them in. In that case, we would have to consider why cat "X" would then go on to kill Gilbert. It's clear from his message that he knew who had killed Hartley, which points to someone much closer to home.'

Tilly yawned. They seemed now to be going round in circles, and she was beginning to think that none of the material they'd gathered so far was going to solve the case. 'Shall I finish reading my notes on Bunty?'

'OK,' said Hettie, adding another shovel of coal to the fire, 'and then I think we should have some supper. My indigestion has nearly worn off now, and we wouldn't want to waste Betty's sausage-meat plait or Beryl's custard cream slice.'

Tilly was pleased that their day was nearly at an end, and made short work of the information that Bunty had given them. There appeared to be nothing in her notes to suggest that the cricketer was involved in any way in Hartley's death, but there was clearly an underlying doubt about whether she'd been entirely forthcoming regarding her own secrets. Hettie was convinced that there was something, but neither she nor Tilly could quite put their paw on it. 'There's just one more thing before we have supper,' Tilly said, flicking back through her notes. 'When we spoke to Tansy, she said that Wilco had told her about Gilbert's death after her show this morning. Well, at one point she mentioned the fact that Gilbert had been stabbed.'

'So what are you saying?' asked Hettie.

'If Jessie didn't tell Wilco how Gilbert had died, how did Tansy know he'd been stabbed?'

'That's a very good point,' said Hettie, laying out the supper, 'and we do have to allow for the fact that no one has been entirely truthful about anything as far as I can see. If we hadn't found out about Tansy renting from Hartley, she'd never have owned up to the blackmail situation. We need to box clever. I think we should go through the stuff we brought back from Hartley's flat first thing tomorrow, and we also need to speak to Marzi Pan and pay a visit to Hilary and Cherry Fudge. I'd like to know a bit more about Gilbert Truffle.'

Chapter Fifteen

'First thing' in Hettie Bagshot's household meant after ten on most mornings, but on Sundays it was hunger rather than time that woke the two cats. Tilly, as always, was first to the kettle, and loaded the toaster with bread while she was waiting for it to boil. As it was Sunday, she decided to break out a new jar of salmon spread – a particular favourite of Hettie's. Tilly was very partial to it as well, and had been known to eat a whole jar with a spoon before it got anywhere near the toast, but today she was exercising a modicum of self-control, and satisfied herself by licking the knife instead.

Hettie's nose had detected the toast long before she opened her eyes, but, as breakfast was now imminent, she sat up and stretched, ready to receive it. The night had been a long one, peppered with suspects coming and going in her dreams, some wearing headphones, others up to their necks in pastry, but nothing seemed any clearer than it had the night before. The salmon spread was a touch of genius on Tilly's part, though, and it lightened Hettie's mood as soon as she took her first bite.

There was more good news to come as the two friends pulled on their Sunday clothes. A polite tap on their door revealed Bruiser, fresh from his bikers' holiday. 'Me an' Poppa saw a bit in the paper about Hartley whatsisname bein' murdered, an' we thought you might need us, so we're back. We was lucky ta see it, as it was wrapped round Poppa's cod 'n' chips. We got in late last night.'

Tilly threw her arms round Bruiser's neck, so pleased to have him home, and even Hettie offered a joyous grin, relieved that The No. 2 Feline Detective Agency had a full complement of staff once again.

'How's Miss Scarlet?' asked Tilly. 'I can't wait for a trip out in her. We've really missed her.'

'Bin runnin' like a dream all week, an' she won first prize in the motorbike an' sidecar class at Bike Fest. We 'ad a really nice time there,' said Bruiser. 'I'm goin' ta give 'er a wash an' polish this morning, an' I'm meetin' Poppa fer Sunday lunch at Bloomers if you two want ta join us – my treat. Unless you need me ter take you somewhere now?'

Hettie shook her head. 'No, we've stuff to do this morning here, but lunch would be lovely and we can bring you up to speed on the case.'

Bruiser left Hettie and Tilly to their work, and went to unpack from his holiday and impose a deep shine on the bright red motorbike and sidecar that Tilly had named Miss Scarlet after a character in her favourite board game.

'I suppose we'd better take a look at Hartley Battenberg's video collection,' said Hettie. 'Let's hope there's something more interesting than a lurch down the high street.'

Tilly pulled the tapes out of the dustbin bag and stacked them next to their video machine, taking the first one off the top and slotting it into the player. It was the one they'd already viewed in Hartley's flat, showing several shops before focusing on a queue at the post office. 'I'm not sure we're any the wiser looking at it again,' said Hettie, 'although two of our suspects are there – but I just can't see the significance of Tarquin or Bunty queuing for Lavender Stamp's services, and I'm not sure why he would want to film Bugs Anderton or Molly Bloom. Let's stick another one in.'

Tilly pressed the eject button and loaded the second video. This time it was very clear what Hartley's subject matter had been. The film opened in a dimly lit nightclub, packed to the rafters with male tomcats, all cheering and clapping. The camera moved to a small stage which housed a three-piece band and a chorus of scantily clad female cats, parading up and down to the delight of their rowdy audience. Suddenly there was a drum roll, and the chorus parted to reveal a cat clad from head to toe in feather boas. The band struck up as the cat proceeded to prance about the stage, shedding the boas and tossing them into the appreciative audience. 'Oh my,' said Hettie. 'Poor Tansy. What drives a cat to do that? I hope she got paid well – just look at those vile Toms. Hartley was clearly a very unpleasant cat with a lot of very unpleasant friends.'

The nightclub video was followed by a series of photographic stills, all showing Tansy in various states of undress. Hartley had put together a montage of all the lowest moments of Tansy Flutter's early life, a life she obviously hoped would be buried for good until it surfaced in the paws of her blackmailer.

Tilly was sickened by the images and ejected the video, choosing the next one on the pile and pushing it into the machine. On first sight, it appeared to be a holiday video, set somewhere along the coast. The camera zoomed in on an idyllic beach, where several families of cats were enjoying the sunshine. Kittens played on the shoreline with buckets and spades, while their parents kept a watchful eye. There were rows of small fishing boats, and a couple of larger craft beached on the sand. A fisher cat sat on an upturned boat, mending his nets, and another was busily unloading a crab pot, as several customers gathered around him waiting to purchase his catch. The video camera moved across the beach; some cats waved, happy to be included in the film, but there was nothing that Hettie or Tilly recognised, including the location, and seemingly nothing in the film that warranted a blackmail note of any kind. The film was a short one, and Hettie hit the fast forward button, stopping occasionally to check that there was nothing more on the tape.

'That video was a bit of a waste of time,' said Hettie, putting it to one side. 'The trouble is, we don't know what we're looking for.'

'Until we find it,' offered Tilly, trying to stay positive.

The next tape featured a location a little closer to home, and the Methodist Hall in Cheapcuts Lane loomed into view. Inside, the camera recorded a pack of young kitten scouts busily practising knots, all gathered around an adult cat with his back to the camera. He moved from one scout to another, issuing praise until he reached the smallest of the kittens and hauled him out from the pack. The kitten began to cry, and the adult proceeded to beat him with a slipper. The tiny scout screamed and begged to be let go as more and more blows were rained down on him. Eventually, the cat tossed the sobbing kitten aside like a discarded rag and chose another scout from the pack. He repeated the attack several times on different kittens, while the others watched in terror, all thinking that they would be next.

Hettie and Tilly watched in horror as the cat indiscriminately meted out his sadistic punishments until the wave of violence was complete. The kittens huddled together while the cat caressed the tops of their heads, as if he would never dream of raising a paw to them. Unwittingly, he turned towards the unseen camera, smiling with satisfaction at his brutal achievement. The cat who stared back at them was Branston Bean.

'Well I never,' said Hettie. 'No wonder he didn't want to own up to that. What a truly horrible creature he is. I just hope Hartley Battenberg took him for every penny he's got. Who'd have thought it? Branston Bean, a top-level sadist with a fancy for beating up little boy cats.'

'And a really good reason for killing Hartley,' added Tilly, wiping a tear from her eye.

There were two more videos left. Hettie rewound the tape featuring Branston and exchanged it for another while Tilly made more mugs of milky tea. The last video had upset her more than Hettie realised: she had been beaten in a similar way when she was a very small kitten by a cat her mother had taken up with. She had run away from home rather than endure any more beatings, and had spent much of her life as a homeless cat until Hettie befriended her. It was a piece of her history that she found hard to discuss with anyone, even Hettie.

The next tape opened in the food hall of Malkin and Sprinkle. It looked busy, as the cats scurried around filling their trolleys with provisions. There were several customers whom Hettie and Tilly recognised: Dorcas Ink, the printer; Marmite Spratt, the town's self-appointed historian; the medium, Irene Peggledrip, and her sidekick, Delirium Treemints. It took a few moments to work out who the camera was focused on, but the very presence of Wilco's niece, Marzi Pan, drew Hettie's attention. Marzi appeared to be loitering in the bread and cakes aisle with a very large bag slung over her shoulder. She stood for several moments, waiting for the aisle to clear of other shoppers, before loading several packets of biscuits and two boxed Victoria Sandwiches into her bag. There was no thought of paying as she headed for the lift to other departments. The video stopped briefly, then resumed in the homecare section, where Marzi was helping herself to an assortment of scented candles and joss sticks; she confidently crammed them into her shoulder bag, before making her way through to cosmetics. It was no real surprise that she homed in on the claw varnish section, taking her time to choose at least half a dozen different shades and securing them with the rest of her shopping before breezing out through the revolving doors into the high street. At this point, the filming came to an end, and Hettie checked that there was nothing further on before rewinding.

'There's no doubt about that one,' she said. 'Marzi Pan caught red-clawed – no argument there.'

'And it looked like it wasn't the first time,' added Tilly. 'She was all set up with that big bag. It looked like a real professional job.'

'Yes, she certainly made it look easy. I wonder how much she had to pay Hartley for keeping that little hobby quiet? I think we should move her up the list of suspects and have a word with her. We need to know where she went to on her day off on Friday, and if she was anywhere near Jessie's shop.'

'And she left the radio station with Gilbert on Thursday night, according to Edward Dexter, so that might mean something – although I don't know what.'

'I've worked up quite an appetite watching Hartley Battenberg's home movies. As Bruiser is paying, I think we should look at this last tape and then skip off to Bloomers.'

Tilly agreed and Hettie hit the play button. The film offered an aerial view inside St Kipper's church, shot from somewhere near the organ loft. The elderly congregation was in full voice, attempting to lift the rafters with the final verse of 'Jerusalem'. The newly arrived Reverend Cuthbert Slink bestowed a blessing, punctuated by the stutter with which God had blessed him, and offered a final encouragement regarding the collection plate. Again, Hettie and Tilly recognised a number of the townsfolk, including Branston Bean and Tarquin Flapjack, and it was Tarquin who now took centre stage as he offered the collection plate from pew to pew. The faithful had been generous, and money was still being added as the congregation filed out of the church. It was clear from the body language that Tarquin was still the celebrity radio presenter in the eyes of the ageing worshippers, who emptied their purses just to share a few brief words with him. The vicar bowed to his altar and snuck off into the vestry to shed his robes, leaving Tarquin to count the booty. He looked from side to side, checking that the pews were empty before sorting through the collection and removing all the paper money, forcing it into his pocket. The coppers and silver that remained were transferred into an ornate box at the door, which held the donations for the church's restoration fund. Tarquin returned the empty plate to the altar and left St Kipper's, slamming the giant oak-studded door behind him. There, the video finished.

'Bravo!' exclaimed Hettie. 'An Oscar winning performance. What a perfect racket, hitting on little old lady cats and stealing from the church all at the same time, while basking in the glory of his misguided celebrity. With him in charge of the collection plate, I can't see St Kipper's church spire being fixed any time soon.'

'I think we should invite all the cats featured in the videos to a special film night at Bloomers,' suggested Tilly. 'We could lock the doors and show the videos, and watch them squirm. It's a shame they won't be exposed now that Hartley's dead, especially Branston Bean. I'd love to name and shame him. Fancy going to church when he's so nasty.'

'Don't start me on that one,' said Hettie. 'There's a certain sort of Christian who thinks that God forgives everything, no matter how cruel their actions may be. Branston Bean has clearly misinterpreted the "suffer the little kittens" bit.'

Tilly knew it was time to change the subject, as Hettie needed to be turned away from her high-horse moment. 'Shall I give Hilary and Cherry a ring to fix a time to visit them before we go to Bloomers?'

'Good idea,' said Hettie, pushing the videos back into the dustbin bag. 'Sometime tomorrow would be good.'

Tilly pulled the telephone out of the staff sideboard. Fifteen minutes passed before she was able to replace the receiver, having endured a long, one-sided conversation with Hilary on the merits of Cherry's triumphant lattice pie challenge and how she was now in the bake off final on Easter Saturday. Tilly finally managed to arrange a meeting, and Hilary insisted that it would include lunch, as Cherry was keen to practise her skills.

'Right, that's all the more reason for us to have a proper lunch today,' Hettie declared, as the two cats padded out into the high street.

Chapter Sixteen

Bloomers was full of expectant diners as Hettie and Tilly pushed their way through to their table, pleased to see that Bruiser and Poppa had secured the space for them. Molly's Sunday roasts were even more popular than her Saturday mixed grills, and she and Dolly were working flat out as they moved round the tables. The menu was simple: beef, pork or lamb with all the trimmings, followed by vanilla, chocolate or strawberry ice cream and the option of catnip wafers. Poppa and Bruiser had already ordered, and Dolly Scollop – at Bruiser's request – added Hettie's choice of pork and Tilly's of lamb to his tab before disappearing into the kitchen to start plating up.

While they waited for their lunch, Hettie brought Poppa and Bruiser up to speed with the case, and Tilly offered her current list of suspects for them to ponder over. Poppa was shocked by the revelations regarding Hartley Battenberg's double life: like everyone else, he'd known him as a folk singer and quite a popular cat, but it was the idea of Bunty Basham being on the list that concerned him most. 'I can't see her killing anything,' he pointed out. 'She's a saint.'

'What do you mean?' asked Hettie.

'Well, they had a burst pipe when we had that big freeze. Bunty called me out to fix it, so I went round there and met the old mother. She's a real piece of work – sits in her wheelchair, shouting out her orders. Nasty, actually. Poor Bunty just took it on the chin, buzzing round the old cat as if she couldn't do enough for her. Mrs Basham sat there chucking insults at her, telling her that she was useless, fat and stupid, and how she wished she'd drowned her at birth – and all that in front of me. Goodness knows what goes on when they haven't got a visitor.'

'They say that old Ma Basham used to cane all them kittens in 'er class every day when she was teachin',' chimed in Bruiser. 'She taught in that posh school in Southwool. I s'pose that sort o' thing's allowed if you're payin', but it's a harsh bit o' discipline.'

'It's a shame she doesn't team up with Branston Bean,' observed Hettie. 'They obviously have a lot in common. It must be difficult for Bunty, having to live with her mother – a real thankless task.'

'And she's always so smiley,' added Tilly. 'You'd never know that things were bad at home for her.'

Their musings on the matriarchal problems of Bunty Basham were curtailed by the approach of four roast dinners, delivered by the very capable paws of Molly Bloom herself. It was noticeable that Poppa seemed to have an extra batter pudding on his plate and at least one extra slice of beef, but no one said anything; it was a known fact that Poppa and Molly were fast becoming an item.

'I'm expecting clean plates, so I am,' Molly said, 'as neither me nor Dolly have a mind for spending the afternoon washing up. Dolly's got to practise for the bake off, so she has.'

'She got through the lattice pie technical challenge, then?' asked Hettie.

'Yes, and a right rumpus it was – too many contestants, not enough ovens, three fainting fits and a violent tantrum,' said Molly. 'Bugs Anderton broke her string of pearls trying to physically eject a cat who'd chained herself to one of the radiators because that Fanny Haddock suggested that her lattice looked more like a section of garden trellising with a bad attack of woodworm. I went down to the hall to collect some bowls I'd lent them, and when I got there it looked like a scene from the Winter Olympics. Flour everywhere – a complete white-out. Me and Dolly helped Bugs to find her pearls, then we beat a very hasty retreat. I dread to think how it will be for the final on Saturday.'

'Who else got through?' asked Tilly, tucking her serviette into the neck of her cardigan.

'Well, let me think,' said Molly. 'That Tansy off the radio, Balti Dosh, Cherry Fudge, Dolly, and that cat with a lisp.'

'Branston Bean?'

'That's the one. I can't help but feel that this bake off competition will be the first and last in the town. It's caused so much bad feeling, setting one cat against another. I've never known such nastiness over a bit of pastry – worse than the troubles, so it is.'

Molly had made her point and returned to her kitchen. Tilly wasn't entirely sure what exactly the troubles were that Molly often referred to; she knew they were something to do with orange cats in her native Ireland, but had never felt the need for a full explanation. It was clear to her, though, that as Molly had chosen to compare the bake off to the troubles, all was not well with Tarquin Flapjack's pet project; with that in mind, she was looking forward to the final showdown on Easter Saturday.

'So who's the money on?' asked Poppa.

'I 'ope Dolly gets it,' said Bruiser, who'd spent several months trying to pluck up enough courage to invite Dolly to go to the pictures with him.

'I just wish it was all over,' said Hettie. 'The prospect of an Easter weekend full of cats doing stupid things is a marvellous smokescreen for a killer. This case is like being given a box of chocolates with all your favourites and having no idea which one to choose. We've got to whittle that suspect list down somehow; every one on it has a motive for murder and, with a little imagination, they all could have been at the crime scenes.'

'Except Wilco,' Tilly pointed out. 'He could have murdered Hartley, but he was on the radio when Gilbert was stabbed and we've found nothing to suggest that he was being blackmailed.'

'Maybe Hartley was getting at Wilco through Marzi?' suggested Poppa. 'Wilco might have stumped up the cash to protect his niece – that would give him a motive for killing Hartley.'

'But that still doesn't explain Gilbert's murder,' Tilly said, 'unless Marzi did it. Wilco did give her the day off.'

'All the more reason to check her out,' said Hettie, 'but not before we've provided Molly with four clean plates.'

There was little conversation as the friends enjoyed their lunch. It was inevitable that there should be a small gravy and batter pudding incident on Tilly's plate that required mopping up with Bruiser's serviette, but her cardigan escaped until the strawberry ice cream she'd ordered set out on a different route from bowl to mouth and turned her bright yellow buttons pink. Generally, though, a good time was had by all – until the cat fight.

When Hettie and Tilly arrived at Bloomers, they'd failed to notice Tarquin Flapjack tucked away at one of the tables, reading his Sunday paper and waiting for his lunch. The arrival of Branston Bean was far less understated. As Hettie pushed her empty ice cream bowl away from her, the door to the café was nearly flung off its hinges, and Branston wasted no time in locating Tarquin and launching himself at him. Bruiser and Poppa responded immediately by leaping up and forcing the two cats apart, but Branston continued to hiss and spit as Poppa held him back. Tarquin lifted his paw up to his head, where blood seeped from a deep gash across his ear, and Branston broke free of Poppa, fully intending on finishing the job. Hearing the commotion, Molly shot out of her kitchen, armed with a non-stick saucepan that she'd filled with cold water. As the two cats tangled in a flurry of fur, claws and teeth, she threw the water over them. Branston gasped and pulled away from his victim, while Tarquin cowered under the table, his paws over his head to protect himself from further injury.

The diners looked on as Molly took control. 'Right!' she shouted. 'You sit there, and you can come out from under that table and sit there. Now then, what in heaven's name is this all about?'

Branston sat where Molly had indicated, flanked by Poppa and Bruiser. Tarquin crawled back onto his chair to lick his wounds. Neither cat said anything until Molly asked again. This time, Branston answered, still shaking with anger. 'Heth taken my thow from me, behind my back. Heth been having meetingth with Wilco, when he wath pretending to be my friend. I wath going back on Monday, but Wilco hath justht told me ith weekendths or nothing, and that Tarquin ith the new mid-morning prethenter. Heth a thnake in the grath, and I'll wring hith neck if you let me at him.'

'Well that's not going to happen, and you've had your say,' said Molly, 'so let's hear what Mr Flapjack has to say.'

Tarquin decided to play to his audience. The entire café had put down their spoons, knives and forks, waiting in silence for him to speak. Forgetting his wounds, which were still bleeding, he got to his feet and addressed everyone, avoiding any sort of eye contact with Branston. 'As many of you know,' he began, 'I have for some years been an important part of our local radio station. My Saturday night shows have achieved very high listening figures, and many of you were upset when my programme was taken off under Wilco Wonderfluff's new ownership. Well, I'm delighted to inform you that I have been offered a weekday show, so you'll be able to enjoy me from Monday to Friday from now on. Wilco has seen the error of his ways, and has begged me to return to Whisker FM. There will always be casualties in radio, and I'm sorry that Branston has reacted in such a violent way, but I'm sure you'll all agree that the best cat won.'

Branston Bean moved forward in his chair, intending to have another go at Tarquin, but Bruiser and Poppa restrained him long enough for Molly to have her say. 'Thank you, Mr Flapjack, for explaining the situation, and now I suggest that you leave us before there's any more trouble. If you and Mr Bean want to continue to fight, you can do it somewhere else. I'm barring you both from Bloomers until after Easter.'

The round of applause that Tarquin expected after his announcement came off the back of Molly's declaration; it was clear that none of the diners in Bloomers were in the slightest bit interested in his return to the airwaves, or Branston's departure from them. Tarquin pushed his half-eaten lunch away, picked up his newspaper and slunk out of the café, leaving a trail of blood behind him. Branston struggled free of Poppa and Bruiser and cursed his way to the door, slamming it behind him and leaving Molly's customers with plenty to talk about.

'Who'd have thought we'd be treated to such a cabaret with Sunday lunch?' said Hettie, as Poppa and Bruiser returned to their table. 'And Wilco must really be on his uppers if he's been forced into taking Tarquin Flapjack back, especially as he didn't exactly rate his broadcasting skills.'

'It's all a bit cut-throat,' Tilly added. 'When we spoke to Branston, he seemed to think he'd been reinstated, so it must have come as a real shock to discover that Tarquin had pulled the show from under him.'

'Yes, and I wonder what changed Wilco's mind? He seemed determined to keep Tarquin away from the radio station, and now suddenly he's a main presenter. It would be interesting to know how Tarquin swung that one, and why Branston has been sidelined.'

Dolly came to clear away the empty dishes, keen to get all the washing up done so that she and Molly could have some time to themselves. Poppa leapt up to help, hoping for a chat with Molly in the kitchen, and Bruiser settled up for the lunches, which gave him the opportunity to suggest a walk in the sunshine with Dolly – but all thoughts of some quiet time were dashed by the arrival of Bunty Basham, bedecked from head to toe in her cricket whites.

'You're back then?' she said, striding up to Poppa. 'Splendid, and thank goodness! I thought we'd have to play the first match of the season without you. We're having a practice this afternoon, and I need you both.'

Bruiser's hopes of a walk in the sunshine with Dolly were dashed. He and Poppa were carried away to the recreation ground on a sea of Bunty's enthusiasm, leaving Hettie and Tilly indecisive about what to do with their Sunday afternoon. 'It's too nice to go home,' Tilly pointed out, 'but you did say that we needed to talk to Marzi.'

'The trouble is we have no idea where she lives, and our transport has just been strong-armed into cricket practice, so how about we take a walk over to the recreation ground and see if Wilco's about at the radio station? We can get Marzi's address, then decide what to do, and I'd like to know why Wilco changed his mind about Tarquin Flapjack and the mid-morning show.'

The two friends set off up the high street. Tilly called in at their room to abandon her ice cream stained cardigan, exchanging it for a T-shirt and picking up her notepad in case she found something interesting to write about.

The recreation ground was a hive of activity. Bunty's call to arms had produced almost a full team, although Hettie suspected that it was the warm sunshine and the fact that Wilfred Whipp's ice cream van was parked next to the pavilion that had encouraged such a good turnout. 'Just look at them! Is it any wonder that we never win anything? What a ragbag – they look like leftovers from a hippy commune. No wonder Edward Dexter worries about them playing on his pitch.'

Tilly had to agree. 'It's such a shame, when Bunty works so hard to keep it all together. At least she's got Poppa and Bruiser back, and Balti Dosh always does her best.'

They watched as Balti took a long run-up and bowled to Marmite Spratt, who took a wild swing at the ball, smacking Dorcas Ink in the teeth. Play was halted while pockets were searched for tissues to stem the blood. Bunty repositioned her fielders so that Dorcas could sun herself on the boundary, out of further harm's way, and Poppa took up the bat, responding to Balti's delivery by knocking the ball for six. Bruiser joined him at the opposite end, and the pair settled into an impressive defence of Balti's assault on the wicket.

Hettie's attention was drawn away from the cricketers to the pavilion, where Wilco had emerged and was getting on his bicycle. 'Come on,' she shouted. 'We might catch him if we hurry.' She took off across the grass, leaving Tilly to struggle on behind her. They were just in time, but Wilco seemed in no mood for conversation, and Hettie's request for a quick word met with very little enthusiasm.

'Can we leave this until tomorrow?' he said, preparing to pedal away.

'Actually it was Marzi we wanted to talk to, but we don't have her address.'

Wilco took his foot off the pedal and got off the bike, leaning it up against the pavilion's veranda. 'Why on earth would you want to drag Marzi into all this?' he asked. 'She's not the brightest match in the box, and I hate to say it, but she makes things up – drives my poor sister up the wall with her fanciful stories. If I were you, I wouldn't bother with her.'

Hettie decided to stand her ground. 'The thing is,' she began, 'we've discovered some evidence which suggests that Hartley Battenberg was blackmailing her, so it's quite important that we talk to her.'

Wilco threw his head back and laughed. 'So where are you going with all of this? Are you suggesting that she murdered him? If that's the best you can come up with, I think we should leave it there.' He reached inside his jacket and pulled out his wallet. 'Here you are – fifty should cover it. I'm sure you've done your best, but all this detective stuff is just stringing it out and upsetting everyone.'

Tilly snatched the money out of Wilco's paw, concerned that Hettie might refuse it under a misguided principle, but Hettie was in no mood to give up the case and hardly noticed the transaction. 'I'm sorry you feel that way, but two cats have been murdered, and – with or without your cooperation – we intend to solve this case. You were very keen for us to get to the bottom of it, and suddenly you've changed your mind. Can I ask why? You seem to be doing that a lot lately.'

'What do you mean?' asked Wilco. 'I've just told you – you're upsetting everyone with your suspicions, and now you want to start on Marzi. She's family, and it's my duty to protect her.'

'And what about your change of heart over Tarquin Flapjack?' countered Hettie. 'We've just witnessed a violent fight between him and Branston Bean, thanks to you. You're rather good at stirring things up yourself, it seems to me.'

'I had no choice in taking Tarquin back. It was that or close the station down, and he asked for Branston's show so I gave it to him. If they choose to fight over it, that's their business. At least you can understand what Tarquin is saying, and I have offered Branston weekend work. It's tough in radio. They need to get over it and move on.'

'Like Hartley and Gilbert?' suggested Hettie. 'They've certainly moved on, and you seem happy to draw a line under that, too.'

'Look,' said Wilco, 'I'm sorry. I just want it all to go away. A week ago I had a thriving radio station, a decent bunch of presenters, and listening figures to bank; now I have two dead presenters, a bunch of amateurs, present company excepted, and a notice to find new premises as soon as possible. It's all too much, and I'm not sure how long I can keep it going. Now, if you'll excuse me, I have to meet Gilbert's sister from the bus station. She's coming to arrange for his body to be taken back to her place, as she wants him buried in her garden.'

Hettie was about to ask why the news hadn't reported Gilbert's death as murder, but Wilco took off like a rocket before she had the chance. He chose the direct route across the cricket pitch, bringing the practice session to a standstill, much to the annoyance of Edward Dexter, who shook his paw at him.

'What do you make of all that?' Hettie asked, settling herself down on a bench seat.

'Fifty pounds!' replied Tilly, joining her.

'That's true, and I suppose it's a good price for silence, but it tells me that we're getting too close to solving these murders. He seems very keen for us not to speak to Marzi.'

'Maybe Poppa was right. Wilco killed Hartley because he was blackmailing Marzi, and Marzi killed Gilbert because he found out – and she can't be trusted to talk to us because she might give it all away. Wilco obviously thinks she's a bit stupid, and Edward Dexter said – just a minute, let me find it – yes, here it is in my notes. He said Marzi was "two puddings short of a beef dinner".'

'Marzi is just my sort of interview,' said Hettie. 'Stupid enough to give the game away. Most of the cats we've spoken to so far on this case are as bright as buttons and clever at concealing the truth. But why is Wilco protecting her if he has nothing to hide? It's as if he's stumbled on the truth and doesn't want it to come out. I wouldn't mind having a word with Gilbert's sister, but I don't suppose we'll get the chance. I wonder if she knows he's been murdered? She didn't give that impression on the television.'

'It sounds like we're carrying on with the case then?' said Tilly.

'Damned right we are,' said Hettie, 'but not before we've had our second ice cream of the day. Lead on to Mr Wilfred Whipp!'

Chapter Seventeen

Monday mornings had never filled Hettie with any great enthusiasm. If it had been possible, she would have abolished the day altogether and gone straight to Tuesday; in fact, there had been a couple of occasions over the previous winter when she and Tilly had actually managed to sleep through Monday, tucked up in their fleecy blankets and taking it in turns to add another shovel of coal to the fire during brief waking moments – but this Monday morning was different.

The sun streamed in through their small window, creating beams of light that made sleep impossible, and the Butter sisters were constantly busy, banging around in their bread ovens and trying to keep up with the demand for hot cross buns. Beryl's contemporary rendition of 'There is a Green Hill Far Away' was clearly too close to bring Hettie any comfort, and the thought of spending time at Hilary and Cherry Fudge's lunch table was almost too much for her to bear.

It was the start of Easter week, a time for reflection, contemplation and rebirth as far as the believers were concerned. For Hettie, it was a time of mixed messages: she found the story of the crucifixion engrossing, but had never been able to find any parallels with her own life; self-sacrifice was something she'd never subscribed to, and life was too short for grand gestures. There were cats slinking round the town who'd denied themselves proper dinners for weeks; now they queued in the Butters' bakery for as many hot cross buns as they could eat in celebration of their self-sacrifice, and no doubt they would go on to devour vast quantities of Easter eggs before the week was over. Hettie had often wondered what Jesus might have thought of such strange behaviour, as his followers marked his passing.

Tilly had no such concerns as she pottered about with their morning tea, enjoying the smell of bread and cinnamon as it permeated their room. She knew when the knock came at their door what it would be, and she wasn't disappointed. 'You'll need to eat these while they're hot,' said Beryl, pushing a plate with two hot cross buns into Tilly's paws. 'Sister has slapped a nice wedge of butter in them, so you can eat them just as they are. She's doing you a small simnel as a treat, but she can't decide on the marzipan balls on account of Judas. We have this every year, and no one seems to care one way or another how many balls they get. I did suggest she put rabbits on instead, but that fell on deaf ears. Anyway, I'd better get on – they're queuing down the high street for these buns.'

Tilly thanked Beryl and carried the buns over to Hettie's armchair, where she was waiting patiently for her breakfast. 'These look lovely, and Betty's even buttered them for us,' said Tilly, taking one of the buns to her blanket and settling down to eat it.

Hettie finished her bun in record time, offering up the occasional chirrup of appreciation as the melted butter covered her paws. 'If Monday mornings all started with a hot cross bun, life would be so much better,' she observed, before starting an intense cleaning session of her face, ears and paws.

Tilly hadn't got off so lightly, and had succeeded in covering herself, her pyjamas and her fleecy blanket with butter. 'I think I might have to freshen up some of our clothes and blankets now the weather's getting warmer,' she said, trying to make light of the mess in which she found herself.

Hettie laughed at her friend's inability to control the behaviour of any food that came her way, knowing that butter, gravy and custard were a nice but hazardous hurdle that Tilly had to overcome. Her large paws were mainly to blame, and her energetic enthusiasm, developed from years of being homeless and hungry. Tilly embraced every meal as if it were her last, and the sheer delight these days of knowing that it wasn't filled her with immeasurable joy.

'Shall I drag the tin bath out into the yard for you?' asked Hettie. 'I've got a couple of jumpers that could do with a wash. I think that hot cross bun was a step too far for your pyjamas, and if I were you I'd stay in them. You could have a bath at the same time.'

Tilly giggled at the prospect and started gathering various items together to wash. Hettie pulled the tin bath out from the side of the bread ovens and set it up in the yard, while Tilly boiled several kettles of water to fill it. Next came the soap powder, and finally Tilly herself. Unlike most cats, she quite enjoyed a bath: for her, it went with the territory; her long tabby fur tangled itself at the slightest excuse, and sometimes a bath was the only option. 'Ooh, this is lovely!' she said, slipping further into the water until only her head was visible above the bubbles. 'If you pile all the washing around me, I'll wiggle my legs and pretend I'm a washing machine.'

Hettie did as she was asked, and Tilly kicked and punched at the blankets and clothes until she was satisfied that they'd all had a good wash. By the time she'd finished, there was very little water left in the tub, and she emerged – still in her pyjamas – looking more like a drowned rat than a long-haired tabby cat.

'I think you'd better go and borrow Betty's hairdryer while I hang this lot on the line,' Hettie suggested. 'You can't turn up at the Fudges' looking like that, and I'd better have those pyjamas – unless you're thinking of wearing them as a new type of wet look fashion.'

Tilly dripped back into their room and emerged minutes later, wrapped in a towel. She passed her pyjamas to Hettie, who was busily rinsing the clothes in the bath with the Butters' hosepipe, then left Hettie pegging out the washing to go in search of a hairdryer. It would take days for Tilly's bouffanted hair to die down, and it presented a number of problems, as her cardigans and T-shirts suddenly didn't fit – but Beryl came to the rescue by offering her a follicle mousse which dampened things down considerably.

Now that their impromptu Monday morning washing session was over, it was time to head out to Snuffle Walk and Hilary and Cherry Fudge's nice, neat semi-detached guest house. Bruiser was waiting in the high street to take them in Miss Scarlet, and was kind enough not to mention Tilly's radical new hairstyle as she clambered into the sidecar. Hettie followed her, and Bruiser kicked the bike into life, opening up the throttle as they set off at speed.

Hettie had enjoyed the brief respite from murder that Tilly's domestic crisis had brought them, but now she was ready to sink her teeth into the puzzle they'd been dealt and bring the killer or killers to justice. Wilco's change of heart concerned her, and she was now more determined than ever to speak to Marzi, but lunch with the Fudges would have to be endured first and might well offer further information on Gilbert Truffle.

Snuffle Walk was a pleasant part of town, untouched by any ugly developments and offering a number of family run guest houses for visitors or cats who worked away from home. Hilary and Cherry Fudge had earned a reputation for offering clean, bright and airy accommodation, a continental breakfast and a modest evening meal, if booked in advance. The mother and daughter combination worked well, and Hilary had made a point of encouraging long stays in her rooms, which meant that the sheets only had to be changed once a week. Cherry balanced her day job with chambermaid duties and anything else that would make her mother proud of her.

As Bruiser pulled Miss Scarlet up outside the house, the lunch that Hettie and Tilly had been invited to was suddenly thrown into doubt by the ambulance that stood in the driveway. 'That's all we need!' hissed Hettie, clambering out of the sidecar. 'Another bloody drama to add to our list!'

Hettie's concern was short-lived. Hilary Fudge loomed out of the driveway wearing the loudest flower print dress they'd ever seen. The garment could easily have won first prize at Wither-Fork Hall's flower and produce show, and Hilary was in full sail. 'My dears! How lovely of you to come,' she said, hugging them both as if they were long-lost friends, and moving on to shake Bruiser's paw. 'Cherry and I have laid on a little surprise for you, haven't we Cherry?'

The double doors of the ambulance burst open to reveal Cherry Fudge done up in her rescue kit, complete with face mask and latex gloves pulled tightly over her paws. Hettie stood back bewildered, Tilly stared with her mouth open, and Bruiser made his excuses and shot off on Miss Scarlet, promising to return to pick them up in a couple of hours. Hettie finally found her voice and asked the obvious question. 'Is someone unwell? If this is a difficult time, we could come back later.'

'Good Heavens no,' responded Hilary. 'We thought you'd like a little demonstration of some of Cherry's new skills before we settle down to lunch. Last time you were here, she was able to offer her Heimlich manoeuvre; well, I'm delighted to say that things have moved on considerably, and she now has her own ambulance. As a very special treat, she's going to show you round, aren't you Cherry?'

Cherry glowed at her mother's pride, although it was hard to see her full reaction as the face mask obscured her nose, mouth and part of one of her eyes. She hauled Tilly up the steps and Hettie was pushed from behind into the main body of the ambulance, while Hilary gave a running commentary. 'As you can see, it's kitted out for every sort of emergency,' she said. 'Show them the oxygen tanks, Cherry.'

To Hettie and Tilly, the tanks were fairly obvious, but Cherry was keen to demonstrate the mask that hung from them; she indicated the tap before forcing the mask over the one she was already wearing and lying down on one of the bunk beds, pretending to be a cat short of breath. Hettie wondered just how long this bizarre medical pantomime was going to last, but the intensity of Hilary and Cherry's demonstration was only just beginning. 'And now we turn to the defibrillator,' Hilary continued. Cherry sprang up, wrenching the oxygen mask from her face and pulling a red plastic box out from under the bunks. Tilly was trying very hard to be interested, while Hettie weighed up the possibility of making a run for it, but Hilary was relentless. 'Now, the model you see here is semi-automatic due to the presence of a manual shock button, which Cherry will now demonstrate.'

Cherry responded by ripping open the box and turning its contents towards Hettie and Tilly. 'If Tilly would like to lie down on the bunk,' Hilary continued, 'Cherry will simulate the action of dealing with a heart attack.'

Tilly had no option but to comply as Hilary gave her a shove and Cherry pulled her down onto the bed. Hettie stood by, helpless, as Cherry unpacked her life-saving kit. 'As you can see,' said Hilary, 'Cherry has just pulled the red handle to open the bag; there are two pads, which Cherry is now attaching to Tilly's chest – normally she would have to take her cardigan off, but as she's not actually having a heart attack, we won't worry about that, will we Cherry?'

Cherry shook her head and stood ready to perform the exciting bit as her mother made everyone jump. 'Stand back! Stand back!' she shouted at the top of her voice, and Cherry pretended to press the shock button. Tilly lay still, completely bewildered by what was happening to her, and Hettie looked on, desperately trying to contrive a way out of the situation they found themselves in. It was clear to her that the demonstration could go on for some time, as the ambulance appeared to be very well equipped.

'And now we turn to splints,' said Hilary. 'Are you happy to be our dummy, Tilly, or would Hettie like a go? We don't want to leave you out, do we Cherry?'

This was Hettie's moment and she took it. 'I'd love to take part, but I think the ambulance is so exciting that I was wondering if we could come back on another day, when we have more time? Maybe Cherry would take us out in it? That would be a really special thing to do.'

Hilary thought for a moment, a little crestfallen, but acknowledged that a whole day would give Cherry much more time to demonstrate her new-found skills. Tilly struggled to her feet, pulling the sticky pads off her cardigan, and Cherry removed her mask and gloves and put them in a locker above the bunk marked 'Cherry'. The four cats clambered out of the ambulance, and Cherry locked the doors. Hilary led the way into the house via the back door, straight into the kitchen. The scrubbed table could hardly be seen under the weight of pies, cakes and breads – enough to fill the Butters' bakery three times over. 'As you can see, Cherry has been practising her considerable skills ready for the bake off, haven't you Cherry?'

Cherry proudly indicated the table with her paw, and Hettie knew that if she didn't take a firm stand now, it was only a matter of time before they would be asked to taste test every single item set before them. 'As you know, we are investigating the murder of your lodger, Gilbert Truffle,' she began.

Hilary put her paw up in front of Hettie's face. 'I need to stop you there,' she said. 'The good news is that Mr Truffle died of a heart attack and wasn't murdered after all, so it's nowhere near as awful as we thought.'

Hettie looked puzzled. Here it was again, a complete denial of Gilbert's murder. 'How do you know it was a heart attack?' she asked.

'His sister called in last night to collect his things with that nice cat from the radio station, Mr Wonderfluff, and they stopped for one of Cherry's marmite and salmon cheesecakes. They didn't stay long after that, but Mr Wonderfluff said that Gilbert had died of a heart attack in the charity shop in Cheapcuts Lane. Much nicer than being murdered, wasn't it Cherry?' Cherry nodded as her mother continued. 'Of course, if we'd known, Cherry might have been able to save him now she's got her defibrillator, but sadly it wasn't to be. He was such a clean cat, too – no trouble at all. Kept to his room mostly, and joined us for supper on Mondays and Wednesdays.'

Hettie felt it was pointless to argue about Gilbert's death, and she was disappointed that his things had been collected as she was hoping to look through them. 'Could we take a look at his room anyway?' she asked.

'Of course you can, although Cherry hasn't had a minute to tidy it up, have you Cherry?'

Cherry shook her head and looked down at her slippers, as if she'd been scolded. She knew that her chambermaid duties had suffered because of her desperation to qualify for the bake off and, for the first time since Hettie and Tilly had arrived, she spoke. 'Please follow me.'

Hettie couldn't wait to get away from Hilary. She and Tilly followed Cherry upstairs and into the corridor where the best guest rooms were. Cherry led them to the end room and threw open the door. 'I'll leave you here to look round while I lay the table for lunch. Just come down when you've finished.'

Hettie shut the door behind them and waited for Cherry's footsteps to recede. 'What a bloody nightmare!' she said. 'This is all a complete waste of time, and we're stuck here until after lunch. Goodness knows how many more of Cherry's accomplishments we'll be treated to.'

'Maybe we should make something up and skip lunch?' suggested Tilly. 'They have kept us waiting with all that ambulance stuff. It's half past one now, so we could say we have to be at Bloomers for an interview.'

'That's tempting, but Bruiser is coming back to pick us up and it's too far to walk home from here. We'll just have to make the best of it. Let's take a look round this room – just our luck that the sister has collected everything. We really do need to get to the bottom of why Wilco is trying to cover up Gilbert's murder by telling everyone it was a heart attack.'

'Except Tansy. She seemed to know he'd been stabbed,' Tilly pointed out.

'You take that chest of drawers and I'll look under the bed,' said Hettie, getting crosser by the minute.

Tilly pulled open the drawers and found them empty except for an unwrapped barley sugar twist. Hettie crawled under the bed, but could only find a single sock covered in fluff. She emerged with it and sat on the bed. 'I don't get any sense of Gilbert Truffle here. Wilco and his sister did a great job of clearing him out.'

Tilly joined Hettie, keen to kill some time before facing the Fudges' hospitality. She sat down and stood up again immediately. 'There's something under the sheets!' she said, pulling the covers back. 'It's a photo album, he must have been looking at it in bed.'

Tilly began to flick through the photographs as Hettie looked over her shoulder. 'It seems to be all about his radio days. That must be the pirate radio boat with all the presenters on deck. There's Gilbert – doesn't he look young? He's labelled that photo "me, George, Harry and Roscoe". And look – there's Roscoe again on his own, and another one with just Gilbert and George.' Tilly carried on turning the pages; there were more photos of the pirate boat studio with Gilbert presenting, and one or two press cuttings showing a list of programmes broadcast from there. The boat was called *The Merry Dance*. 'They all look like they were having a lovely time.'

'Yes, but look at this newspaper clipping,' said Hettie, reading out the headline. '"Tragedy Strikes *The Merry Dance*. DJ Roscoe Sunbeam drowned in storm out at sea." It says that he fell overboard in high seas and his body was washed up three days later. Gilbert has given a quote to say that he was one of the most promising DJs he'd ever trained. Out of respect, *The Merry Dance* was decommissioned and put into dry dock.'

'Maybe that was one of the boats in Hartley's video!' said Tilly excitedly. 'That would explain something, although I don't know what.'

'We'll take a look at it again when we get home, but I'm not sure where this leads us. Maybe Hartley was blackmailing Gilbert for some reason, or maybe Gilbert was planning to buy another boat for Wilco's radio station. It would make sense, as he's been told to quit the pavilion. I wonder what Gilbert's sister took away with her? I really think she could be the key to everything. Let's get this lunch over. I want to see if the Fudges can remember anything about the morning Gilbert died. We know he made that call to us, but did he speak to anyone else? Perhaps even his killer?'

Tilly gathered up the photo album and the two cats made their way downstairs to the kitchen. Hilary ushered them through to the dining room, where they took their places and waited for the food to arrive. There was much banging and at least one sizeable crash from the kitchen before Cherry emerged, offering a beaming smile and two full plates. 'Cherry has chosen to give her individual beef Wellingtons,' said Hilary, following on behind with two more lunches. 'She's served them with butter creamed potatoes and petty poises to add a touch of green to the plates, haven't you Cherry?'

The food looked good, although Hettie couldn't help but think that one day something inside Cherry would snap and she would turn on Hilary with catastrophic consequences. At this point in time, Hettie would cheerfully have assisted by holding Hilary down long enough for Cherry to do her worst, but she currently had two murders still to solve without embarking on another.

They enjoyed their beef Wellingtons very much, and the apple dumplings with ice cream and custard were equally delicious. The lunch was easier than Hettie had feared, as Hilary felt unable to talk with her mouth full, and Cherry rarely said anything anyway. As soon as Cherry began to collect up the empty plates, Hettie swooped on Hilary regarding Gilbert's final morning and asked if there was anything out of the ordinary about his behaviour.

'Not really,' she said. 'He had his continental in his room as usual, then he came down and asked if he could make some calls.'

'And did you happen to hear anything that was said?' asked Hettie, feeling sure that Hilary rarely missed anything.

'Well, he did shout at one point. I think he said "I can't go through all this again", or something similar. I got the feeling that he was making an arrangement of some sort. After he came off the phone, he seemed a bit upset, but I put that down to the heart attack he had later. He went back upstairs to pack his case for the weekend and left without another word.'

'And did he take his case with him?'

'I assumed he had, but after Tilly told me he'd died, I checked in his room and it was still there. He did take his tape recorder, though – he kept it on the hall table, and it had gone when he left. I just hope it wasn't Cherry's lime and lemon preserve that did for him. I mean, you never know, do you?'

Hettie chose not to engage on the merits of Cherry's jam-making abilities, and asked another question. 'Did he have any visitors while he was with you?'

'Only that Marzi cat. Cheeky little minx! She turned up quite often, but he always seemed pleased to see her. They'd spend hours up there in his room. Goodness knows what they were doing.'

Hettie had the benefit of a perfect view of the street through Hilary's net curtains, and she noticed that Bruiser had just arrived on Miss Scarlet. It was perfect timing. She rose from the table and tugged at the sleeve of Tilly's cardigan, indicating that they were leaving. 'It's so kind of you to give us such an excellent lunch and a marvellous insight into Cherry's work as an ambulance driver,' she said, moving towards the front door. 'We really must go, though, as we have several appointments this afternoon. Next time we'll be able to stay longer.'

Tilly marvelled at Hettie's exit strategy, and Hilary and Cherry stood at their front gate to wave their visitors off, announcing that they would see them at the weekend, when Cherry would be on duty with her ambulance at the recreation ground. It was as well that they didn't hear Hettie's instruction to Bruiser as she clambered into the sidecar with Tilly. Bruiser's response was to give Miss Scarlet full throttle as he took off at speed down Snuffle Walk.

Chapter Eighteen

On Hettie's instructions, Bruiser stopped off at Malkin and Sprinkle so that they could stock up with provisions from the food hall. It was unsettling when their cupboards were bare, and Tilly delighted in filling their trolley with lots of things to try. Due to the money they'd received from Wilco, Hettie announced that Tilly could be as lavish as she liked, and left her to the shopping while she and Bruiser sat in the small coffee shop and read the papers. The fuss over Hartley Battenberg's murder seemed to have died down, but it had been replaced by glowing column inches on Gilbert Truffle and his radio career. Only one paper reported the heart attack, and none of them so much as insinuated that he'd died of anything but natural causes.

Tilly was in her element. The Butters supplied their supper each day with the vouchers that came free with their rent, so a shop in Malkin and Sprinkle was for treats, which made it extra special. Since Bloomers had opened, cooked breakfasts and lunches were often catered for, but it was those in between snacks that Tilly focused on, as well as the basics like tea, milk, and cheese triangles. The food hall was busy, so she decided to queue at the pre-packed meat counter first, where Doris Lean reigned supreme. For years, Doris had longed to move upstairs to haberdashery, but both Mr Malkin and Mr Sprinkle felt that her strengths remained in the operation of their bacon slicer, and it had to be admitted that she was also very adept with a cheese wire. The problem with Doris was her mood swings: unlike her bus conductress sister, whose sunny disposition made her instant friends, Doris hated everything about her life, and it showed in every cat she served. When Tilly's turn came, Doris huffed and puffed at each request: the cooked turkey slices that Hettie liked were thrown onto greaseproof paper with bad grace; and the wedge of Edam that Tilly pointed to – asking for half of it – met with the violence of an executioner determined to remove a head in one blow. Tilly added four prawn spring rolls and a pork pie for Bruiser to her order, and was pleased when her items were slammed onto the counter, freeing her to enjoy the rest of her shopping.

Next came the basics. Tilly added sugar lumps, tea and a tin of condensed milk, which she particularly enjoyed with a spoon. The canned fish section offered sardines, tuna and pilchards in tomato sauce, and Tilly made a point of stocking up on a variety of potted meats, choosing salmon, chicken and beef.

Sweet biscuits came next: custard creams, jammy dodgers and iced Playbox biscuits. Just as Tilly was reaching for the chocolate fingers, Marzi Pan loomed into sight with her shoulder bag. She looked terrible: her eyes were puffy and her paw was shaking as she loaded several packs of garibaldi biscuits into her bag. The theft was blatant, with no thought or concern for being seen, and Tilly suddenly felt sad for her.

Knowing that a conversation with Marzi was vital to the case, Tilly decided to approach her. 'Hello,' she said. 'Remember me? I do "Tea Time with Tilly" on Whisker Radio.' Marzi looked at Tilly with a vague recognition, but said nothing. 'I was wondering whether you'd like to join me for lunch at Bloomers tomorrow? You seem a bit upset. Perhaps you'd like to have a chat?'

Tilly expected Marzi to run a mile from her invitation, but she was wrong. 'I'd like that,' she said. 'It would be really nice to have someone to talk to.'

'Lovely,' said Tilly. 'Shall we say one o'clock? Or I can fit in with your lunch hour at the radio station?'

'One o'clock's fine. I've finished with that job. It didn't suit me. I'll see you tomorrow – and thank you.'

Marzi took off and headed for the lift, and Tilly – delighted that she'd finally netted the interview – finished her shopping and delivered the glad tidings to Hettie and Bruiser in the coffee shop. Bruiser was delighted with his pork pie, and decided to save it for his supper to go with the jar of pickles he'd treated himself to on his holidays. Hettie was ecstatic about Tilly's arrangements with Marzi, and praised her for grabbing an opportune moment. The three cats loaded themselves and the shopping into Miss Scarlet, and got home minutes before the heavens unleashed another torrential downpour. Seeing the ominous black clouds gathering, Tilly sprang out into the garden to haul in the washing that Hettie had pegged out earlier, pleased to have some clean pyjamas and cardigans to put away in the bottom drawer of the filing cabinet.

Bruiser ambled down to his shed at the bottom of the Butters' garden to enjoy his pie, pickles, and the latest edition of *Biker's Monthly*, while Hettie and Tilly settled in for the evening with a small fire and the prospect of Betty's salmon turnovers for their supper. Cherry Fudge's beef Wellington and apple dumplings still weighed heavily on them, so Hettie decided that they should put their shopping away, then pull together the newly acquired strands of the case before considering another meal.

One of the joys in Tilly's life was a well-stocked food cupboard, and just as she was standing back to admire the fruits of her labours, the telephone rang. 'Bugger!' she exclaimed, clambering into the staff sideboard and dragging the phone out of its nest of cushions. 'Hello, Tilly speaking. How may I help?'

Hettie waited with interest, hoping that the call wasn't going to wreck their evening, and was relieved to discover that it was Bugs Anderton on the other end. 'She wants us to help with the setting up of the marquee and film screen at the recreation ground tomorrow,' said Tilly, putting her paw over the phone in case Hettie's reaction was explosive.

'Well, it might be a good idea to be up there tomorrow,' said Hettie, looking thoughtful. 'I'd quite like another crack at Wilco, so tell her we're busy but we'll do our best to be there at some stage – and we'll try and rope Bruiser and Poppa in as well.'

Tilly delivered the message, and Bugs offered her grateful thanks and rang off.

'Let's hope this weather improves,' said Tilly, putting the kettle on. 'It'll be a complete washout if it doesn't – there's no shelter up there for the film night on Thursday or the cricket on Sunday. At least the bake off will be inside the marquee, but they've got to take that down on Saturday night as it's taking up half the cricket pitch.'

'The way Bunty's team plays, they might as well leave it up and just run round it – or through it if they keep the side flaps open.' Tilly giggled at Hettie's lack of faith in the Basham eleven, and stirred two sugar lumps into each milky tea. 'Let's take another look at that video with the boats,' Hettie suggested, pulling it out of the dustbin bag and slotting it into the machine. The beach scene was a welcome distraction from the rain that was lashing their window, and Tilly turned to the photo of the pirate boat in Gilbert's album to make a comparison.

'There it is!' she squealed triumphantly. 'Look – that old boat pulled up on the sand is called *The Merry Dance*. It's the pirate radio boat!'

Hettie paused the video for a longer look at the image. The boat was old and neglected, beached where the tide couldn't reach it and clearly of great interest to Hartley Battenberg. The big question was why. She rewound the tape, putting it to one side and choosing another from their own collection. 'I want to see that news report on Gilbert's death again,' she said, spooling through an episode of *Thundercats*, a favourite of Tilly's.

The newsreel of Gilbert's pirate radio days confirmed that the boat had been *The Merry Dance*, and this time Tilly looked a little closer at some of the other DJs in the film. The cats Roscoe and George were there in the studio, beaming at the camera, and Tilly went right up to the screen for an even closer inspection of their faces. 'Can you show me that bit again?' she said with some urgency.

Hettie did as she asked and Tilly waited for the presenters to appear again. 'Yes! I thought so. Look!'

Hettie paused the tape and followed the direction of Tilly's paw on the screen as she pointed to the cat named George. 'Well I never! Well spotted. Mr Wilco Wonderfluff. You did well to recognise him – he's barely out of dungarees. Well done!'

It was always a special moment for Tilly when she received praise from Hettie, and twice in one day was almost too much. She'd started as Hettie's office junior when The No. 2 Feline Detective Agency was in its early days of business, but had quickly proved herself to be a rather good sleuth, thanks to continuous encouragement from the works of Agatha Crispy and the twists and turns of Nicolette Upstart's plots. Although she might never admit it, Hettie was of the opinion that their detective venture couldn't exist without Tilly's analytical talents and her attention to the smallest of details, and this time she'd really come up trumps.

Hettie let the tape run on to the bit where Gilbert's sister was featured, wanting to get another look at her. She came across as one of those cats you knew and liked instantly: an attractive, open face; honest in her grief for her brother; and shy of the camera that was being thrust at her. 'I'm sure I've seen her before,' Tilly remarked. 'Maybe she was in the town visiting Gilbert. She looks nice, anyway.'

'We'd better concentrate on Wilco – or should I say George?' said Hettie. 'There's clearly a connection with Gilbert, Wilco and Hartley Battenberg that goes back to *The Merry Dance*, and my money would be on the DJ who went overboard. It must have been something serious enough for blackmail.'

'Do you think Roscoe's death wasn't an accident?' suggested Tilly.

Hettie thought for a moment, weighing up the possibilities, and Tilly waited patiently as her friend reached for her catnip pipe and filled it, lighting it with a taper from the fire. 'It seems to me,' she said eventually, 'that Wilco is rather good at telling half a story. He told us he'd trained under Gilbert, but didn't say it was on the pirate boat. He's obviously changed his name, and I suspect that he knew Gilbert much better than he's admitted to. He's also suddenly very keen for us to drop the case, and that was sparked by our wanting to talk to Marzi. Then we need to consider what Hilary Fudge told us about Gilbert's last morning. She said she'd overheard Gilbert saying that he couldn't go through all this again, so what did he mean?'

'Well, we know he knew who murdered Hartley because he said so in his message,' said Tilly, 'so if he was actually talking to the murderer, it means that cat might have killed before.'

'Precisely! And if he was talking to Wilco, he might have been referring to the death on the pirate boat all those years ago. Perhaps he helped to cover up what really happened to Roscoe to protect Wilco, or maybe he was responsible for the death himself and Hartley found out and blackmailed both of them. There's a wall of silence in all this, and it's time we kicked it down. I keep coming back to the fact that Wilco had no opportunity to kill Gilbert in Jessie's shop, though.'

'Do you think Marzi knows what happened? She looked terrible when I saw her today, and she'd obviously been crying, I really felt sorry for her.'

'I think Marzi Pan is the key to everything, and I suggest you meet her on your own tomorrow. We don't want to scare her off, so we need your soft paw approach for this one. I'll go to the recreation ground and see if I can have another word with Wilco. I think I might start by discussing his halcyon days on *The Merry Dance* – perhaps that might improve his memory of certain events.'

Tilly was pleased to be trusted with such an important interview, She decided to prepare a few notes on how best to approach Marzi while Hettie set out their supper, adding a pawful of crisps to the salmon turnovers. The two cats enjoyed their food, convinced that they had made a real breakthrough in the case – but time was running out for one of the suspects on Tilly's list.

Chapter Nineteen

The rain lashed their window all night, keeping Tilly awake into the small hours. She was nervous about taking on Marzi, and her mind was racing; she knew how important the conversation would be, and it would take all her diplomacy to gain a successful outcome. There was another worry that sat on her shoulder: she'd hardly had a moment to consider her next radio show, and had made no preparations for it. She sprang out of her blankets the moment she heard the Butters' bread ovens being fired up, and pulled out a selection of books from her bookcase, trying to decide which one to feature on her programme. She had enjoyed several Agatha Crispys recently, but her paw fell on the latest book by Polly Hodge, who was almost local. Tilly loved her books and had been to several of her events, as well as booking her for the town's literary festival. *Death in Holey Cardigans* was right up Tilly's street, and she decided to make it the subject of this week's book review. She was relying on Hettie to offer something on true crime and to put the music together for her, so that just left the fill-in bits to find. She turned to some old copies of the *Daily Snout* for local interest pieces; the newspaper had a local history section, and she jotted down a few 'did you knows?' to entertain her listeners with. Satisfied now that she would have something to say on her Thursday 'Tea Time with Tilly' slot, she made herself a milky tea and ran through her notes on Marzi Pan.

Hettie woke an hour later, oblivious to Tilly's early morning labours and ready for several rounds of toast spread thickly with their newly acquired potted-meat paste. The breakfast was soon over, and she decided to strike out for the recreation ground in hopes of catching Wilco at the radio station. Tilly decided to have 'a bit of a clean-up', as she put it, before setting out for Bloomers; their room had become a dumping ground for all the evidence they'd gathered on the current case. She collected the various bits and pieces and added them to the dustbin bag that contained Hartley Battenberg's blackmail videos, pushing it all out of sight under the desk.

She noticed that the pots were building up on the draining board, so she filled the sink with soapy water and washed, dried and put them all away, taking care to wipe her surfaces down when she'd finished. She folded her blankets and hung Hettie's dressing gown on the back of the door, then stacked the things she needed for her radio show in a neat pile on the staff sideboard. The sudden burst of domesticity had helped to channel her thoughts, and now, as she stood back to admire the tidied room, she felt ready to face Marzi and whatever revelations she might offer. She called in at the bakery to order two Cornish pasties and a pair of cream horns for their supper, then made her way to Bloomers to get herself set up for the interview.

Hettie's hopes of a word with Wilco were dashed by his absence from the radio station, but speakers had been set up to broadcast Whisker FM across the recreation ground, offering the dulcet tones of Tarquin Flapjack in his new weekday role as mid-morning presenter. She was frustrated at not being able to discuss Wilco's pirate radio days with him, but Bugs Anderton was delighted to see her and immediately welcomed her into her enthusiastic band of helpers. Hettie made the mistake of asking what she could do to help, thinking that she could keep half an eye on the pavilion in case Wilco turned up, but Bugs didn't mince her words. 'These are the jobs available currently,' she said, reading from a growing list on her clipboard. 'Bunting, folding chairs, cinema screen, egg hunt, bonnets, marquee, tea tent and market stalls. There are several areas that need marking out – lost and found, the ambulance station, and Greasy Tom's burger van. Mr Dexter has kindly offered his line-marking machine to set out those areas, but he can't do it himself because he's helping Bunty with the arrangements for the cricket match.'

It was quite a list, and Hettie was clearly spoilt for choice, but she did like the idea of line-marking and was instantly referred to Edward Dexter for a demonstration. Edward was in deep conference with Bunty Basham outside The Stumps as Hettie approached. The two cats were discussing tactics, which impressed her as there had been very little evidence of them in the game she'd witnessed the previous summer, when the town's team were all out for fifteen runs, ten of them scored by Bunty herself and the other five shared between Poppa and Bruiser.

Edward lifted his cap in greeting and Bunty peeled away to swing the bat for Balti Dosh, who was keen to practise her bowling in the nets area. 'Well lass, how are you gettin' on with this murder?' he asked, offering Hettie a sherbet lemon from the bag in his paw.

Hettie accepted the sweet. 'I think we may be making progress,' she said, 'but Bugs Anderton has asked me to mark out some lines and I gather you have the machine to do it.'

'I most certainly do,' said Edward. 'I've got a prime piece of kit: me Dimple Line Marker, with – wait for it – pneumatic tyres, no less. The question is, are you up for handling her?'

Hettie's thoughts were as far away from line markings as any cat's could be, but she played along as Edward hauled his machine out from under a cover in his front garden and trundled it through his gate, returning briefly to lug a plastic bottle of white paint to join it. Hettie watched, trying to look interested, as Edward filled the box on top of the line marker, offering a running commentary until he eventually stood back and pronounced that she was 'ready to go'. Hettie moved towards the machine, but Edward raised his paw. 'Now hold your horses! There's nowt to be done in haste. I've a plan here of the areas we've got to cover, and we'll need my line twine and corner markers to do a proper job.'

Hettie looked bewildered as Edward pulled a map of the site out of the pocket of his cricket trousers, forcing it into her paws before disappearing into his house and returning minutes later with a reel of twine and a bag of brightly coloured markers. 'Now you take care how you handle these corner markers,' he cautioned. 'You'll not want one of them through your foot or you'll know about it. Best to leave that to me. I thought we'd start with the ambulance station as it's next to me house. I gather we have Cherry Fudge in attendance this year – grand lass, although there's not a deal goes on between her ears.'

Hettie stared down at the collection of machinery, paint and accompanying paraphernalia, and realised that Edward needed no help from her; he clearly intended to do the job himself. She chose to ignore his comment about Cherry and sucked loudly on her sherbet lemon while Edward marked out a large square with his twine and corner markers, then proceeded to apply the white paint with his Dimple Line Marker. In Edward's paws, the machine behaved impeccably, producing perfectly straight lines, and Hettie wasn't in the slightest bit interested in having a go herself. Just as she was wishing that she'd chosen the bunting from Bugs's list, she saw Tarquin Flapjack coming out of the pavilion and left Edward marking out the area allotted to Greasy Tom's burger van.

Tarquin seemed in a hurry, but Hettie caught up with him as he reached the area where the bake off marquee was being erected. 'I was wondering what time Wilco is due in today?' she asked.

'He isn't,' snapped Tarquin. 'I don't know where he is. He left a note for me in the studio to put his show on after mine – that's it going out now on those speakers. He seems to think I'm some sort of continuity announcer. Now, if you'll excuse me, I've got things to do. The marquee is nowhere near finished and the kitchen equipment is arriving any minute.'

Tarquin attempted to push Hettie to one side, but she stood her ground. 'Just a minute,' she said. 'What do you mean by "put his show on"?'

Tarquin shrugged. 'I'd have thought that was obvious. He's pre-recorded his afternoon show on tape, so I put it on air before I left. Now, if you'll get out of my way, I'm really too busy for this.'

This time Hettie allowed Tarquin to go about his business. She stood looking back at the pavilion, suddenly flooded with an understanding that had, until now, eluded her.

***

Tilly had been waiting for some time in Bloomers, and was beginning to think that her lunch date with Marzi wasn't going to happen. She'd filled the time by reading Molly's extensive menu from cover to cover until she knew it by heart, and she was just considering ordering some takeout sandwiches and joining Hettie on the recreation ground when Marzi blew in through the café door, looking like she was being pursued down the high street. Locating Tilly, she made a beeline for her and slid into the seat opposite, keeping an eye on the door. 'Sorry I'm late,' she said, getting her breath back, 'but I was delayed in Malkin and Sprinkle.'

Tilly was about to respond when Marzi suddenly dived under the table, dragging her large shoulder bag with her. Mr Malkin himself had just come into the café and was looking round as if he'd lost something. He spent a minute or two looking at the diners, before shrugging his shoulders and leaving. By now, Tilly understood perfectly what was happening: Marzi's form of retail therapy had backfired on her at last. 'You can come out now,' she said, peering under the table. 'Mr Malkin has gone. You're safe.'

Marzi emerged slowly, furtively checking the door to make sure her pursuer had really left the café. She sat up and faced Tilly searching for an excuse for her odd behaviour; instead she burst into tears and Tilly waved Dolly away as she was fast approaching with her notepad to take their order.

Marzi was the picture of misery. The tears fell thick and fast, forming a puddle on the table in front of her, and Tilly reached for her paw, looking for words of consolation but finding only platitudes. 'I'm sure things aren't as bad as you think,' she offered.

'Yes they are,' sobbed Marzi. 'I've never felt so alone. Everyone thinks I'm stupid except Gilbert, and now he's gone there's no one.'

'What about your uncle Wilco?' suggested Tilly. 'You've still got him and your mother. You live at home, don't you?'

'I hate them both,' sobbed Marzi. 'She never wanted me, but I'm forced to live there because I can't afford to move out, and he keeps secrets from me.'

'What sort of secrets?'

'Secrets like Gilbert – all those years when I could have felt wanted, and just when I was getting to know him, he's snatched away from me and I'm not even supposed to be sad.'

'It's always sad when a friend dies,' said Tilly, 'but we have to remember all the happy memories. Nothing can take those away.'

'You don't understand!' protested Marzi. 'Gilbert wasn't my friend; he was my father! I only found out a few weeks ago. He was the family secret, and no one thought to let me in on it. My mother was ashamed, and Wilco didn't seem to think it mattered to me, although I don't know why I'm calling him Wilco

– he's really my uncle George. Who'd want an uncle called Wilco Wonderfluff?'

It was a question that Tilly neither wanted nor needed to answer, but she was keen to keep Marzi talking to see if there were any other revelations that she was willing to share. 'It must have been a real shock to discover that Gilbert was your father. How did you find out?'

'I was sorting through a load of stuff at home and I came across some photos of Gilbert and my mother. George was in some of them, too, and they were dated the year I was born. I asked my mother about them, and she just kicked off big time, telling me to keep my nose out of her business. She took them off me and burnt them on the fire. I discovered later from Gilbert that she was walking out with a cat called Peter Pan at the time, and that I was a mistake. He said that Peter found out I wasn't his kitten and left shortly after I was born. Gilbert told me that he wanted to be with my mother and bring me up, but she refused, so he went off to make his fortune as a radio presenter.'

'And what about Gilbert and George? Did they stay friends after that?' asked Tilly, keen to get to the main part of her investigations.

'I'd never heard of Gilbert until George took over the radio station. He introduced him as an old friend. It was shortly after I met him that I found the photos, and, as my mother didn't want to discuss them, I went round to see Gilbert. He was so pleased to see me and he admitted that he was my father. The only reason he'd taken the job on the radio station was to get to know me better. He became my secret. I visited him a lot, but he warned me not to let George know that I knew the truth.'

'Why do you think that was?'

'I'm not sure, but he did ask me if Uncle George had been kind to me over the years. He said when George was young he had a quick temper, which got him into trouble, and he made me promise that if ever he raised his paw to me I'd tell him straight away. Gilbert was such a lovely cat. I felt loved for the first time in my life, and now he's gone forever.'

'Did Gilbert say what sort of trouble George had got himself into?' asked Tilly.

Marzi shook her head. 'Not really, although I overheard them having a row at the radio station. Gilbert said something like "violence solves nothing", and he told George that he wasn't willing to stand by him again.'

'And can you remember when this was?'

'Oh yes, it was last Thursday. I remember because it was the day that Hartley Battenberg died.'

'You left with Gilbert that day to come to my party, didn't you?'

'That's right. Gilbert stormed out of Wilco's office and said he wasn't happy about me working at the radio station. He wanted me to come to his sister Elvira's for the weekend, as she was keen to meet me. I was so excited. I went home after your party and packed my case. George called me early on Friday morning to say I could have the day off, and I told him I wouldn't be working there any more anyway. I'd arranged to meet Gilbert after his show outside the post office. I waited and waited, but he didn't come so eventually I went home. That's when my mother told me that he'd died of a heart attack that morning.'

Marzi began to cry again, and this time Tilly decided to change the subject. She knew that Hettie would be pleased with her investigations, and felt that she was now only adding to Marzi's distress. 'Shall we order something nice from the menu?' she suggested brightly.

Marzi shook her head. 'I'm not really hungry, and I think I should go soon.'

'Not even a few chips?' encouraged Tilly. 'They do lovely chips here.'

Marzi smiled through her tears, and Tilly instantly realised why she'd found Gilbert's sister so familiar: she resembled her niece, and the smile was Gilbert's. 'Maybe we could share some?' Marzi suggested.

Tilly was pleased and left the table to put her order in with Dolly, who was busy behind the counter making frothy coffees. When she returned, Marzi looked a little better and was sorting through her shoulder bag. Tilly could see that it contained quite a few items, but she said nothing, and it was Marzi who decided to raise the shoplifting issue. 'I suppose you're wondering why I do it?' she said, putting the bag down on the floor.

Tilly was a little taken aback, but tried not to show it. 'I imagine it's because you're unhappy?'

'That's true, but it's more than that. I feel powerful while I'm doing it, and until today I've got away with it. I just love pretty things – anything to cheer that drab old house up. The trouble is, I can't resist helping myself. I know it's wrong, but it doesn't feel like stealing. I explained that to Hartley when he tried to get money from me; he said he'd filmed me doing it, and I told him I didn't care.'

'So what did he do?'

'I don't know, but he didn't get a penny out of me. He threatened to tell Uncle George, but I don't think he did, and anyway, I'm off the hook now he's dead. I never liked him. I don't know why George took him on, really – he was a bag of nerves and couldn't do anything live on the radio, not like Gilbert.'

Tilly sat up as if Marzi had given her an electric shock. 'What do you mean? I thought his show was live?'

'No, he always recorded it and then sat there watching it go out. I think he liked the sound of his own voice.'

Tilly could have hugged Marzi, but their chips arrived instead and the two cats enjoyed them with very little conversation. Marzi promised to catch up with Tilly at the cricket match on Sunday, and went on her way a little less burdened than when she'd arrived. Tilly skipped off in search of Hettie, bursting to bring her up to date on the case with the revelations that Marzi had shared with her.

Chapter Twenty

The recreation ground was in chaos when Tilly arrived. Bunty Basham was using a loudhailer to put her team through a series of exercises; Tarquin Flapjack was shouting his head off at a group of cats attempting to erect a marquee; Bugs Anderton was wobbling round on an ancient bicycle, offering ineffectual words of support to Edward Dexter and his line-marking machine; and in the centre of the commotion, Hettie, Poppa and Bruiser were attempting to unroll a giant cinema screen, ready to show Julie Android's ascent up a mountain at Thursday's open air movie spectacular. The mechanism that released the screen had eluded them so far, and Hettie had adopted the tactic of brute force to go with their ignorance.

'Can I help?' asked Tilly, approaching with caution.

'I doubt it. We've been at this for half an hour now, and all we've got to show for it is six bruised paws!' said Hettie waspishly.

'The one Turner Page uses at the library for his travel talks has a catch on the side,' said Tilly, 'like this one – you just have to release it and it should… there we are.'

The screen shot up into the sky, and Bruiser and Poppa grabbed the sides and secured them to the supports. Hettie looked on in sheer admiration, grateful for Tilly's timely intervention, as Betty and Beryl Butter arrived in their Morris Minor and parked in front of the screen. 'Have you any idea where they're putting us?' Betty called. 'Sister and me have come to spy out the land.'

'We're supposed to be marked out, but we've driven round four times now and we can't make head nor tail of it,' added Beryl.

'I think the tea tent is supposed to be next to Greasy Tom's burger van, over there where Edward Dexter is,' said Hettie. 'He's marking it out now.'

'Well that won't do, will it, sister?' said Beryl indignantly. 'Cream teas and cut sandwiches don't go with hot dogs and burgers!'

Hettie couldn't see the problem, but she directed the Butters towards Bugs Anderton, who appeared to have crashed her bicycle into Edward Dexter's cricket bat fence and was temporarily concussed. 'Just the fold-up chairs to go, then I think we can call it a day,' she said, casting her eye across to the pavilion for the hundredth time in the hope of seeing Wilco.

Tilly followed Hettie's gaze as Wilco announced another record on his show, which boomed out from the speakers across the field. 'Did you get to talk to him before he went on air?' she asked, unfolding a chair from the stack in front of her.

'No, I didn't,' said Hettie, 'and what you're hearing is a recording, which puts a whole new spin on the case. It would appear that Mr Wonderfluff can be in two places at once, which means...'

'That he could have murdered Gilbert!' said Tilly excitedly.

'But we've still got to figure out how he might have murdered Hartley,' cautioned Hettie.

'That's easy,' said Tilly. 'Marzi just told me that Hartley never presented his shows live. He always recorded them, so Wilco could have murdered him before he left for my party, then gone back later to pretend to find the body, even though he knew it was there already.'

It was a rare thing to see Hettie Bagshot dance a jig, but there was a time and a place for everything. Bruiser and Poppa looked on as she spun Tilly round in celebration of there being a very bright light at the end of what had been a long dark tunnel.

Tilly indicated to Hettie that there was more to come from her conversation with Marzi, and Hettie decided that the recreation ground wasn't the best place to discuss the case further, as half the suspects on their list were milling around. The four friends put up the chairs in record time, ready for the film night, and Hettie and Tilly elected to walk home, leaving Poppa and Bruiser still in the thick of preparations for the Easter events.

Tilly had quite forgotten the spring cleaning session she'd undertaken earlier in the day, and it was a joy to return home to find everything tidy and in its place. The Butters had left the pasties and cream horns just outside their door, and Hettie threw herself into her armchair, pleased to be home with a good supper in prospect. Tilly put the kettle on and reached for two clean mugs out of the cupboard, while Hettie put a match to the fire and took up her pipe, filling it with Hartley Battenberg's catnip. 'Come on, then – fill me in. What did Marzi have to say besides the fact that Hartley recorded his shows?'

Tilly delivered a milky tea and a jammy dodger to Hettie's armchair, and settled herself on her blankets to enthral her friend with the saga of Marzi's parentage, Gilbert's concerns over Wilco (now known as George), and Hartley's attempt to blackmail Marzi over her obsession with pretty things. Hettie listened carefully, blowing the occasional smoke ring into the air but saying nothing until Tilly had finished her account; eventually, she spoke. 'Excellent work, and well done you! I imagine that Marzi isn't the easiest cat to talk to, but it makes perfect sense now to assume that Wilco is at the heart of all this. The big question is – where is he? Does he know we're on to him? Or could we be horribly wrong about it all, and find out it was Bunty Basham instead?'

Tilly giggled, before pointing out that that was three big questions. 'I'm a bit worried about Marzi,' she said, on a more serious note. 'If Wilco finds out she's been talking to us, she might be in danger. I'm not sure her mother would stand by her. I don't think there's much love lost there.'

Hettie agreed. 'And what about Elvira Truffle, Gilbert's sister? If Wilco was happy to bump Gilbert off, what might he do to her? Depending on what she knows, she could be in danger, too. I think we need some concrete evidence to prove that Wilco was involved in Roscoe's death, and that he subsequently murdered Hartley and Gilbert to keep his secret.'

'Short of a confession, how can we prove anything?' said Tilly, dunking her jammy dodger in her tea.

Hettie thought for a moment. 'Do you still have that key to the pavilion?'

'Yes. I've put it here, under my blankets, for safekeeping. I thought we might need it to get in to do the show.'

'How do you feel about paying a quick visit now? We could take a look round and save the pasties for a late supper. We might even bump into Wilco if he's turned up.'

The last thing Tilly wanted to do was to go out again, but she could see the sense in Hettie's plan. She banked up the fire, put the pavilion key in her cardigan pocket, and hooked her mac down from the back of the door, pushing her notepad into one of the pockets.

'We'd better take the stuff you've prepared for your show to make it look like we're meant to be there,' suggested Hettie. 'Just in case Tarquin or Branston turn up.'

Tilly loaded the book and her programme notes into her satchel, and the two cats set out for Whisker FM. By the time they reached the recreation ground, the light was failing but there was still plenty going on. A substantial marquee now stood against the darkening sky, with several shadowy figures darting in and out of it, putting the finishing touches to what would be the home of the bake off competition on Saturday. Two giant sets of floodlights had been erected next to the cinema screen, ominously still in darkness, while the generator they were connected to spluttered and coughed unhelpfully. Greasy Tom had set himself up on his designated area and seemed to be doing a roaring trade already, as Bugs Anderton's army of helpers sought him out for takeaway suppers.

The radio station was also in darkness, its outdoor speakers silent as Hettie and Tilly approached. Letting themselves in, they fumbled their way through reception to the studios, where Hettie found a light switch. Both studios were unoccupied. 'Let's start in Wilco's office,' whispered Hettie. 'He might even be in there.'

They moved forward down the studio corridor, knocking gently on the door. There was no response, so Hettie turned the door handle. 'Bugger! It's locked,' she said, giving the door a bad-tempered shove with her shoulder. 'Now what shall we do?'

'I could see if Bruiser or Poppa are still around, and get them to break it down like they do on *Z Cars*,' suggested Tilly.

'I'm not sure causing wilful damage to the town's pavilion would go down very well with the elders of the parish, so I think we'd better abandon our search and go home for supper. If by any chance we're wrong about Wilco, we'd look pretty stupid breaking into his office.'

Tilly agreed, and they retraced their footsteps back to reception and out onto the recreation ground. They were about to make tracks for home when Tilly suddenly remembered something. 'Last summer I helped with the cricket teas by collecting up the trays of empty pots, and I had to take them round the back of the pavilion to the kitchen door.'

Hettie was puzzled. 'So what are you saying?'

'Wilco's office is where the kitchen is, so maybe the back door opens with the same key as the front door.'

Hettie was doubtful, but thought it was worth a look. They made their way round to the back of the pavilion and were in luck. The door was locked and Tilly's key proved to be useless, but the window next to it was slightly open. Hettie slipped her paw through the gap and lifted the catch, allowing the window to swing wide. She sprang through in a rare show of athleticism, helping Tilly to follow on behind her.

As Tilly had said, Wilco's makeshift office was the pavilion's kitchen. His desk took up half the space, with a tall metal filing cabinet jammed in beside it. Above the desk was a drying rack, which looked a little incongruous as it still had last summer's tea towels draped across it. On the opposite wall was a chart of the broadcasting week, and Hettie smiled to herself as she noted all the crossings out. Hartley's and Gilbert's names had a thick black line through them, and Branston had a re-routing arrow against his name, showing that he'd been moved from weekdays to weekends. The return of Tarquin Flapjack had been marked by his initials on each day of the week, and the only names that hadn't been tampered with were Tilly's, Tansy Flutter's and Morbid Balm's, all still in their original slots.

'You take the desk drawers and I'll have a look in this filing cabinet,' said Hettie, switching on the anglepoise desk lamp.

The drawers offered nothing more than a selection of presenter cards, assorted pens and stationery, but Hettie had significantly more luck with the top drawer of the filing cabinet. 'Well, that solves the mystery of Gilbert's tape recorder,' she said, pulling the small reel-to-reel out from under a nest of papers. 'No mistake there – he's got his name stencilled on the lid, and unless his ghost brought it back here, we can only assume that his murderer removed it from him. There's nothing else of interest, except… ouch!' Hettie pulled her paw out of the drawer, revealing a nasty cut across her pad which proceeded to bleed over Wilco's desk.

Tilly let the rack down and snatched a tea towel from it. She ran it under the tap at the kitchen sink, and wrapped it around Hettie's paw. 'That's a nasty cut,' she said. 'Did you catch your paw on the filing cabinet?'

'No. There's something sharp in the bottom of that drawer where I found the tape recorder,' Hettie said, nursing her injury.

Tilly clambered onto Wilco's desk to take a closer look inside the drawer. She carefully dug down below the papers and, to her horror, pulled out a long-bladed knife. The two cats looked at each other, knowing they had found the weapon that was used to kill Gilbert Truffle. Tilly put the knife down on the desk and pulled out a pawful of papers that had been used to hide it. They were mostly old hazard assessment forms, used for outside broadcasts, but there was a note that drew her attention. 'Look at this – it's from Hartley Battenberg to Wilco, and it says "Time is running out. Either you pay up or I'll make sure the truth comes out about Roscoe. Gilbert can't protect you this time."'

'It looks like we were spot on,' said Hettie, running her paw under the cold tap to try to stop the bleeding. The problem is what do we do about it? Do we remove the evidence and face him with it, when and if he turns up? Or leave everything as it is and see what he does next? He's got to turn up soon. This radio station won't run itself, and as far as he's concerned, he's paid us off and silenced Hartley and Gilbert, so there's nothing to stop him carrying on as normal.'

'I think we should put all the stuff back in the filing cabinet and pretend we haven't seen it,' said Tilly. 'He's bound to turn up soon. He's taken over the afternoon show from Gilbert, so he'll probably be here tomorrow. I think we should ask for a meeting with him about doing more shows. He'll think we've given up on the murders.'

'Unless Marzi tells him we're still digging around,' Hettie pointed out.

'I don't think she'll say anything, and she probably won't see him, anyway, as she doesn't work here any more.'

'OK, stick it all back in that drawer and we'll get out of here, but be careful with the knife,' said Hettie, binding her paw up in the tea towel again. 'Let's hang on to that note from Hartley; it's actually all the proof we need.'

Tilly put the tape recorder, the knife and the papers back in the filing cabinet, wiped Hettie's blood off Wilco's desk, and hoisted the tea towel rack back up, leaving it the way she'd found it. She switched off the lamp and they climbed back through the window, pulling it almost closed behind them and satisfied that they'd left no sign of their nocturnal visit to Wilco's office.

All was quiet on the recreation ground. The marquee and the giant cinema screen stood out against the night sky as a promise of things to come. It was cold now, strange and eerie as the moon peeped in and out of the clouds, throwing long shadows across the grass. Hettie shivered, and winced with the pain from her injured paw; she plunged it into the pocket of her business mac for comfort, only to discover that the pocket was already stuffed with Hartley Battenberg's final programme script, which she'd removed from the dead cat's paws and quite forgotten about. Tilly took it from her for safekeeping, and the friends wended their way homeward.

The fire offered a welcoming blaze when they got in and Tilly busied herself with the supper, while Hettie applied some antiseptic cream to her cut and – with Tilly's help – stuck a plaster over it. She settled in her armchair and amused herself by reading Hartley's programme script out loud. There was no doubt that he had a talent for satirical humour: the first part was a darkly amusing conversation on the merits of killing birds or mice, swiftly followed by a sketch on the bake off, in which Hartley voiced all the characters, including Fanny Haddock, who admitted that she was slightly worse for the gin she'd treated herself to. Branston Bean's impersonation had Hettie in fits of laughter, but the programme notes ended on a rather more sinister note. The final sketch, called 'All At Sea', featured two characters on a pirate radio boat called *The Merry Chance*. The cats had seemingly got into a fight about who should put the next record on; they were throwing biscuits at each other, until eventually one threw the other overboard. Hartley finished his script in the style of the old-fashioned radio adventure series, leaving his audience to ponder over whether the cat would survive or not, and promising to continue the story the following day. That, of course, never happened, because by then Hartley was dead.

'If I'd heard that programme a week ago, I'd have laughed my head off,' said Hettie. 'Harmless fun aimed at the community, but very uncomfortable listening for Wilco, I imagine.'

'I wonder if Wilco heard him recording it that afternoon, when we were doing my programme?' suggested Tilly. 'Perhaps that was when he decided to kill him.'

'And I wonder if this particular show ever went out at all? If Hartley always pre-recorded, Wilco might have swapped it for another show altogether – it really is a little too close for comfort. Maybe Gilbert knew, too, and that's what he was arguing with Wilco about. Maybe Wilco threatened to kill Hartley, and Gilbert thought history was repeating itself. Killing Hartley would have implications for Gilbert, as he'd kept his silence to protect Wilco in the past. That's why

Gilbert called us when he knew that Hartley had been murdered – to put the record straight.'

Tilly agreed and offered another question. 'I'd like to know why both murders included pies in their pockets? That seems a pretty strange thing for a murderer to do.'

'If you think about it, when we first started this case, it was all about Tarquin and his bake off. My guess is that Wilco decided to incriminate Tarquin by leaving a trail of pastry at the murder scenes to throw us off the scent. Wilco's big mistake was to underestimate our talent for investigation. He spent a lot of time telling us how awful Tarquin was – and Branston, for that matter; he was almost pointing us in their direction, and when we didn't take the bait and started to look closer to home, he thought fifty pounds would be enough to have us back off. His second big mistake was to tell Tansy Flutter that Gilbert had been stabbed. He'd obviously not thought through the wider implications of another murder at that point, and then he toned it down into a heart attack and offered that up for public consumption.'

'Perhaps he was trying to soften the blow for Marzi and Elvira Truffle,' said Tilly, delivering Hettie's supper to her armchair. 'He probably didn't want to kill Gilbert, but felt he had to to protect himself.'

'I think we should call it a day and do some damage to these Cornish pasties and cream horns,' said Hettie, pulling her plate towards her. 'Tomorrow, as they say, is another day.'

And as things turned out, there would be very few tomorrows left for Wilco Wonderfluff, formerly known as George Tibbs.

Chapter Twenty-One

Hettie and Tilly spent Thursday morning putting the finishing touches to Tilly's radio show. Hettie pulled together a good selection of music from her singles collection, and Tilly brushed up on her local history nuggets and her book review. For her true crime slot, Hettie decided to feature the Milky Myers case that she and Tilly had solved to great acclaim a couple of years before.

'Well, we're ready to hit the airwaves,' Hettie announced. 'I think we should strike out for the radio station and pick up a sausage bap from Greasy Tom's on the way, then wait to see if Wilco turns up to do his show. He can't stay away much longer, unless he's run away altogether.'

'And if he has run away, what will we do?' asked Tilly.

'I don't see any point in trying to hunt him down – he could be anywhere. My guess is that he'll try to brave it out. Until we found that stuff in his filing cabinet, we had no firm evidence against him, and if we hadn't found out about the recorded shows, he'd have strong alibis for both murders. I think his passion for Whisker FM will do for him in the end. It seems to me he's spent the whole of his broadcasting life waiting for the moment when he could run his own radio station. He's killed twice to keep it, or maybe even three times if Roscoe got in the way of his future prospects all those years ago.'

Tilly agreed, and packed her satchel with all the things she needed for her show. They called in at the bakery to order their supper and made their way to the recreation ground. Greasy Tom was doing a roaring trade with Bunty Basham's cricketers when they arrived. Hettie sent Tilly to queue for their sausage baps, while she called in at the radio station on the off-chance of bumping into Wilco. To her surprise, it was Morbid Balm who was warming up for the afternoon show in studio 1A. 'I didn't expect to find you here,' she said. 'I was hoping to have a word with Wilco before he started his show.'

'He called me first thing and asked me to cover for him,' said Morbid. 'He was in luck as it's my day off, but I'm not sure I can handle his afternoon listeners. I don't think they'll take too kindly to thrash metal and progressive rock. I've tried to tone it down, but once a Goth always a Goth.'

'They're lucky to have anything coming out of Whisker FM at the moment,' Hettie pointed out. 'Did Wilco say why he couldn't make his show?'

'Not really. He said something had come up, but he did say he'd be in later, as he was looking forward to the open air cinema this evening. I can't wait, either. All those black robes and crucifixes – right up my street! Are you and Tilly going after her show?'

Hettie had quite forgotten that Tilly had bought them tickets for *The Sound of Music*. She'd resisted at first, suggesting that Tilly went with Jessie, but as things were turning out, it could now be the perfect opportunity to corner Wilco. 'Did you meet Gilbert Truffle's sister?' she asked. 'I gather she was in town to organise his burial the other day.'

'Yes, nice cat,' Morbid said. 'She turned up with Wilco. She's having Gilbert buried in her garden. It was all a bit odd, really – Wilco took me to one side and asked me not to mention how he'd died. He said that he didn't want to make things worse by upsetting Gilbert's sister even more than she was already. He'd told her it was a heart attack, which I suppose it was in a round and about sort of way – if you factor in the knife that attacked his heart.'

Hettie held her damaged paw up. 'Well, I can report that we found the murder weapon all right. Nice and sharp – sliced straight through my paw.'

'Ouch! Occupational hazard in your game, I imagine. Dare I ask where you found it?'

'I'm not quite ready to say, but I'm sure it will all come out in the wash very soon. Is Hartley Battenberg still taking up space in your freezer?'

'No, we waved him off yesterday. A bunch of very odd-looking cats turned up to carry him away. They were all dressed as undertakers, but I just knew that they weren't. A couple of them actually shied away from the body – wide boys, if you ask me. London gangland written all over them. They left a substantial cheque with Mr Shroud for our trouble, and loaded Hartley into the boot of a shiny black Daimler. It was just like a scene from *The Godfather*.'

Morbid suddenly stiffened in her presenter's chair, as Tarquin Flapjack came to the end of the one o'clock news bulletin in studio 1B. She pressed the on-air button to take control and fired in her jingle, following up with one of her favourite tracks from The Sisters of Mercy. Hettie left her to it, and went to find Tilly and a sausage bap with her name on it.

Tilly had parked herself on a bench outside the pavilion with two of Greasy Tom's extra-large sausage baps and two bottles of Vimto with straws. 'I thought I'd bring them over here, because Cherry Fudge has just turned up in her ambulance,' Tilly explained. 'I didn't think we could cope with another demonstration so soon after the last one, and to make matters worse, she's camping out in it right across the weekend, so there's no getting away from her: she's sandwiched between the marquee and the Butters' tea tent. Greasy Tom's van has had to be moved, as Cherry told Edward Dexter that she needed extra space for a field hospital, just in case there was a major disaster. He's marking it out at the moment, and Bugs Anderton is threatening to resign from the steering committee for not being kept in the loop, whatever that means.'

'All that and *The Sound of* Bloody *Music*!' said Hettie. 'I do wonder sometimes why the cats in this town can't stay at home and watch TV instead of causing chaos with their outdoor events – and all this in the middle of a murder enquiry.'

Tilly sensed Hettie's frustration. 'Did you have any luck with Wilco?'

'No, but he'll be here later according to Morbid, who's doing his show this afternoon. I'll be ready for him, no ifs, no buts. I intend to run him to ground and see what he has to say for himself. It's time this particular nightmare was over.' With that declaration, Hettie took a healthy bite out of her sausage bap, allowing the tomato sauce to trickle down her chin.

The two cats enjoyed their lunch and stayed on the bench in the sunshine, watching the chaotic preparations for the Easter weekend unfold until it was time for them to head for studio 1B to get ready for 'Tea Time with Tilly'. Morbid waved from the other studio, relieved to pass the broadcasting baton on after the four o'clock news. Tilly laid out her bits of paper and loaded her jingle, while Hettie cued up the first two records, ready for the beginning of the show. She passed Tilly a scribbled list of her music choices in the order she intended to play them, just as the teleprinter in the corner of the studio suddenly sprang into life and spewed a raft of papers out onto the floor. 'It's the weather and the five o'clock bulletin, and there's some travel news as well, so you won't be short of things to say.'

Tilly was pleased to have the weather and travel to read out, but was quite upset at the thought of having to read the news. 'You have to have such a posh voice for that,' she said, 'and it's got to sound really strict. I'm not sure I can do it justice. Wilco did it last week for me.'

'There's nothing wrong with your voice,' said Hettie, trying to be encouraging. 'It's all part of being a presenter, and I'm sure you'll get the hang of it. Listen to Morbid – she's about to read the four o'clock news.'

Morbid's delivery of the news was slow and precise, and she adopted her graveside manner throughout. Tilly listened carefully while Hettie took control, ready to fire in Tilly's jingle. The news was over in a trice, and Tilly's second radio show was underway. Hettie followed the jingle with Nashville Cats, and Tilly picked up at the end of the record with her introduction. 'Welcome to "Tea Time with Tilly" on Whisker FM,' she announced. 'We've got lots of nice things in today's show, and I hope you can stay with us until six. And now for those who've been bothered by fleas lately, here's The Faces with "Itchycoo Park".'

Tilly's confidence grew with every disc that Hettie played, and she chatted about the town's local history to her listeners. She made a good job of the weather on the half hour, and Hettie delivered a spine tingling account of the Milky Myers case in her true crime spot. Tilly's mouth became very dry as she headed for the five o'clock news, but with only thirty seconds to spare, Wilco Wonderfluff appeared and slid into one of the contributor seats, relieving her of the news script and jamming a set of headphones over his ears. Hettie fired the news jingle and Wilco delivered a perfect bulletin, taking the show into the second hour.

Hettie lined up 'American Pie' out of the news, as it was a long record and she hoped to be able to pin Wilco down to the conversation she'd been trying to have with him for a couple of days. He was full of apologies, and said that he'd meant to be there at the start of Tilly's show. He seemed almost back to his normal, affable self, and agreed to see Hettie and Tilly after the show in his office. He left them to it, promising to return to read the six o'clock news.

Tilly gave a helpful run-down of the events taking place across the Easter weekend on the recreation ground, trying hard to contain her excitement over the prospect of seeing Julie Android in the evening's open air cinema. Hettie had taken the trouble to borrow Betty Butters' soundtrack album, and played out the title track much against her better judgement. Tilly followed up with her book review of Polly Hodge's *Death in Holey Cardigans*, and before they knew it, Wilco was back to read the six o'clock bulletin before plumbing the station into FWS for the night.

Tilly was elated with her performance, and Wilco was very complimentary as he led them into his office. Hettie was almost sorry to spoil the moment by raising the subject of murder, but she knew it had to be done. Wilco sat at his desk, offering stools to Hettie and Tilly. 'Now then,' he began, 'what can I do for you? Have you reconsidered my offer of more shows? I'd really like you both on board if you have the time, and I'm happy to fit you into the schedules on days that suit you. Just say the word.'

Hettie stared open-mouthed at Wilco, who seemed to have airbrushed the events of the last week completely out of his mind. He was relaxed and friendly, and gave no indication of the dismissive abruptness he'd shown at their last meeting. 'I'm afraid we're not here to sign up for more shows,' she said. 'Our investigations have moved on considerably since we last saw you, and we think it's time to wrap up the case – don't you, George?'

Wilco's shoulders sank as he bowed his head, and suddenly his whole body began to shake uncontrollably. 'I'm so glad it's all over,' he said, more to himself than to his accusers. 'I've carried this weight all my working life. One stupid mistake in a fit of anger, and now it's all caught up with me, just as I knew it would.'

Hettie needed to clarify the situation, and decided to prompt Wilco into offering some details. 'So you killed Roscoe on *The Merry Dance*. Why?'

Wilco looked up, avoiding Hettie's eye and stared into the distance instead, into his own past. 'Gilbert kept a happy ship. Me and Roscoe were his model students, and we had such a great life on that boat. One day I overheard Gilbert tell Roscoe that he was going to give him his own show. He said that it was hard to choose between us, but that Roscoe's presentation was better than mine. I was furious, and later that night Roscoe joined me up on deck just as a storm was brewing. He was full of how Gilbert had chosen him and not me to head up the new show, and I just snapped. I attacked him and we rolled about the deck until a wave hit us. Roscoe got washed overboard, but I caught hold of his paw and dragged him out of the water. As soon as he got his breath back, he came at me. I punched him back into the water and another wave swallowed him up. Gilbert had just come up on deck to check the radio mast and he saw me do it. I tried to make out that it was an accident, but he knew the truth.'

'So why did Gilbert let you get away with it?' Hettie asked.

'It was complicated. Gilbert had been seeing my sister and he didn't want to rock the boat with her, so he said he'd keep my secret. He was sure that I didn't mean to kill Roscoe.'

'And did you mean to kill him?'

'No, but I was so angry, and I did save him the first time he went overboard. We were both so young and full of ourselves. Roscoe and I were always fighting – just a bit of delinquent fun until that night.'

'So Gilbert kept your secret until Hartley Battenberg came along? prompted Hettie.

'Yes. Hartley turned up just after I'd taken over Whisker FM and started digging into mine and Gilbert's past. Tansy Flutter told me to watch out, as he was blackmailing her, and she thought he had something on Bunty Basham and Marzi, too. I told Gilbert that I thought Hartley would try and blackmail me as well, but he said he had nothing on us as long as we stuck together. When Hartley was recording his show last week, he was doing a sketch on a pirate radio boat and I knew he'd guessed what had happened to Roscoe. I found a note on my desk, asking me to pay up, and I showed it to Gilbert. We had a row. Gilbert said I was to do nothing, but I told him I was going to put a stop to Hartley's little games once and for all. Gilbert left with Marzi, and I went into Hartley's studio and strangled him with his headphones. His show was going out, so I cross-faded it into one he'd recorded last week, and I left him there thinking my troubles – and everybody else's – were over.'

'And what about the steak and kidney pie?' asked Tilly.

'He was just about to eat it when I went into the studio. He said he'd had to skip lunch, so I shoved it in his mouth while he was dying. It was probably the first time in his life that he'd eaten humble pie. I stuck the rest of it in his pocket.'

Hettie was surprised by Wilco's attempt at humour, but keen to get to the end of the story. 'You went back to the studios after Tilly's party and called us, pretending you'd discovered the body and asking us to take on the case in a double bluff. Didn't it occur to you that we might just find out that you were the murderer?'

'Not until Gilbert phoned me on Friday morning, after he'd heard about Hartley's death. He told me he wasn't going to stand by me this time, and I had no choice but to kill him before he gave me away. I knew he was doing some recording at the Methodist Hall that morning, so I pre-recorded the middle hour of my show and went down there. I caught up with him during the storm and killed him in the charity shop. He didn't even know it was me – there was such a crush in there. I grabbed his tape recorder and legged it back here to present the final hour live.'

'That was a big mistake,' said Hettie. 'Why didn't you leave the tape recorder with the body?'

'I just didn't think. Tape recorders like his are very expensive, but why do you say it was a mistake?'

Hettie stood up and pulled open the top drawer of the filing cabinet. She reached inside, carefully this time, and retrieved Gilbert's tape recorder, putting it in front of Wilco, then reached in again and pulled out the knife. 'We paid a visit to your office and found these, along with the blackmail note from Hartley. Sadly, it was the proof we'd been looking for. Your mistake was that you didn't get rid of the evidence.'

Wilco put his head in his paws, realising that the murder which had haunted him for most of his life finally needed to be acknowledged. 'I've been so stupid,' he said. 'I just can't believe what I've done. When I look back on this past week, I don't see myself in any of it. It's like watching a nightmare unfold in front of me. In my head, I'm still wondering who did murder Hartley and Gilbert.'

'Why did you tell everyone but Tansy that Gilbert had died of a heart attack?'

'I was about to put Gilbert's murder into the news bulletin after the breakfast show and I mentioned it to Tansy, then changed my mind. I suddenly thought about Gilbert's sister, Elvira, and how she would take it. I even thought that Gilbert might have told her that he suspected me of killing Hartley, so I needed Gilbert's death to be from natural causes. And then there was poor Marzi. You see, Gilbert was her father and she'd only just found out. She's a difficult cat at the best of times, and the last thing I wanted was to give her even more grief by thinking he'd been murdered. For my sins, I completely underestimated your detection methods. I honestly thought I could get away with it by pulling the wool over your eyes, but clearly I should have known better.'

Hettie took great satisfaction from the fact that Wilco's account of what would become known as the Whisker FM case was so close to their own solution. It would seem that The No. 2 Feline Detective Agency had triumphed once again, but Hettie felt sad for Wilco: the stain of murder had spread into an uncontrollable torrent of lies and deceit, compounding the original sin. She looked across the desk at him, conscious now that his options were very limited.

Without another word, she stood up and nodded to Tilly to make it clear that they were leaving. Their work was done, and Wilco's story was almost complete.

Chapter Twenty-Two

There was an air of anticipation on the recreation ground as Hettie and Tilly made their way to their seats for the first event of the Easter weekend. Poppa, Bruiser and Jessie had reserved them all chairs on the front row – much to Hettie's annoyance, as she had never felt the need to get close to Julie Android. To make matters worse, Jessie, Molly and Dolly had all dressed up as nuns to enter into the spirit of the film they were about to see. Even Bruiser was wearing his best waistcoat, although that was more for Dolly's benefit than from a need to emulate anyone in the von Trapp family. The Butter sisters had both dressed as mother superiors and dominated the second row, where Betty was treating the cats around her to a medley from the soundtrack long before the first mountain appeared on the giant screen.

Hettie stared at the screen but saw nothing. Her thoughts were still with Wilco, as he sat at his desk in the fading light; she hoped that – at last – he would do the right thing. Suddenly, Tilly's paw brought her back to reality, reaching out with a complete understanding of the situation; the two friends were playing a waiting game, and *The Sound of Music* was the perfect distraction.

Normally community singing got on Hettie's nerves, but tonight she allowed herself to be carried away by the sheer force of the voices around her. The town's cinema fans chorused their way through Maria's problems, drowned Julie Android out during the title track, and hit the ground running with a magnificent rendition of 'The Lonely Goatherd', yodelling their way through an extra chorus that wasn't even in the film. Betty and Beryl Butter entertained the second row with their own interpretation of 'My Favourite Things', in which they both stood on their chairs and added mimed actions to the words. None of the cats seemed the slightest bit interested in the plight of Maria or the von Trapps in general, but Tilly was fascinated by the Nasty Party, as she called them, and she clapped her paws with delight every time a snow-covered mountain appeared.

By the time the real Mother Abbess offered a reprise of 'Climb Every Mountain', everyone in the audience was standing on the chairs, lifting their voices into the night sky, and even Hettie had to concede that the moment was a truly magical one. Now, as the cats dispersed and made their way home, it was time for her and Tilly to return to the radio station.

Using Tilly's key, they let themselves in and made their way through to the studio corridor. Hettie's heart began to beat loudly in her chest as they approached the door to Wilco's office. There was a hastily scribbled note pinned to it, which simply said 'sorry'. The door was unlocked, and Hettie stood for a moment before pushing it open. At first sight, the office was empty, with just the monotonous dripping of a tap in the sink. The room was dark, and she fumbled with the lamp on the desk, cursing the fact that Wilco appeared to have made a successful bid for freedom. She was right and wrong. As the light filled the room, it was clear that Wilco had settled his debts.

The cat hung motionless from the drying rack above his desk, his head lolling to one side where his neck had broken. It appeared to have been a quick and effective execution, and Hettie and Tilly bowed their heads in respect for the bravery that Wilco had shown in his final act.

Good Friday

There was nothing good about the day so far. Hettie and Tilly were woken abruptly by the telephone in the staff sideboard. Hacky Redtop, editor of the town's *Daily Snout* newspaper, had never been known to shy away from a good story. The No. 2 Feline Detective Agency had certainly supplied him with plenty of front-page column inches in the past, and the suicide of the owner of the local radio station was now his top priority, bumping the bake off competition on to page four. Hettie spent some time giving her account of Wilco Wonderfluff's fall from grace, taking care to demonise Hartley Battenberg as a blackmailer, and sidestepping any reference to Gilbert Truffle's death.

Hettie and Tilly had talked long into the night on how they might present their case when asked, and had decided that there was nothing to be gained by discussing Gilbert or Roscoe's demise publicly. Hartley Battenberg had proved the villain of the piece, and – as Tilly pointed out – he'd got what was coming to him, with Wilco paying the ultimate price.

After keeping Hettie on the phone for over an hour, Hacky was satisfied that he had a real scoop and went away happily to write the story up in time for his lunchtime edition. Hettie crawled back into her armchair to catch up on some sleep, while Tilly did a ring round to shore up their story. It was only Jessie, Morbid and Tansy Flutter who knew the true circumstances of Gilbert's death; Morbid could always be trusted to be discreet; Jessie loved to gossip, but was also very good at keeping secrets; and Tansy Flutter was keen to draw a line under the whole sorry business, so all agreed with Tilly not to complicate matters.

Tilly had managed to get hold of Tansy after her breakfast show at the radio station. She presented her programme with no knowledge of Wilco's death, as Morbid Balm had collected him on Hettie's instructions the night before. Tansy was shocked by Tilly's news, but she also had some news of her own, having been invited to join a national station in the north; she had decided to take up the offer and start a new life. She was relieved not to have to let Wilco down, but sad that Whisker FM was now in danger of closing altogether. Wilco had saved her from a wicked blackmailing ring, and to her he would always be a hero.

After her acts of diplomacy, Tilly toyed with the idea of going back to bed, but the sudden eruption of both Butter sisters into a full-scale reprise of *The Sound of*

Music as they snatched batch after batch of hot cross buns from their bread ovens put paid to any chance of peace. They offered a particularly lively version of 'Do-Re-Mi', turning it into a duet which lasted for some time, before Betty launched into a passionate, if out of tune, rendition of 'Edelweiss'. Tilly had always loved the film, but was gradually coming round to Hettie's way of thinking: perhaps Julie Android had always been a little too much of a good thing.

With the smell of freshly baked hot cross buns now filling their room, Tilly realised that she was actually very hungry. Hettie seemed to be sleeping through the Butters' concert, so she pulled on some clothes and tiptoed out of the room and round to the front of the bakery to join the lunchtime queue. As the cats waited patiently to be served, there was only one topic of conversation, and Hilda Dabbit from the dry cleaners waved the latest edition of the *Daily Snout* for all to see. Hacky Redtop had chosen just three words as his bold front-page headline – 'BLACKMAIL! MURDER! SUICIDE!' – and Tilly was impressed by how easily he had summed up one of the most complicated cases that she and Hettie had ever dealt with. Hilda enthralled the queue with the details, making it impossible for Tilly to escape with her hot cross buns without a multitude of pats on the back for a job well done. Once again, it would appear that The No. 2 Feline Detective Agency had been bucketed into the limelight, with another triumph under their belts and another reason for the town to celebrate its resident sleuths.

Hettie was wide awake when Tilly got back to their room, and had actually managed to put the kettle on. 'I hoped you'd gone to the bakery,' she said. 'I'm starving, and to make matters worse, Bunty Basham has just phoned. She's seen the piece in the paper and needs to talk to us urgently.'

'Did she say what about?' asked Tilly, wielding the butter knife.

'No, but she sounded upset – or a bit panicky, actually. She wants us to go round to her house as soon as we can.'

'You'd think she'd be up on the recreation ground, practising with her team – such as it is. I'll be interested to see where she lives, though, and to meet her nasty mother. Where have we got to go?'

'She's out on the road to the Much-Purrings, near Irene Peggledrip's house,' said Hettie, taking a huge bite out of a hot cross bun.

'We'd better spruce ourselves up, then. Those houses are all quite posh.'

Tilly tackled her bun head-on, allowing the butter to seep out and cover her paws and the corner of her newly washed blanket. There was much licking and cleaning to be done after they'd finished, followed by a detailed assault on the bottom drawer of the filing cabinet to find some suitable clothes; Bunty's mother's reputation as a tyrant went before her. Hettie eventually chose a plain, long sleeved T-shirt to go with her business slacks, and Tilly went for one of her less flamboyant summer cardigans.

When both cats were looking almost presentable, Hettie went to ask Bruiser to drive them to Bunty's in Miss Scarlet. She was in luck, and found him planting potatoes in the Butters' vegetable patch. Since moving into the purpose-built shed at the bottom of the sisters' garden, he had happily become their lad about the yard, taking on gardening and any odd jobs that the sisters couldn't manage in exchange for a comfortable life with pies and pastry on tap. His days of wandering the highways were over: age and a general weariness of being nomadic had convinced him to put down some roots. Now, he was content to be a useful part of the community, while still maintaining an independent life of sorts, and there was no shortage of adventure in his work for The No. 2 Feline Detective Agency.

Half an hour later, Hettie and Tilly clambered into Miss Scarlet's sidecar and Bruiser headed for the open road, passing the recreation ground where Tarquin Flapjack was embroiled in a major stand-off with Bugs Anderton and Edward Dexter over the plumbing-in of kitchen equipment for the bake off, now less than twenty-four hours away. On hearing the news of Wilco's suicide, Tarquin had cancelled his mid-morning show, realising that the days of Whisker FM were over. He'd decided instead to sink his energy into putting the finishing touches to what he regarded as being the main event of the Easter weekend, disrupting any sensible plans put in place by Bugs or Edward.

***

Basham House was set back from a frontage of cherry trees, gloriously burdened with pink and white blossom. Bruiser drove through the open double gates and parked Miss Scarlet on the gravel, close to the front door. Bunty had clearly been looking out for them, as she was waiting on the doorstep. Bruiser elected to stay with the motorbike, settling down to enjoy the bag of Easter biscuits that Beryl had pushed into his paws as a thank you for planting potatoes. Bunty ushered Hettie and Tilly into the hallway, full of apologies for taking up their time. She steered them into a very pleasant front room, full of books, an ornate fireplace, and a piano peppered with sheet music, giving the impression that it was loved and well played. 'Make yourselves at home,' she said, waving her paw at the sofa. 'I'll go and put the kettle on.'

Tilly sat down, but Hettie – in true detective style – decided to take a closer look at the room and its contents. She realised that she knew nothing about Bunty except for her passion for cricket and the fact that she cared for her elderly and cantankerous mother. The bookshelves revealed an interest in travel, and there was a whole row of what Tilly would call 'difficult' books by foreign authors; there were no Agatha Crispys, or anything else that could be described as popular fiction. Hettie was pleased to see that Bunty had taken ownership of a whole shelf, assuming that the difficult books were her mother's and the impressive row of Wisden Almanacks belonged to her cricket-mad daughter; stacks of books on the floor looked as if they'd been ousted to make way for the Wisdens. The sheet music on the piano also suggested that Bunty enjoyed her music; it was an arrangement of Kat Bush's latest hit, 'The Cat with the Kitten in His Eyes'.

'No sign of the mother yet,' said Hettie, joining Tilly on the sofa. 'Not that I mind. I've always found schoolteachers intimidating, even the nice ones.'

The sound of a tea trolley rattling down the hallway made both cats sit up straight and decide that best behaviour was the order of the day, especially if old Mrs Basham was pushing it. They needn't have worried, as it was Bunty who steered it into the room. 'I've got ham rolls and angel cake if you'd like some with your tea,' she said. 'I wasn't sure if you'd had lunch.'

'That's lovely,' said Tilly, noting that there were only three cups. 'Won't Mrs Basham be joining us?'

'I hope not,' said Bunty, taken a little off guard.

Tilly considered Bunty's reaction and put it down to the fact that there was clearly a rift between mother and daughter, which made her even more keen to meet the formidable Mrs Basham; in good time, her wish would be granted.

Bunty passed round the plates and then the ham rolls. She poured the tea, and settled on a footstool next to the tea trolley. The three cats ate their lunch in silence; a strange shyness had descended upon them, as if they were meeting for the first time, and no one wanted to push herself forward into a conversation. Aware of the awkwardness, Bunty eventually broke the silence by offering a slice of angel cake to her visitors. Hettie and Tilly's plates clashed as they both offered them up at the same time, which made Bunty jump and drop the cake on the carpet. She looked to the door, as if someone was about to scold her for her clumsiness, then back at Hettie and Tilly. 'I'm so sorry,' she said. 'You must be wondering why I've got you here today, but when I read the paper, I knew it was time for me to tell the truth. I feel so sad about Wilco. I owe him a great debt in getting rid of that vile creature.'

'You mean Hartley Battenberg?' asked Hettie, keen to clarify the situation.

'Yes. He tricked me into doing something really stupid, and the longer it went on, the worse it got. I gave him money, but he just kept coming back for more. Now I've got to confess and take my punishment, just like Wilco. I can't live with myself any longer.'

Tilly reached down to pick the cake up off the carpet and put it back on the trolley. She collected the empty plates and cups, and stacked them while Bunty sat staring at her plimsolls. When all was tidy, Hettie decided to move things on. 'Why don't you start from the beginning?' she suggested. 'We're here to help in any way we can.'

Bunty took strength from Hettie's invitation, and suddenly the floodgates opened. 'All my life has been dominated by my mother,' she began. 'I think I disappointed her from the moment I was born. There was no room in her life for anyone else. Don't get me wrong – she fed and clothed me, I had this nice house to live in and a private school education, but she was in charge of every breath I took. She ran the school in Southwool with a rod of iron, humiliating me at every opportunity in front of the other pupils, and they bullied me because I was the headmistress's daughter. When she finally retired, I was little more to her than an unpaid servant, and when her health failed, I had to do everything. Cricket was my escape – a chance for me to be good at something that she neither understood nor cared about. It was easier when she became wheelchair bound. It meant that I could leave the house without being followed, which gave me a certain amount of freedom, but it all came crashing down on me thanks to Hartley Battenberg.'

Hettie was intrigued and found herself watching the door, waiting for Bunty's mother to roll in over the threshold. She said nothing, keen not to interrupt the story. 'Several months ago, at my mother's insistence,

I had to clean all the silver in the dining room,' Bunty continued. 'She made me do all the cutlery as well. When I was putting it all back in the Welsh dresser, I came across a bundle of papers, and one of them was my mother's will. I was horrified to discover that she'd left all her money *and* this house to her old school in Southwool. It even mentioned me by name, and said that under no circumstances was I to benefit in any way from her estate. On her death, I was to leave this house and pass the keys over to the current head of the school, making sure to remove only my personal possessions.'

Tilly offered a sharp intake of breath, and Bunty – appreciating her reaction – moved on with her tale. 'I hardly knew my father, but I've inherited his love of cricket and music, and when he died, he left this house to my mother on the understanding that it would eventually become mine. It's probably the only thing that stopped me from running away – knowing that this would always be my home – and I went through hell and back caring for my mother, which proved to be a thankless task, even on a good day. I was so angry, and I decided to face her with my discovery later that evening. I served her dinner on a tray as usual and watched her eat it, wishing with every mouthful she took that I had poisoned it. Then fate intervened, and she choked before I could even mention the will. I would like to say that I tried to save her, but I didn't; I just watched her struggle. For the first time in my life she reached out to me, but I left the room and let her die.'

'What happened next?' Tilly asked.

'I left the house and walked blindly out into the rain. It was cold, and I didn't have a coat, so I just wandered around, not thinking straight and knowing what I would find when I got home. It was then that I bumped into Hartley, and I blurted out the whole thing. He seemed very kind: he even gave me his coat and walked me home. He came in with me, and I was about to call the undertakers when he suggested that there was another way. He reminded me that as soon as my mother's death became public, I'd have to walk away from my inheritance and I'd be left with nothing. He convinced me to pretend that she was still alive in order to carry on living here.'

Bunty paused, as if she found the next part of her story difficult to tell. Seeing her distress, Hettie offered some encouragement. 'So what did you do with your mother?'

Bunty stood up on shaky legs and invited Hettie and Tilly to follow her. She moved down the hallway, which opened out into a spacious, farmhouse-style kitchen. The back door led out to a utility room, well equipped with a twin-tub washing machine, an old-fashioned mangle, and a very large chest freezer. Hettie knew even before Bunty lifted the lid that they were about to be introduced to the late Mrs Basham.

The corpse was barely visible, obscured by packets of fish fingers, beef burgers and frozen peas. The body appeared to be wrapped in a tartan blanket, but they could just make out the head, with the mouth set in a rictus grin, made more horrific still by the lack of teeth.

'So now you know, and I'm ready to take my punishment,' Bunty said firmly, shutting the lid on her frozen matriarch and ushering them back to the front room.

The three cats resumed their sitting positions, and Hettie decided to take control of the situation. 'The thing is, as far as I can see, no real crime has been committed. Your mother choked on her dinner, and you've merely been preserving the body – perhaps until getting round to making the arrangements?'

Bunty nodded in hopeful agreement, but then her face fell. 'The problem is the pension. I've been collecting it for her every week since she died.'

'So that's why Hartley made a video of you in the post office queue!' said Tilly, a little too triumphantly under the circumstances.

'Yes, and he took a photo of her the night we put her in the freezer. He sent me a print of it with his first demand for money.'

Hettie sat deep in thought, digesting the full impact of Bunty's predicament. Eventually, she broke her silence. 'It seems to me that there's an easy way out of this. Only you and Hartley Battenberg knew that your mother was dead, so there's no reason why she couldn't have died last night, or even this morning. It's a good way of covering up the pension issue, and I'm sure Morbid Balm would turn a blind eye to the length of time that Mrs Basham has been in your freezer. The only stumbling block is the house. She may have lodged a copy of her will with a solicitor, who will be keen to execute it as soon as her death is announced, and that means you'll be homeless.'

'I don't really care about that any more. I've been saving her pension, and I have enough money to find a flat or a room somewhere. I just want this nightmare to end.'

'But that's so unfair,' said Tilly indignantly. 'You've looked after her for years, putting up with her cruelty and nastiness, and it's not what your father would have wanted for you.'

'That's a very good point,' added Hettie. 'Did your father actually make a will?'

'I'm not sure, but I do have a stack of his papers under my bed. I rescued them when my mother was having a burning session, shortly after his death. I'd quite forgotten about them until now. I'll go and fetch them.'

Bunty returned with a plastic box stacked with papers, and emptied them out onto the hearthrug. Tilly and Hettie joined her on the floor, and together they began to sift through Basil Basham's life. There were greetings cards, postcards from exotic locations, receipts for lawnmowers, cars and even a greenhouse, but it was Tilly who struck gold. 'Here it is!' she shrieked, refusing to contain her excitement as she passed it to Bunty.

'I hardly dare look at it,' said Bunty, passing it to Hettie.

Hettie broke the wax seal on the document and opened it out on the floor. She ran her claw across the legal jargon until she came to the bequest section. 'This is the bit that matters. "I, Basil Montague Basham, leave all my worldly goods, property and chattels to my wife, Enid Basham, for the duration of her lifetime, in safe keeping for my beloved daughter, Bunty Doris Basham." There you are,' said Hettie. 'It appears that your mother had no right to will anything to anyone but you.'

For the first time for months, Bunty Basham allowed herself to cry with the sheer relief of having such heavy burdens lifted from her shoulders. Tilly joined in, and even Hettie allowed a single tear to escape and trickle down her nose. 'I think we'd better give Morbid a call and get her to come and collect your mother as soon as she can,' she said. 'Now we've got everything sorted, we can't risk a power cut, can we?'

Tilly giggled, and Bunty offered an appreciative smile before showing Hettie the telephone in the hallway. Hettie discreetly explained the details to Morbid, who adopted her usual sympathetic tone when she arrived, making no comment about the fact that the body had clearly been suitable for home freezing. Mrs Basham was waved off with all the pomp and ceremony of a newly deceased, and Bunty hugged her two detective heroes before returning to repack her freezer and dance a jig around the kitchen that was now truly hers.

Bruiser drove Hettie and Tilly home, where they celebrated yet another triumph with a girls' night in, a steak pie, crisps, and an iced custard slice each.

Easter Saturday

Now that they were free from any further investigations, Hettie and Tilly decided to make the most of the Easter weekend by enjoying themselves. They joined Betty and Beryl on the pavement outside the bakery to watch the bonnet parade pass by *en route* to the recreation ground, had an all-day breakfast at Bloomers with Poppa and Bruiser, and were now all set to enjoy – if that was the right word for it – the bake off final.

The contestants had been busy all morning with their culinary tasks, away from the scrutiny of the general public, with only Fanny Haddock and Tarquin Flapjack for company in the giant marquee. Tansy Flutter, Balti Dosh, Cherry Fudge, Dolly Scollop and Branston Bean were all intent on winning first prize in what had proved to be a keenly fought battle around the town. The five finalists had spent the morning chopping, mixing, baking and decorating their final entries. Fanny Haddock had devised three categories to test them on: a savoury pie, a celebratory cake, and her own Easter trifle as the 'difficult challenge'.

The marquee was due to open to the public at two o'clock, and Tilly was keen to get a good seat for the judging. It was no surprise to find Tarquin Flapjack stationed at the entrance to the tent, greedily collecting the ticket money. 'I can't believe that he's actually charging us to watch Fanny Haddock eating pastry!' said Hettie, grumpily pulling some coins out of her pocket. 'We should have gone with Poppa and Bruiser to have a look at the vintage car display.'

'I think it's going to be much more fun in here,' said Tilly, 'and just look at that sky – it's going to chuck it down any minute. At least we'll be dry in the marquee.'

Hettie had to agree; the sky was suddenly black and the wind was getting up. Grudgingly, she forced the coins into Tarquin's paw and followed Tilly to an area right in front of the judging table. The chairs next to theirs had reserved notices on them, and Hettie was horrified to discover that the seat immediately by hers was earmarked for Hilary Fudge, who took up her position just before Tarquin called everybody to order. The tent was packed to the gills due to the sudden threat of rain, and Bugs Anderton voiced her concerns regarding the health and safety aspect of an overcrowded marquee, but Tarquin batted away her objections, delighted to have made even more money from the ticket sales. Defeated, Bugs slumped in the chair next to Tilly as the heavens opened and the rain beat down on the canvas roof.

There was confusion at the start of the judging. The contestants brought their savoury pies forward to the judge's table and nervously returned to their seats. Tarquin looked expectantly in the direction of the makeshift dressing room that he'd created with several windbreaks for the comfort of Fanny Haddock, but there was no sign of the celebrity. After several minutes, the audience became restless and Bugs left her seat to see what was causing the delay. The reason for the holdup was in the champagne tent, seated on a bar stool and in danger of falling off; Fanny Haddock had got bored with watching the contestants create their masterpieces, and had decided on a light lunch of crab sandwiches and Moët & Chandon, running up a tab that would give Tarquin Flapjack convulsions. After four glasses, she'd lost all sense of time; after two more, she'd lost all sense. As the audience waited for her thoughts on savoury pies, she was propositioning the bartender into spending more time with her and another bottle of his best vintage. Luckily for all concerned, he declined her invitation just as Bugs came to the rescue, having scoured all the other attractions in search of the TV cook.

By the time Bugs had marched Fanny through the rain to the marquee, the audience was in uproar and some were demanding their money back. Hettie and Tilly loved every moment of the chaos, watching Tarquin squirm as his big event threatened to turn into a major disaster. The coldness of the rain had helped to sober Fanny up to the extent that she could now stand unaided. Bugs delivered her to the judging table, put a fork in her paw, and beat a hasty retreat back to her seat. On the arrival of the star of the show, the audience fell silent and waited for Fanny to begin tasting the pies.

Tarquin hovered nervously as she broke the first pie open and plunged her fork into the filling. She missed her mouth by a mile, allowing Tansy Flutter's chicken and ham mix to fall off the fork onto the floor. Undeterred, she moved on to Balti Dosh's lamb masala dosa, which looked more like a pancake than a pie; she prodded it with her fork, sniffed it, and finally fell onto it, forcing the filling out onto the table. Tarquin watched in horror as Fanny moved on to Cherry Fudge's ambitious flaky pastry sausage plait; this time, she actually managed to find her mouth, having abandoned her fork in preference to her paw. She crammed a sizeable piece into her mouth before spitting it out into the audience, where it landed in Hilary Fudge's lap. The audience gasped as one, and Hilary attempted to wipe the pie stains off her second-best summer print frock. She was visibly angry, and was about to challenge the cook over her daughter's offering when Hettie put her paw out to restrain her, keen not to have the fun spoilt by a premature cat fight.

Fanny turned her attention to Dolly Scollop's entry, a Stargazy pie to celebrate her Cornish roots. Fanny hesitated as four pilchard heads stared at her from out of the pastry. Thinking that she was hallucinating, the cook backed away from the table, muttering to herself, before moving on to Branston Bean's game pie. She took up the fork again and broke the crust with it, then forced it into the mixture; successfully reaching her mouth this time, she chewed and even swallowed before announcing to the audience that it was the worst pie she had ever tasted. As an encore, she promptly sicked it up again all over Tarquin Flapjack's best blazer, with the added bonus of a crab sandwich and a lot of champagne.

Branston Bean could contain himself no longer. He leapt from his seat, intent on challenging the cook who had humiliated him. In his keenness to reach the judge's table, he tripped on one of the main cables tethering the marquee to the ground. There was a sudden crack as the framework gave way, and the tent billowed out in all directions like an out of control blancmange. The rain poured in and the crowd, having no concern for the danger, revelled in the turn of events. Hettie and Tilly watched as food was tossed into the air and trampled underfoot. The Easter trifles proved the most popular missiles, and one of them scored a direct hit on Fanny Haddock as she exited the marquee. Soon, everyone was covered in pastry, cake and cream, as the contestants shrank away from their desecrated dishes to seek sanctuary in the Butters' tea tent.

It would later be said that the bake off was the best entertainment the townsfolk had ever witnessed. Hettie and Tilly certainly enjoyed the spectacle, but for them the best moment was still to come. After the hordes had left to go in search of more Easter fun on the recreation ground, Tarquin Flapjack had removed his blazer and retired to a corner of what was left of the marquee to count his money. 'Looks like you did all right, in spite of everything,' said Hettie, making him jump. 'There must be a couple of hundred there at least – not a bad haul for the church restoration fund. The Reverend Cuthbert Slink will be delighted.'

'I don't know what you mean. This isn't for the church,' Tarquin said, pushing the notes and coins into a bank bag.

'Well, that's where you're wrong. I think you'd better hand that over to us for safekeeping, don't you?'

Tarquin stood his ground, clutching the bag of money as Poppa and Bruiser entered the tent. 'This is daylight robbery. I don't intend to hand anything over to you. What gives you the right to demand money from me?'

Realising that there was a situation unfolding, Poppa and Bruiser flanked Tarquin as Hettie went in for the kill.

'And what gives you the right to steal from the church collection every Sunday? I suppose you think that now Hartley Battenberg is dead, there's no one to tell tales. The fact is, we have a lovely little film of you helping yourself to the collection plate, and we're more than happy to show it to the congregation you've robbed. What would your faithful listeners think when they find out that you're nothing but a thief?'

Tarquin blinked at his accuser. There was nothing he could say: he'd been caught out, and his days of calling the shots in the community were over. The only thing left to do was to hand over the money and shrink away into obscurity.

Easter Sunday

Easter Sunday dawned bright and sunny. As the town's kittens scampered round in search of hidden chocolate eggs, Bunty Basham was putting her team through a final nets session before facing the might of the squad from Much-Purring-on-the-Rug. The bake off marquee that had become such a disaster area the night before was now cleared away, and Edward Dexter had been up since six o'clock, rolling the cricket pitch and removing anything lying on the grass that might impede the field of play. By the time Algernon Frisk's team arrived in their charabanc, all was set for a glorious afternoon of cricket.

The Butter sisters had been up half the night, preparing sandwiches and scones for the cricket teas. Delirium Treemints had dusted off her samovar as head of beverages, and Cherry Fudge had borrowed Edward's hosepipe to wash down her ambulance, which had taken a few direct hits from Fanny Haddock's Easter trifle. For the first time over the weekend, Bugs Anderton was feeling confident that all was going to plan – except for the awful noise coming from Whisker FM.

It was a hot topic of conversation when Hettie and Tilly arrived to take up their seats for the match. It appeared that Branston Bean had barricaded himself inside the pavilion the night before, and had embarked on a non-stop, on-air marathon, broadcasting the worst music he could find. Some said that his humiliation at the paws of Fanny Haddock had tipped him over the edge; others thought that he was making a one-cat takeover bid for the radio station now that Wilco was dead. In any event, Hettie and Tilly were met by Bugs at the gate to see if there was anything they could do to restore the recreation ground to the traditional peace of Easter Sunday.

Tilly still had her key and tried to gain entry to the pavilion with it, but it was clear that Branston had made a very good job of his barricade. The music was deafening, and Algernon Frisk had already put in a formal complaint to Bunty, suspecting her of a ruse to put his team off. Hettie moved to the back of the pavilion to see if they could gain entry via the window again, but it was shut tight and locked. 'I don't see what we can do,' she said. 'I suppose we could try disconnecting the speakers on the roof, but the cricket's about to start and it would take too long.'

'We could smash the window,' suggested Tilly.

Hettie's thought process was interrupted by Edward Dexter, who was marching the town's scout troop past her to their spectator seats. The kittens looked like a pint-sized military army, resplendent in their uniforms and all carrying small cricket bats like rifles. Suddenly, she remembered the horror of the video showing Branston Bean and his sadistic attacks. 'That's it!' she cried, leaping after them.

Tilly watched as Hettie shared a short conversation with Edward, who in turn issued the scouts with an instruction. The kittens turned on their heels and, in perfect formation, marched back to the pavilion. Edward collected a cricket bat from his front garden, and joined them as they assembled by the window that Hettie had indicated. 'Stand back, lads! This won't tek a minute,' he said, taking a perfect swing at the window, much to the delight of Hettie, Tilly and the scouts. The glass fell out almost in one sheet; without further conversation, the kittens leapt in through the window one by one and bounded over to the door to what had been Wilco's office. Hettie, Tilly and Edward watched through the window frame as the scouts gained entry to the studio corridor.

Several minutes passed before the speakers were silenced, but the noise now coming from the studios was much worse than any of Branston Bean's music choices. It was the screeching of an animal in distress, as the scouts set about their abuser with their kitten-sized cricket bats. Eventually, Branston made a bid for freedom, using the back door as his escape route, only to run into Hettie and Tilly. The scouts followed him out, still wielding their bats, and Edward congratulated them on a very fine innings, then marched them away to watch the match.

Hettie stood over Branston while he cowered on the ground, licking his bruised and beaten paws. One of his eyes was swollen and closed, and he appeared to have fewer teeth than when Hettie had last seen him. 'So,' she began, 'did you enjoy that? You should be proud of those lessons you taught the scouts when you were in charge of them, but I think you may have underestimated their strength in numbers, don't you? It's so easy to take a big stick to a small kitten, especially when he's frightened, but I think your days of abusing kittens are over. As for your broadcasting career, it's time you stopped making a fool of yourself in public and crawled back under whichever stone you call home. You're lucky to get away with a beating, and if we ever catch you lifting a paw to a small cat again, we'll get the scouts to finish the job. Understood?'

Branston Bean used whatever strength he had left to stagger to his feet. He limped away across the recreation ground to the capable paws of Cherry Fudge and her ambulance, just as Bunty Basham was winning the toss and electing to bowl first.

Hettie and Tilly joined a happy crowd of spectators as the teams took to the pitch. Jessie had saved them deckchairs outside The Stumps, giving them an excellent view of the wicket and easy access to the Butters' tea tent, with the added bonus of continuous commentary from Edward Dexter as the cricketers took up their places in the field. 'I'm not sure Bunty has done right by electin' to bowl first,' he said, settling in his deckchair. 'That Indian lass has a lot to do to knock out the Much-Purrin' lot, and I'm not keen on her fielding positions. They need to come in a bit and hope for catches.'

Edward's words of cricketing wisdom went straight over Hettie's head, much like the first balls struck by Much-Purring's opening bats as they aimed at the boundaries, clocking up more runs than Elsie Haddock could keep pace with in her scoring tower. Bunty looked on in dismay from her short square leg position as history began to repeat itself. Greasy Tom and Dorcas Ink opened the bowling, offering no trouble to the opposing team and allowing them a brisk fifty before Bunty decided to make a change at the pavilion end, calling upon Balti Dosh to do her worst.

The sleek and very beautiful Indian cat received a rousing cheer from the home crowd as she fired her first missile at the wicket, and was instantly rewarded with an LBW decision in her favour. Her victim left the crease without argument, only to be replaced by Algernon Frisk himself. Algernon was a celebrated all-rounder and deserved his place as team captain, but today was not to be one of his finest. Balti adjusted her cap, spat on her paw and polished the ball before taking a long run-up. Algernon positioned his bat a fraction too late as the ball hit the wicket, sending the bails spinning in every direction.

The joy from the home crowd was deafening as the visiting captain slunk off the field; even Hettie woke from her snooze in the sun, and Tilly had now moved to the edge of her seat in sheer excitement. In spite of another early dismissal, victory was a long way off and the match settled into what was almost a sideshow as more of the townsfolk arrived to sit in the sunshine, drink tea and exchange news. By three o'clock, Algernon's team had declared on two hundred for six, leaving Bunty and her team everything to do.

Hettie was pleased when someone announced that tea was being served, and it came as a welcome diversion from Edward's comments on the mistakes being made at silly mid on, short square leg and long off. Tilly delighted in the fielders' positions, especially the ones with 'silly' in them; just like the radio job, it was a whole new vocabulary to her and she vowed to write some of them down in her notebook when she got home.

The Butters' tea tent was heaving as they joined the queue. Betty could hardly keep up with the demand for creaming and jamming the scones, and Beryl had joined forces with Delirium Treemints, constantly topping up the samovar with water from Edward's kitchen. As Hettie stood in the queue, a paw was pushed into her back and she turned to see Marzi Pan. 'I hope you don't mind, but I thought you might like to meet my aunt,' Marzi said. 'She's spending the day with me.'

Elvira Truffle stepped forward, looking much better than she had on her recent TV appearance. She offered her paw to Hettie and Tilly. 'I'm very pleased to meet you both,' she said. 'I don't think I've ever met real life detectives before, and Marzi has told me so much about you. I gather you were kind when Gilbert died.'

Tilly beamed and Hettie decided to change the subject, not wishing to complicate things further by discussing the details of Gilbert's demise. 'It's good to know that you and Marzi are getting to know each other,' she said. 'It must be nice to discover that you have a niece?'

'It's better than that,' said Marzi, before Elvira could respond. 'I've just found out that Gilbert left me all his money, and Aunt Elvira has invited me to live with her in the Fens. I'm to have an old barn on her land, and with Gilbert's money I can convert it and fill it full of lovely things. I can even pay for them now, and I can't believe that I'm to have a place of my own.'

'Well, it's the least I could do, my dear, and it's only what Gilbert would have wanted for you,' said Elvira. 'I'm so pleased to have some young company about the place. Perhaps when your barn has been converted, you'd like to invite Hettie and Tilly to stay?'

'I'd love to,' said Marzi, 'and I just want to say thank you for everything you've done.' She turned to Tilly and took her paw. 'I've never had a proper friend, and you rescued me when I was lost. I'll never forget that.'

Marzi and Tilly both blinked back tears, as Elvira filled a tray with sandwiches and scones ready to return to their seats. Hettie did the same, and the four cats promised to stay in touch as they took up their places for the final showdown on the cricket pitch.

Algernon led his team out to take up their fielding positions, and Bunty sent Poppa and Bruiser out as her openers. No sooner had the first ball whizzed past Bruiser's ear than play had to be temporarily suspended, as Fanny Haddock streaked onto the pitch wearing nothing but her spectacles and a champagne bucket on her head. Her sister Elsie had to be called from the scoring tower to bring her elder sibling under control, and it was quickly decided for the sake of decency and the match that she should be bundled into Cherry Fudge's ambulance until she'd sobered up. Play resumed ten minutes later, and, for the next hour, Poppa and Bruiser put on an impressive partnership, chipping away at Much-Purring's total until Poppa received a rather nasty knock on the side of his head from an overly aggressive bowler. He retired on seventy, leaving Bruiser to partner Morbid Balm. The two put on another thirty runs before Morbid succumbed to a catch at silly point, much to Tilly's amusement. Next came a succession of Bunty's hopeful middle order: Marmite Spratt was out for her usual duck; Molly Bloom added ten to the scoreboard before bowing out; Balti found it difficult to adjust from ball to bat; and Dorcas Ink was stumped on her third delivery. Bunty's team were in disarray, and Elsie Haddock's scoreboard gave Much-Purring the advantage with only thirty minutes of play left. Poppa had officially retired with mild concussion, which gave Bunty the option of a substitution, and she was just considering her options when Bruiser was caught and left the field to rapturous applause for a truly magnificent effort.

The late spring sun was now beginning to sink, along with Bunty's hopes of victory. They were thirty runs behind, and she was ready to concede defeat as she padded up to join Greasy Tom who was caught on the next ball. It was Tilly who saved the day. She had listened with great delight to Edward's commentary throughout the match, and he had explained the rule regarding substitution in more detail than anyone needed – so much so that she suggested that Edward himself should be the substitute for the injured Poppa.

He needed no further encouragement than a claws-up from Bunty. Minutes later, Edward strode out to take his place at the crease. Edward faced the bowler and hit the first ball for six right over the top of the pavilion; he played a safety shot to the next delivery, before settling in to a quick succession of boundaries, making the fielders scatter like nine pins. By the end of the over, the crowd was on its feet, and Elsie's scoreboard announced that only six runs were needed to level the match, and seven for a win. The next ball offered just two runs, keeping Bunty on strike as Edward watched nervously from the other end. The sun had gone down and the umpires looked concerned as the light began to fade. Algernon Frisk took up the ball, polishing it on his trousers and taking more time than he really needed, before starting the long run-up. This was Bunty Basham's moment: she thought of her father and how proud he would have been; all she had to do was hit the ball for six. She swung with all her strength as the fielders closed in, and some would say later that the ball grew wings in that moment, taking flight as the crowd watched it climb high over the field. The boundary was no obstacle as it finally came to rest in Miss Scarlet's sidecar, parked at the back of the pavilion.

The crowd roared and engulfed the pitch, carrying Bunty and Edward off on their shoulders, and leaving Algernon and his team to clamber back onto their charabanc, defeated.

The celebrations carried on well into the evening, with Greasy Tom offering cowboy suppers from his van as the townsfolk gathered round their cricketing heroes. Bunty announced that Mr Edward Dexter had agreed to become the team's official coach for the season, and Bugs Anderton – who'd allowed herself a celebratory shandy – gave a vote of thanks to all those who had helped to make the weekend a success, announcing that due to unforeseen circumstances the pavilion would no longer be the temporary home of Whisker FM, and would now be returned to the cricket and rugby club.

Tilly sighed, realising that her broadcasting days were probably over, but she brightened as one of her jokes came into her head. 'I've just thought,' she said, 'if Fanny Haddock's Easter trifle had ended up on the cricket pitch, we'd have been batting on a sticky wicket!'

'Nothing new there, then,' said Hettie, before biting into her sausage.

Tilly giggled. 'Maybe next year we should invite Prudence Leaf and her trifle?' she suggested.

THE END

Acknowledgements

I always knew that I would eventually write about my broadcasting career – after all, it has taken up nearly a third of my life – but this book is really about the competitive spirit that drives us on and the fact that some folk will stop at nothing to get what they want, even murder!

In my experience, the life of a radio presenter is always precarious: you never know when the next bright spark will turn up to take your show away, or, in many cases, when the newly appointed manager will take his or her broom and sweep the airwaves clean of voices that – although familiar – have served their time. It is a strange profession, where most of your time is taken up with sitting behind a microphone in a soundproof studio talking to yourself, but for most broadcasters it is a passion which is very hard to relinquish. I hope in this book I've given a small insight into the competitive nature of the job and the jealousies that can often create monsters. I would like to thank all the talented broadcasters and monsters I have worked with over the years for the rich seams of inspiration which have found their way into Hettie and Tilly's world.

Although these days we are now overrun with TV cooks and baking competitions, I will always remember watching Fanny and Johnnie Cradock as a child. They were larger than life and somewhat brusque in their delivery of the culinary arts; by today's standards, their shows were lacking the creativity and presentation we've come to expect, offering a much more brutal stuffing of the turkey than perhaps Nigella would go for. This memory was a gift in the writing of this book, and wherever Fanny Cradock is resting her rolling pin, I hope she'll forgive me for any liberties taken.

Finally to cricket, and for this I must thank my partner, Nicola, who steered me through the perils of actions and language which I still do not truly understand. For me, the game conjures up a village green mentality that due to its competitive nature could so easily end in murder, and what would be more perfect for a book of crime fiction?

May the pastry be with you x

About the Author

Mandy Morton was born in Suffolk and after a short and successful music career in the 1970s as a singer-songwriter – during which time she recorded six albums and toured extensively throughout the UK and Scandinavia with her band – she joined the BBC, where she produced and presented arts-based programmes for local and national radio. She more recently presents The Eclectic Light Show on Cambridge 105 Radio. Mandy lives with her partner, who is also a crime writer, in Cambridge and Cornwall where there is always room for a long-haired tabby cat. She is the author of The No. 2 Feline Detective Agency series and also co-wrote *In Good Company* with Nicola Upson, which chronicles a year in the life of The Cambridge Arts Theatre.

Twitter: **@hettiebagshot** and **@icloudmandy**
Facebook: **HettieBagshotMysteries**

Also available

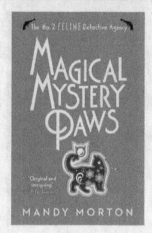

The No. 2 FELINE Detective Agency

MAGICAL MYSTERY PAWS

'Original and intriguing'
P.D. James

M A N D Y   M O R T O N

All aboard for the Summer of Fluff!

Meet Hettie Bagshot, a long-haired tabby cat whose whiskers twitch at the first sign of a mystery, and her best friend Tilly Jenkins. Together, they run The No. 2 Feline Detective Agency, and nothing will stop them from untangling each brain-teasing case that comes their way.

In scorching temperatures, Hettie Bagshot and her sidekick Tilly set out on a road trip to catch a killer cat amid a sea of entertainers. As Psycho Derek's bus lurches from one venue to the next, the killer strikes again. The big question for The No. 2 Feline Detective Agency is who will be next?

Will it be Patty Sniff, the ageing punk star? Or Kitty O'Shea from the Irish dance troupe? Or perhaps Belisha Beacon's days are numbered. As the fur flies and the animosity builds, Hettie and Tilly become embroiled in a world of music, mayhem and murder. As matters draw to a terrifying conclusion, will Magical Mystery Paws finally top the bill?

OUT NOW!

Also available

What mysteries lie beyond the gravy?

Psychic cat Irene Peggledrip is being visited by a band of malevolent spirits who all claim to be murderers. Not only is their message disturbing, but they cause chaos with indoor snowstorms, flying books and the untimely demise of a delicious Victoria sponge. Irene calls in Hettie and Tilly of The No. 2 Feline Detective Agency to help, but they're not sure how far their skills reach into the spirit realm.

Meanwhile, Lavender Stamp, the town's bad-tempered postmistress cat, has some good news to deliver to Tilly: she has won a competition to take afternoon tea with renowned mystery writer Agatha Crispy at her Devon home, Furaway House.

Will Hettie and Tilly finally lay the ghosts to rest? Can Molly Bloom's new café survive the seance? And will the moving claw give up its secrets before the gravy congeals? Find out in this latest adventure of our favourite feline sleuths.

OUT NOW!

Also available

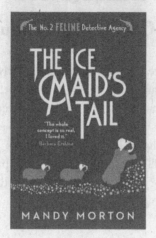

**Hettie and Tilly are called in to investigate as the
town's kittens disappear into the snowbound woods…**

The town is gripped by a big freeze, and blizzard after blizzard
has engulfed the feline community, leaving shops and businesses
snowbound. Hettie Bagshot and her sidekick, Tilly Jenkins, have
found sanctuary by their fireside but soon they are bucketed into a
terrifying nightmare, called to investigate the disappearance of the
town's kittens as – one by one – they are taken in the snow.

Who are the strange cats living in Wither-Fork Woods?

Will the ancient prophecy of the Ice Maid's Tail become a
reality?

And can Hettie and Tilly defrost the fish fingers in time for tea?

Join them as they slip and slide their way through another frost-
biting case for The No. 2 Feline Detective Agency.

OUT NOW!

Coming soon

The Cat and the Pendulum

When the celebrated crime writer Agatha Crispy engages Hettie and Tilly in the search for a stolen manuscript, our detective duo are plunged into a Dickensian world of street cats, thieves and murderers.

Will they survive the perils of London's cruel and vicious underbelly? Or will they end up under the pastry crust in Mrs Croop's Pie Shop? Find out in the next dark and hilarious adventure for The No. 2 Feline Detective Agency.

Note from the Publisher

To receive updates on new releases in The No. 2 Feline Detective Agency series – plus special offers and news of other humorous fiction series to make you smile – sign up now to the Farrago mailing list at farragobooks.com/sign-up.